BEETLE BOY

M. G. LEONARD

BEETLE BOY

Chicken House

Scholastic Inc. / New York

Library of Congress Cataloging-in-Publication Data

Leonard, M. G. (Maya Gabrielle), author.
Beetle boy / by M. G. Leonard.—First edition.
pages cm
Summary: Darkus Cuttle had taken care of his father ever since his mother died, but one day his father vanished from a locked vault at the Natural History Museum, and now he lives with his eccentric uncle—but one day he finds a large and unusually intelligent and self-aware beetle, and soon he and his two friends are caught up in a struggle to protect an intelligent superspecies of beetles.
ISBN 978-0-545-85346-0
1. Beetles—Juvenile fiction. 2. Insects—Juvenile fiction. 3. Missing persons—Juvenile fiction. 4. Fathers and sons—Juvenile fiction. 5. Uncles—Juvenile fiction. 6. Best friends—Juvenile fiction. [1. Mystery and detective stories. 2. Beetles—Fiction. 3. Missing persons—Fiction. 4. Fathers and sons—Fiction. 5. Uncles—Fiction. 6. Best friends— Fiction. 7. Friendship—Fiction.] I. Title.

PZ7.1.L46Be 2016
[Fic]—dc23

2015028492

10 9 8 7 6 5 4 3 2 1   16 17 18 19 20

Printed in the U.S.A. 23

First edition, March 2016

Book design by Carol Ly

For Arthur, Sam,
and Sebastian

"*I feel like an old war-horse at the sound of a trumpet when I read about the capture of rare beetles . . .*"

—CHARLES DARWIN

CHAPTER ONE

The Mysterious Disappearance of Bartholomew Cuttle

*D*r. Bartholomew Cuttle wasn't the kind of man who mysteriously disappeared. He was the kind of man who read enormous old books at the dinner table and got fried egg stuck in his beard. He was the kind of man who always lost his keys and never took an umbrella on rainy days. He was the kind of dad who might be five minutes late picking you up from school but he always came. More than anything else, Darkus knew his dad was not the kind of father who would abandon his twelve-year-old son.

The police report stated that September 27 had been an unremarkable Tuesday. Dr. Bartholomew Cuttle, a forty-eight-year-old widower, had taken his son, Darkus Cuttle, to school and gone on to the

Natural History Museum, where he was the Director of Science. He'd greeted his secretary, Margaret, at nine thirty, spent a morning in meetings discussing museum business, and eaten lunch at one o'clock with an ex-colleague, Professor Andrew Appleyard. In the afternoon, he'd gone down to the collection vaults, as he frequently would, via the coffee machine, where he'd filled his cup. He'd exchanged pleasantries with Eddie, the security guard on duty that day, walked down the corridor to the vaults, and locked himself in one of the entomology rooms.

That evening, when his father didn't come home, Darkus alerted the neighbors and they called the police.

When the police arrived at the museum, the room Dr. Cuttle had entered was locked from the inside. Fearing he may have suffered a heart attack, or had an accident, they produced a steel battering ram and smashed the door open.

The room was empty.

A stone-cold cup of coffee sat with some papers on the table beside a microscope. Several Coleoptera specimen drawers were open, but there was no sign of Dr. Bartholomew Cuttle.

He had vanished.

The vault had no windows or doors other than the one he had entered by. It was a sealed chamber with a controlled atmosphere.

The puzzle of the disappearing scientist made the front page of every newspaper. The unsolvable mystery drove journalists crazy, and not one of them could explain how Dr. Cuttle had gotten out of that vault.

SCIENTIST DISAPPEARS! headlines screamed.

POLICE ARE OUTFOXED! newspapers cried.

ORPHANED BOY PLACED IN CARE! they reported. *HUNT IS ON FOR ONLY LIVING RELATIVE, FAMOUS ARCHAEOLOGIST MAXIMILIAN CUTTLE.*

And the next day: *ARCHAEOLOGIST LOST IN SINAI DESERT!*

BOY ALONE! they wailed.

Outside the foster home, journalists stopped Darkus in the street, taking pictures and shouting questions:

"Darkus, have you heard from your dad?"

"Darkus, is your father on the run?"

"Darkus, is your dad dead?"

Five years earlier, when his mother died, Darkus had retreated inside himself. He stopped playing outside with friends or inviting anyone over. His mum, Esme Cuttle, had been taken away suddenly by pneumonia. The shock was terrible. His dad was overcome with grief. Some days—blue days, Darkus called them—his father lay in bed and stared at the wall, unable to speak, tears rolling down his cheeks. On the bleakest blue days, Darkus would bring tea and biscuits and sit beside his dad, reading. It was doubly hard, losing Mum *and* Dad being so sad all the time. Darkus had to learn to take care of himself. At school, he got along with everyone, but he didn't have close friends. He kept to himself. The other children wouldn't understand and he wasn't sure he could explain it. The only thing that mattered was taking care of Dad and helping him get happy again.

Finally, four years after Mum's death, the blue days got fewer and farther apart, and Darkus watched with cautious joy as his father awoke from his long sleep of sadness. He became a proper dad again, playing soccer on Sundays, smiling at Darkus over the breakfast table, and teasing him about his unruly hair.

No, Darkus was sure his dad wasn't suicidal, or on the run, or living a double life. Something else had happened in that vault, and that made him sick to his stomach with fear, because he couldn't think what that something else could possibly be. So when the reporters asked their stupid questions, he jammed his hands in his pockets, scowled at their notebooks, and refused to answer.

Boy with Broken Heart Stops Speaking! the papers told the world.

When Darkus's uncle, Professor Maximilian Cuttle, was finally tracked down in Egypt, he flew straight back to London to look after his nephew. The papers, unable to solve the mystery of the disappearing scientist or make up new stories about Darkus, lost interest and left him alone. Uncle Max brought Darkus home to his flat above Mother Earth, a health food store in a row of shops between Camden Town and Regent's Park.

"I have to warn you, my boy," Uncle Max said as they climbed the stairs, "I've always lived on my own. Travel a lot, you see. Never much liked England; it's all this blasted rain—dreary, and not much fun on a dig, I can tell you. I'd rather be in the Sinai Desert, riding a camel." He paused to catch his breath. "Anyway, long and short, not much good with guests. Like them, just not sure what to do with them; same goes for children."

Darkus followed his uncle silently through the front door, enjoying listening to a voice so similar to his father's.

"Kitchen." Uncle Max first pointed to a bright orange room on his left and then up some steps to his right. "Living room."

As they passed the living room, Darkus stared at a series of long-faced wooden masks hanging on the midnight-blue walls, and they stared back at him. Climbing another flight of stairs, to the second floor, they arrived outside Uncle Max's bedroom and a large pink bathroom.

"Because I work abroad most of the year, the university won't give me an office, so this is my office as well as my home," Uncle Max said as they climbed a third flight of stairs into the loft, "and up until now, the room you'll be sleeping in has been my—um, well—my filing cabinet."

When they reached the low-ceilinged landing of the third floor, Uncle Max leaned against the wall and made a show of being tired. Pulling a handkerchief from his shirt pocket, he nudged up his safari hat with the swollen knuckles of his right hand and mopped his tanned, leathery forehead.

"Phew," he grimaced, "whatever you do, don't get old, lad. Lord only knows how I'll make it back down. You may have to carry me!" He chuckled heartily to show he was joking, but when Darkus failed to join in, he smiled sadly and shook his head. "You might look like your mother, but you're Barty through and through. Esme would always laugh at my jokes, especially the unfunny ones."

Darkus tried to be polite and smile, but it came out like a grimace. Conscious of Uncle Max studying him, he hugged his oversize green sweater to his body and looked down to see that his scruffy jeans were torn at the knee.

Because of his dark skin and hair, and coal-black eyes, people said he had his mother's Spanish looks, but when he thought of Mum, it was her wide smile that filled his head. His mouth was shaped like hers, but when he realized his smile made Dad sad, he'd stopped doing it.

"What happened to your hair?"

"They shaved it off at the foster home." Darkus rubbed his hand over his stubble. He didn't want to tell his uncle about the bully who had shaved a stripe into his hair on his first night in that unfamiliar house. "There were nits," he muttered.

"I see. Sensible precaution, I suppose." Uncle Max frowned, returning his handkerchief to his pocket. "Righty-ho." He pointed at the door in front of them. "That's a bathroom." Then he walked along the landing: "And this is your room." Uncle Max gave Darkus an apologetic grin before pushing the door open. "Ta-da!"

A piece of paper, covered in scribbled notes, floated into the hall and landed at Darkus's feet. The room was tiny. Piles of paper hid the floor and boxes were stacked clumsily on top of one another. Objects wrapped in yellowing newspaper hung out of half-opened packages, and the air was thick with the aroma of mildew and dust.

Darkus sneezed.

"Gesundheit," said Uncle Max, reaching inside the doorway and switching on the light.

Beyond the boxes was a wall of black filing cabinets. Several drawers were half open, paper spewing out. On the top, rows of hardback atlases and loose-leaf maps slumped against one another. Darkus noticed a skylight in the roof, its external pane spread so thick with grime that it filled the room with shadows.

"You must hate filing," he said.

"Well, yes, I suppose it has been some years." Uncle Max coughed. "Come to think of it, I'm not sure when I last came up here. It might have been before you were born."

Darkus smiled weakly, not wanting to appear rude. Pleased that his nephew was warming, Uncle Max picked up a book from an open box. "*An Intellectual History of Cannibalism*—I've been looking for that." He raised his eyebrows twice and dropped the book back down.

A cloud of dust erupted from the box and broke over Darkus's face.

Uncle Max laughed as Darkus frantically waved the dust away with one hand, sneezing, and then—unable to resist the infectious nature of his uncle's roars—laughing.

"The upshot, lad," said Uncle Max, offering Darkus a clean handkerchief from his back pocket, "is it needs work. However, if we put our backs into it, I'm certain we can make this into a bedroom of sorts."

Darkus put his suitcase down in the hall. "It'll be fine, Uncle Max. Thank you."

"Of course it will." Uncle Max clapped Darkus on the back, knocking him forward. "It'll be a rum old place when we're done." He took off his safari hat, his hair springing up above his tanned scalp like a cloud of silver thoughts. "First, I suggest we move everything out into the hall, because there's some cleaning to be done before this room is fit for human habitation."

Darkus got to work. He pushed up the sleeves of his green sweater, exposing dark skinny arms, and dragged a heavy box across the room. As he hauled it through the doorway, he stumbled backward, ripping the carton open to see a stack of folders marked *Fabre Project* and scattering what looked like human teeth on the floor.

"I—I'm sorry, I . . ." he stammered.

"Ah, the teeth of Nefertiti." Uncle Max knelt down and carefully gathered the teeth into his hand. "Let's put these somewhere safe, shall we?"

"The actual teeth of Nefertiti?" Darkus asked, wide-eyed. "Are you serious?"

"Deadly serious." Uncle Max nodded. "I discovered her tomb. People will tell you it's still lost, but I found it. These teeth"—he held up his hand—"are plucked from the casket of the infamously beautiful Egyptian queen."

"Did you pull them out of her skull?"

Uncle Max shrugged. "Well, she wasn't using them."

Darkus picked up a stray tooth. "Shouldn't they be in a museum?"

"They *would* be in a museum, lad, if anyone had listened to me," Uncle Max said. "But no, they wouldn't hear of it. A junior archaeologist making such an important discovery? A mere boy? They said it was impossible, but they were wrong. Just because a person is young doesn't mean they don't have the curiosity, determination, and grit to do what a grown-up can do, eh?" Uncle Max sniffed. "When they finally decide to find the thing—and they will, because I've told them where it is—old Nefertiti will be toothless, and these beauties will prove categorically that I was there first." He carefully poured the teeth into an envelope. "The past always has a way of catching up with you, lad, even when you don't want it to." He folded down the flap and sealed it. "It was one of my first Egyptian excavations, you see. I was fresh meat, newly qualified, and didn't understand the rules of the game. Grown-up life can be awfully dull, Darkus; it's full of politics and compromise . . ."

Uncle Max rambled on about the trials and tribulations of being an archaeologist, and Darkus nodded or shook his head as they cleared, swept, and dusted the room together. A brightly colored Moroccan cloth was thrown over four boxes of books to make a table, and three empty containers were stacked one on top of the other to make shelves for clothes.

Uncle Max climbed onto a stool and scrubbed the inside of the skylight with vinegar-soaked newspaper. As he reached up to open the window and clean the outside, Darkus saw something black sitting on the glass. A creature . . . with seven legs . . . or was it six legs . . . and a horn?

"Wait!" Darkus called out.

But Uncle Max pulled the window toward him, and the creature leapt into the air, zooming away.

"What was *that*?" Darkus pointed, wanting to scramble up onto Uncle Max's chair and get a proper look.

"What was what?" Uncle Max looked up, but whatever the beast was, it had gone.

Six legs meant an insect, didn't it? No animal had seven. Maybe it was a bat or a small bird, or two. But bats didn't have horns, and even two birds only had four legs. It must have been an insect, but he'd never seen an insect that big before.

"The sun is setting," Uncle Max said, his head out of the window. "It's not an Egyptian sunset, but I must admit the city has a beauty of its own."

Darkus surveyed the tiny room. "Uncle Max?"

"Yes, lad?"

"Where am I going to sleep?"

Uncle Max popped his head back into the room.

Darkus threw his hands out. "I don't think a bed will fit in here."

"And I don't have a spare bed, even if one would fit, which it wouldn't." Uncle Max nodded in agreement.

"I suppose I could sleep on the floor."

"Or on the ceiling," said Uncle Max.

"Right." Darkus scratched his head, unsure if Uncle Max was joking again.

"In a hammock," Uncle Max said. "A hanging bed sort-of-a-thing. Sailors and archaeologists use them all the time. They're very useful for avoiding the deadly sting of a fat-tailed scorpion—not that there are any scorpions here, you understand . . . well, not ones that are alive, at any rate. So, how does a hammock sound?"

"It sounds good."

"Excellent, because I have a spare one of those." Uncle Max went out into the hall and returned with a blue bag. Inside was a sandy yellow stretch of canvas gathered around two large copper hoops. "I thought we could hang it up there." Uncle Max pointed to the roof space above the filing cabinets.

Darkus nodded eagerly, and Uncle Max reached into the bag and pulled out two brass hooks and a mallet. "Run down to the living room, lad, and grab the sleeping bag—it's on the leather armchair—and bring up a cushion from the sofa."

When Darkus came back upstairs, Uncle Max had hung the hammock. He eagerly clambered onto the cabinets and flopped into his new bed, which rocked him gently from side to side. Cocooned in the canvas, he was completely hidden.

"I love it!" he said, poking his head out.

Uncle Max passed him the sleeping bag and pillow. "Not bad," he agreed, looking around with a satisfied smile. "Now then"—he picked up Darkus's suitcase and placed it on top of the filing cabinets—"we should see about getting you some clothes."

"I've got clothes."

"Some new ones." Uncle Max smiled. "That sweater wouldn't look out of place on a tramp."

"This is Dad's sweater," Darkus said quietly.

"Oh." Uncle Max looked crestfallen. "Forgive me, Darkus. I'm an old fool." He cleared his throat. "Terribly insensitive of me."

"Uncle Max . . ." Darkus swallowed. He couldn't look his uncle in the eye. "Now that you're back . . . the police will have to start looking for Dad again, won't they?"

Uncle Max nodded. "I have an appointment with Scotland Yard tomorrow."

"Tell them"—Darkus leaned out of the hammock—"he wouldn't run away. He'd never leave me, not with Mum gone. Something must have happened to him in that vault. Something bad."

"Yes, that's exactly what I'm going to tell them." Uncle Max looked up with an apologetic grimace. "Darkus," he paused, "I'm truly sorry it took me so long to get back to you." He put his hat back on his head. "I feel terrible about it, and I will do my level best to find out what's happened to your father and bring him home. But if, as I suspect, the police aren't going to be very helpful, we may have to do a bit of investigating on our own—and that will require grit and determination from both of us."

"You can count on me," Darkus said earnestly.

"I knew I could." Uncle Max smiled. "Dinner's at seven." He stepped out of the room and saluted. "And it'll be fish and chips."

Darkus listened to his uncle go downstairs. Then he leaned down and pulled his suitcase up onto his lap. Opening it, he swept his clothes aside and took out a framed photograph of his father. Looking down at Dad's sandy hair and smiling blue eyes, he felt his chest tighten and his stomach twist. He stroked the glass. He missed his dad so much it hurt like a stitch in his chest.

Darkus lay back in the hammock and propped the picture on the pillow beside him. Gazing up through the skylight, he watched the first stars appear. Tracing the constellations his father had taught him to recognize, he wondered if somewhere under this night sky his father was looking up and thinking of him.

CHAPTER TWO
King Ethelred Hall

*D*arkus peered through the spiked railings that ran along the front of King Ethelred Hall School. It was an enormous Gothic building with brooding gargoyles sprouting from its many corners. Darkus took in the narrow windows, soot-stained brickwork, and graffiti. The playground looked like the exercise yard from a prison film. His old school wasn't perfect, but at least it had a playing field.

He hoped this school would be better than the one he was dumped in for three weeks while staying at the foster home. That had been rough. Uncle Max had said that you didn't get to choose which school you went to if you applied at the wrong time—you got sent to a school that had room for you. Darkus had learned that the schools with free spaces tended to be the bad ones.

He stared at King Ethelred Hall. If you counted his old one, this was his third school in five weeks.

Five weeks since Dad had last walked him to school.

Darkus clenched his teeth. He couldn't get upset just before going into a new school: People would stare. He thought about what Uncle Max had said. "Grit and determination," he whispered to himself, and, taking a deep breath, he walked through the school gates.

At morning registration, Darkus was made to stand at the front of the class and introduce himself to a sea of uninterested faces. A tall girl called Virginia Wallace was appointed to look after him. Her hair was pulled into eight black pigtails, each held tight by a brightly colored elastic band. She pouted as she looked him up and down, obviously unimpressed with her new duty. Sitting next to her was a small boy who was so pale he looked ill. He wore large-framed glasses and had a shock of frizzy white hair. The boy held out his hand and shook Darkus's as he sat down at the empty desk behind them.

"Hi, I'm Bertolt Roberts."

Darkus mumbled his name, taken aback by the boy's formal handshake and keen smile.

At recess, Darkus was the first out of the classroom. He strode onto the playground, finding himself wandering toward a giant tree. The trunk of the solid oak was tattooed with hearts and names carved into the bark by knives and compasses, and leaning against it was a muscular boy with the hair rising from his forehead like a rhino's horn. His shirt was unbuttoned at the neck, framing a chunky gold chain.

The knot of his purple-and-black-striped tie hung at his waist. A gaggle of smaller boys clamored around him, trying and failing to lean against the tree in the same casual manner.

"Have you figured out who the losers are yet?" he called out.

"Yeah! You don't want to get stuck with Big Bird and Einstein," sneered a red-haired boy with a mouth full of braces.

The gaggle of boys snickered.

"Wanna come for a puff?" the boy with the rhino's horn asked, cocking his head.

"No thanks." Darkus walked on.

The red-haired boy ran up and fell into step beside him. "All right. I'm Robby."

"All right, Robby, I'm Darkus."

"Yeah, I know. Listen, it ain't clever to turn down an invite from Daniel Dowie, see. You won't get asked twice. I'm only tellin' yer 'cause you're new."

"Thanks, but I don't smoke."

"Maybe you should take it up." Robby grinned a mouthful of metal.

"No thanks."

"Don't know why Daniel's interested in you anyways. It probably ain't true what they're sayin'," Robby said, watching Darkus move away.

"What's not true?" Darkus stopped.

"About your dad."

Every muscle in Darkus's body tensed.

"That he's dead." Robby leaned forward, searching Darkus's face for a response. "Is he? Is he dead?"

"He's *not* dead."

"Then where is he?"

"I–I don't know," Darkus stammered.

"P'raps he got tired of being your dad?" Robby laughed, nastily. "Nah, we reckon he's dead. Probably murdered."

Darkus clenched his fists. "Say that again and I'll thump you."

"Oooo, I'm really scared." Robby cowered away from Darkus and then laughed. "Darkus's dad's dead. Darkus's dad's dead."

Darkus felt a surge of fire in his chest and he lurched forward, but before he could swing his fist at Robby's face, two strong hands grabbed his upper arms, holding him back.

"Easy, tiger," Virginia said without loosening her grip.

"You're a loser, just like your friends," Robby said to Darkus as he backed away from Virginia, looking scared. "You're all a bunch of LOSERS!" He ran back to the tree and the raucous chattering of the other boys.

"Are you okay?" Virginia let go of Darkus's arms.

Darkus glared at her. "You should've let me hit him."

"*He* made me stop you." She nodded over her shoulder to where Bertolt was standing, blinking at them. "But you should thank him. He did you a favor."

Bertolt shuffled forward to stand beside Virginia, smiling shyly.

"Robby's a snitch," Virginia explained. "You'd have spent your first week outside the headmaster's office, and that little rat would have laughed in your face every day."

"She should know," Bertolt piped up. "She walloped him a couple of weeks ago."

Virginia grinned like the Cheshire cat, and then, seeing something over Darkus's shoulder, said, "Uh-oh, Robby's talking to the clones. C'mon, let's get out of here before he returns with backup."

"Robby likes pushing people around," Bertolt explained in a series of squeaks as they hurried away. "Virginia clobbered him because he threw me in one of the big trash cans down Stink Alley and wouldn't let me get out." He stumbled, and Darkus caught his arm. Bertolt smiled gratefully. "Thanks."

"There isn't a boy in this school I can't whup in a fight," Virginia said defiantly. Darkus believed her.

"Thanks for stopping me—you know, from getting into trouble."

"If you weren't new, I'd have let you smack him," Virginia growled. "Robby's a weasel."

"Would you like to have lunch with us?" Bertolt asked.

"Sure." Darkus nodded. "Thanks."

Bertolt and Virginia were as different as peanut butter and jelly, but as tight as friends can be. They finished each other's sentences and spoke to each other with looks. Darkus had never made that kind of friend, because he couldn't talk about the things in his head. He couldn't explain the chasm of fear that had opened up inside him when Mum had died, or the terrible nightmares he had about Dad. But as he listened to their banter, he envied Bertolt and Virginia's closeness.

Virginia had the build of a featherweight boxer and skin the color of cinnamon sticks. She was loud, animated, and talked very rapidly. As they entered the dinner hall, she told Darkus about her family: her three older siblings, David, Sean, and Serena; and two younger, Keisha and Darnell.

"I'm the middle child." She pulled her lunch box from her satchel. "Mum says I've got the syndrome." She threw it down on the table with a clatter and slid onto a chair.

"What syndrome?" Darkus asked, sitting opposite.

"The one where you have to be a famous explorer or sail around the world to get noticed."

"She's not frightened of anything," Bertolt said proudly as he took out his blue Tupperware lunch box and sat down beside Virginia. "Or anyone."

"My brothers are why I can fight," Virginia explained, stuffing her mouth with chips. "Sean's always trying to beat me, but he can't," she went on, spraying chip crumbs across the table.

"Unfortunately," Bertolt said, one white eyebrow arched with disapproval, "she hasn't any manners."

Darkus soon realized how Bertolt had gotten the nickname Einstein—he was the ultimate science geek. He described his hobby as "constructing working prototypes of new inventions that throw fire, or explosives." Like Darkus, Bertolt was an only child. He lived with his mother in a compact flat on a block not far from the school.

"Bertolt nags a lot." Virginia poked him. "Hates it when I talk with my mouth full. He has dinner round ours when his mum's working, and that's all I hear: 'Only pigs eat with their mouths open.'" She mimicked Bertolt's high-pitched voice.

Bertolt blushed, and Darkus, seeing his unhappy face, changed the subject. "Your mum works at night?"

"She's an actress," Bertolt explained. "Her name's Calista Bloom; have you heard of her?"

"Um, no, sorry." Darkus shrugged apologetically.

"No one has." Bertolt fed small bits of a Marmite sandwich into the side of his mouth. "You won't have seen her on TV unless you watch adverts about people who fall over at work, although you might have heard her. She does the voice of the annoying bunny rabbit on *Bazonka's Bath Time.*"

Darkus shook his head, pulling a knotted carrier bag from his backpack. "I don't really get to watch much TV."

"Mum mostly does theater. She was in a play when she had me. I'm named after a playwright."

"Pity she didn't think how it might ruin your life and get you thrown in trash cans," Virginia snorted.

"I don't think that was because of my name." Bertolt frowned.

"I like it," Darkus said. He pulled a spoon from his coat pocket and tore a hole in his lunch bag. "It's unusual, but in a good way."

"Thanks." Bertolt beamed, and then looked puzzled as Darkus dipped his spoon into the hole in the lunch bag. "What are you eating?"

"It's my uncle Max's special fried rice. Try some. It's really tasty." Darkus held the spoon out toward Bertolt. "I told him a packed lunch should be sandwiches, but there was no time to make them this morning, so he gave me a bag of rice."

Bertolt refused the rice with a little shake of his head.

"So"—Virginia cleared her throat—"what happened to your dad, then?"

"Virginia!" Bertolt gave her a thump and looked apologetically at Darkus. "I'm so sorry."

"What? Oh, c'mon! Everyone's talking about it." Virginia threw her hands in the air. "If I don't ask, somebody else will."

"It's okay. Perhaps if I tell you, people will ask you about it instead of me." He sighed. "I'd like it if they'd stop staring at me."

"You were in the papers, and on the news," Bertolt pointed out. "That makes you kind of famous."

"Yeah, well, not anymore." Darkus looked at the table. "They can't keep writing about a mystery that has no solution."

"So tell us. What happened?" Virginia leaned in, all ears.

"There's nothing much to tell. My dad went to work, like normal, and at some time in the afternoon—no one knows when—he vanished," Darkus said in a matter-of-fact way. "I realized something was wrong when he didn't come home."

Bertolt sucked in his breath.

"There must be more to it than that," Virginia prodded.

"No one knows what happened," Darkus continued. "The police found no clues. And that's all there is to know. My dad just disappeared."

"Perhaps he's a spy," Virginia suggested helpfully. "He could be saving the country from terrorists right now."

Darkus shook his head. "He's not a spy. He's the Director of Science at the Natural History Museum."

"Wow!" said Bertolt, his eyes lighting up. "I love the Natural History Museum. Do you get to go there a lot?"

Darkus nodded. "During the school holidays."

"It'd be better if he was a spy," Virginia grumbled.

"Tell that to your own dad!" Bertolt scolded. Turning back to Darkus, he added, "He's an accountant."

"I'm just saying, if he was a spy it would have explained the whole disappearing thing," Virginia huffed.

"I've got to stay with Uncle Max until Dad comes back," Darkus said. "That's why I'm at this school. When Dad comes home, everything will go back to the way it was before."

"What about your mum?" Bertolt asked. "Why aren't you staying with her?"

"Mum died of pneumonia when I was seven," Darkus replied quietly.

"Oh no!" Bertolt cupped his hands over his face in dismay. "That's awful."

"You think your dad will come back?" Virginia asked.

"I know he will." Darkus felt so certain of this fact that he sat bolt upright. "People say he ran away, or he's dead, but he's not. I know he's not. There was no packed suitcase, no note. Nothing's missing, there's no dead body, and he's *my* dad. I know him. He would never leave me, not like that." He heard his voice become muffled with emotion and knew if he said any more he'd cry. He paused and swallowed. "Wherever he is, he's worried sick about me."

"Of course he is," Bertolt agreed furiously. "And I bet he's an excellent dad."

"But there's something else." Darkus looked at Virginia and lowered his voice. "I know my dad is alive, because Uncle Max isn't acting like he's dead."

"What do you mean?" she whispered back.

"Uncle Max looks worried, and like he's thinking about things, but he isn't sad at all. In fact, sometimes I think he's more angry than anything else."

"So what do you think *did* happen?" Virginia asked, leaning across the table, keeping her voice low.

"I think he's been kidnapped." Darkus checked both their faces to see if they believed him.

"Kidnapped!" Bertolt gasped.

"Brilliant!" Virginia's eyes grew wide. "I mean, obviously not for you, but—a real-life kidnapping? That's brilliant!"

"The police don't believe me. They've added his name to a missing persons list and stopped looking. They say some people don't want to be found, but . . ." He paused, thinking about whether or not he should tell them the rest.

"But what?" Virginia pressed.

"Me and Uncle Max, we've started our own investigation." Darkus looked deathly serious. "And we're going to find Dad ourselves."

"I'll help!" Virginia sat up. "We both will, won't we, Bertolt?" She tugged at his sleeve.

"If you want us to, that is." Bertolt shot Virginia a disapproving look.

"This is fantastic, a real adventure! I've always wanted to be a detective." She jumped to her feet and pulled her homework notebook from her blazer pocket. "We should interview you now and get your story of what happened the day your dad disappeared, just in case you get amnesia and forget everything."

"Virginia might be good at fighting," Bertolt said to Darkus, "but she's as blunt as a spoon." He shook his head. "It's that middle-child syndrome."

"Ha-ha!" Virginia stuck her tongue out at Bertolt.

Darkus laughed. It felt good to have people finally believing him. He looked at Bertolt and Virginia quarreling on the other side of the table and realized it had been a long time since he'd shared anything with children his own age.

It couldn't hurt to let them help. The more people there were looking for his father, the better.

"Okay, okay," Darkus said. "You're in."

"YES!" Virginia punched the air. "You won't regret it."

Bertolt stood up beside Virginia.

"We will do our very best to find your dad."

Looking from Bertolt to Virginia, an unfamiliar warmth blossomed in Darkus's chest, and he surrendered to the smile tugging at the edges of his mouth.

"Thanks," he said.

CHAPTER THREE
The Eye-Gouger

*D*arkus stuck with Virginia and Bertolt for the rest of the afternoon. At three thirty, when the school bell rang, they went their separate ways, and Darkus returned to Uncle Max's place alone.

Nelson Road was mostly residential. Tall row houses lined the street, grubby with exhaust fumes. The road was a busy thoroughfare for London buses taking people into town. The shopping area was halfway down and made up of eight shops, four on each side of the road.

The entrance to Uncle Max's flat was through a cherry-red door to the left of the health food shop. Through it was a flight of stairs, which took you up to the flat's front door and a hallway out to the backyard, which Uncle Max shared with the shop.

Standing on the doorstep, Darkus pulled at a shoelace hanging around his neck and fingered the two keys Uncle Max had given him ten days earlier, when he'd first arrived. Uncle Max didn't get back from work till six, and his home wasn't equipped for kids; he didn't even have a TV. The front room was crammed with books, mismatched furniture, and strange objects Uncle Max had brought back from his travels. Darkus felt out of place when his uncle wasn't there, and it was in those moments that he missed his father most.

He dropped the keys back inside his shirt. Instead of going inside, he crossed the road and sat down on the curb opposite, a little way from the bus stop and a trash can.

He looked at the boarded-up shop next door to Mother Earth. Half of a broken EMPORIUM sign hung down wonkily over the wood-covered windows. Darkus guessed the shabby gray door between the two shops was like Uncle Max's door and led to the derelict-looking flat upstairs. Uncle Max had warned him to stay away from the men who lived there. They were cousins who'd inherited the building, he said, each planning to open a different type of shop downstairs, and because neither would give way, the Emporium had remained closed for five years.

Darkus decided he'd go and sit in the Laundromat opposite Mother Earth and read his Spider-Man comic until Uncle Max got home. Darkus liked the Laundromat. People were always coming and going, and the heat from the dryers made it warm.

As he stood up, a thin man in ill-fitting clothes came charging through the gray door, his eyes bulging out of their sunken sockets. His mouth was stretched wide, emitting a loud shriek and displaying a higgledy-piggledy collection of yellow teeth.

Darkus heard a series of crashes coming from inside the Emporium, and a man the size of an ogre thundered out of the same door, sweating and roaring. Darkus shuffled backward as the two men collided and began to grapple with each other.

"*You're* the health hazard!" the thin man screamed.

"Nonsense! It's *your* rubbish in the backyard that's the health hazard."

"That's stock for my shop."

"It's rotting junk, Pickering."

"What about your room, Humphrey? It's infested with bugs, and it stinks! People can probably smell it from out here!" He raised his beaklike nose in the air. "Yes! Yes! I can smell it now! Poo!"

Darkus sniffed, smelling nothing but exhaust fumes and trash-can juice.

Mr. Patel from the newspaper store came to the door of his shop to see what the fuss was about and rolled his eyes when he saw Pickering and Humphrey fighting. An elderly couple paused to watch the two men and then crossed the road to avoid them.

"I found beetles in my hair after being in your room for only five minutes—and the council knows what a slob you are, because I wrote to them and sent them those bugs as proof!" Pickering let out a shriek of laughter.

"*YOU'RE* THE FILTHY ONE!" Humphrey roared, his chins wobbling. "I've never found beetles in *my* hair."

"You don't HAVE hair!" The veins on Pickering's forehead bulged purple.

"You think you're *so* clever," Humphrey sneered at his cousin. "But the joke's on you, because I wrote to the council, too, complaining about all that trash you've piled up in the yard." He made a satisfied gurgling sound. "I even sent photographs."

"Idiot!" Pickering snapped.

"*I'm* an idiot?" Humphrey's head bobbed from side to side in outrage.

"Yes! Look what you've done!" Pickering threw his hands in the air. "You've got us evicted."

"What *I've* done?" The big man bared his bottom teeth. "It's your obsessive litter collecting that got us the eviction notice."

"That's stock for my antiques shop." Pickering pointed a wiry arm at the boarded-up shop. "It's the gargantuan mass of squalor up in your room that's caused this trouble."

"Antiques shop? I don't think so, rat face. This shop will sell PIES." Humphrey slammed his hand against the window board, making a loud bang.

"It will sell *antiques*!" Pickering pressed his body against the shop and stretched out his arms as if he were trying to hug it.

"PIES!" Humphrey pulled at his waist.

"ANTIQUES!" Pickering clung on tight.

"Pies, pies, PIES. This shop will sell PIES!"

"Over my dead body, Humphrey!"

"That, my dear Pickering, can be arranged."

Pickering wriggled out of Humphrey's grasp and, dodging under his arms, ran into the road. His fat cousin came thundering after him.

Darkus jumped to his feet, stumbling back from the curb as cars and buses screeched to a halt.

"PIES!" Humphrey hollered.

"*ANTIIIIIIIQUES!*" Pickering screamed, spinning around and hurling himself at Humphrey. Grabbing his neck, he leapt up onto his back and pummeled his face with his knuckles.

A thickset teenager leaned out of his tricked-out car and shouted for the men to get off the road.

Humphrey trumpeted like an elephant and shook his legs, trying to break free from Pickering's grip. As he did so, a gigantic black beetle dropped out of his trouser leg and landed on the road, right-side up.

Darkus blinked and leaned forward to get a better look. The beetle looked deadly—like a ninja warrior. A fierce tusk, sharp as a tiger's claw, stuck out of its head, flanked by two smaller horns on its thorax.

He looked about. No one seemed to have noticed the incredible insect that was now crawling toward him. Mr. Patel was standing in his doorway with his arms crossed, scowling at Humphrey and Pickering. Angry drivers were blasting their car horns, and the customers in the Laundromat had spilled onto the street to watch the wrestling men. But the beetle continued its advance toward him, slow and steady, like a miniature tank.

As it got closer, Darkus realized it was easily the size of a hamster. He wanted to get closer, but it was so alien looking that he was a bit scared to approach it. He didn't know if it might bite or sting—and that horn looked sharp.

Humphrey roared, and Darkus glanced up to see him grabbing hold of Pickering's ankles, rotating and spinning like an Olympic hammer thrower, faster and faster, until finally he let go of his cousin's feet, sending him flying into the windshield of a parked car and setting off the alarm.

Pickering's eyes were wide with shock as he slid down the hood and dropped onto the tarmac, smacking his head on the ground. Humphrey dusted off his hands and strode back into the Emporium flat, leaving his unconscious cousin in the road. The onlookers flocked to Pickering and began rolling him toward the gutter, out of the way of the traffic.

Darkus looked down. The giant insect was sitting right at his feet, and before he could think about whether it was a good idea or not, he was reaching down to touch the tip of its horn. It *was* sharp.

"Whoa, you're cool!" he said, realizing his heart was thumping in his chest.

Mesmerized, Darkus watched the beetle scramble up from the road onto the pavement, its body glistening like wet oil. He found the way it crawled fascinating. He'd never thought about the way he walked—upright on two legs—and he wondered what it would be like to have six legs, and to move around so close to the ground. The beetle walked by lifting three legs at a time—the front and rear legs of one side of its body together with the middle leg of the other.

When the insect reached his shoe, it started climbing, heading for his ankle—as if it was trying to get up his trouser leg, too!

"Hey! Stop!" Darkus fell backward, flicking out his foot and flinging the beetle away.

It landed on the pavement and paused, like it was thinking. Darkus was astonished to see it lifting its hard outer wings and unfolding a second semitransparent, rust-colored pair. It flew straight back to him. The giant beetle landed on his knee, clinging on to his trousers with its claws.

Darkus yelped and shook his leg again, rolling back onto his elbows, but the beetle wouldn't let go.

Beside the trash can next to him was a cardboard box. Darkus grabbed it and, sitting up, knocked the beetle into the box with the back of his hand. Embarrassed, he looked around to see if anyone had seen him flailing on the pavement, but everyone was crowded around the unconscious man on the other side of the road, discussing what they should do with him.

Peering into the box, Darkus saw the beetle on its back, legs thrashing about frantically as it tried to get back on its feet. He immediately felt bad for hitting it. He reached in and flipped the poor creature the right way up.

"I'm so sorry. I hope I didn't hurt you," Darkus said softly. "It's just you gave me a bit of a fright."

The beetle scrambled into the corner of the box, pulling at the walls of the temporary prison with its front legs.

"Calm down, little fella. I'm not going to hurt you."

But the beetle kept tearing at the walls, so Darkus decided to set it free. Crouching down, he held the box on its side on the pavement. The beetle scurried out of the box, but instead of running away, it clambered onto Darkus's hand and stood still, looking up at him expectantly.

It took a second for Darkus to realize he was okay with the beetle being on him. The gentle scratch of its claws against his skin was almost pleasant. What surprised him was the weight of the insect— he'd assumed it would be light, but it felt solid and reassuring, like a pebble. He carefully lifted his hand. "Hello there."

Looking up from underneath, he could see the features of the beetle's face. He couldn't have said why but it looked somehow . . . friendly. Its bulbous eyes glistened like blackberries, and it was hold-ing its mouth open as if it were trying to smile. Although the beetle appeared to be pitch-black from above, underneath it had red hair sticking out of the gaps between its joints and body. It was almost cute. And then he realized: This was the creature from Uncle Max's window, the day he'd moved in. The six legs, the horn, the size—it all fit.

"I've seen you before, haven't I?"

As if to answer his question, the beetle began crawling up Darkus's arm.

"What are you up to?" Darkus asked, intrigued now.

The beetle crawled along to his elbow and up to his shoulder.

"Hey, where are you going?" He laughed. He was beginning to like this insect.

Turning to face forward, the beetle hunkered down on Darkus's shoulder, exactly where a pirate would have put a parrot.

Darkus stood up carefully. "You're the freakiest beetle I've ever met!" he said.

"Well, well. Look who it is!"

Darkus froze, and his heart sank.

"It's the sniveling orphan," Robby called out. "And Big Bird's not here to protect you this time."

Darkus turned around. Standing at the bus stop were Daniel Dowie, Robby at his elbow, and three of the other boys who'd been standing by the tree earlier. What had Virginia called them? The clones. They all glared at him, shoulders hunched and hands wedged deep in their pockets. "Clones" was a good name for them—but whatever he called them, they were standing between him and the door to Uncle Max's flat.

"What do you want?" he asked, sounding more confident than he felt.

"Shut up." Robby spat on the ground at Darkus's feet. "You ain't fit to lick Dowie's boots, let alone talk to him. In fact—yeah, lick his boots."

The clones gibbered and grunted with pleasure.

Daniel Dowie put one foot forward and smiled meanly at Darkus.

"If your boots need cleaning"—Darkus looked Daniel Dowie in the eye—"ask Robby to do it. He puts so much effort into kissing your butt, he's sure to do a good job."

Daniel Dowie snorted with anger and looked at Robby, who rolled up his sleeves.

"Fight! Fight! Fight!" the clones chanted.

Darkus's insides ran cold as he watched Robby strut backward and forward. He knew he was about to take a beating.

Robby moved in on Darkus. "I'm going to knock your teeth right down your throat," he jeered.

Darkus narrowed his eyes and did his best to look unbothered, but his heart was beating hard and his palms were clammy. Being a solitary kid, he'd been picked on plenty of times. Usually, he managed to walk away, but sometimes he'd have to stand and fight, so he knew how to defend himself. Not that that would help him here; even if he managed to knock Robby down, there were four more of them waiting to pile on.

Without warning, Robby ran at him.

Unprepared, Darkus raised his fists as Robby plowed into him, punching him in the stomach. His legs gave way, the air ripping from his lungs as he sank to the ground. He landed on the cardboard box, flattening it against the pavement. As he gasped for air, all his eyes could focus on was the Baxter's soup logo printed white on red on the side. Pain ricocheted around his body, and as Robby whooped and closed in to kick him, a fleeting wish that he was stronger shot through his head.

Darkus pulled his knees to his chest, curling up into a ball. He saw the sole of a shoe come speeding toward his ribs and braced himself— but instead of the pain he was expecting, he heard an explosive hiss.

He looked up. The giant black beetle rocketed up into Robby's face and was flying at him, hissing—almost spitting—like a king cobra.

"What the heck is THAT?" Robby sprang backward as if he'd been Tasered.

"What does it look like?" Darkus scrambled onto his knees, thinking quickly. "It's my beetle."

"Bloody hell!" Daniel Dowie's eyes were locked on the enormous hissing insect. Robby stumbled back to the clones, and all five boys shuffled backward.

The beetle hovered in the air in front of Darkus, its soft wings vibrating so fast they were barely visible. It hissed again, like a piston valve on a steam engine.

"Get away! Stay back!" the boys shouted at the beetle, grabbing on to one another in fear.

"You're not scared of a beetle, are you?" Darkus barked out a laugh, his arm wrapped around his aching stomach as he dragged himself up onto his feet. He pulled out the keys to the flat from around his neck. If he could just get across the road and open that red door, he'd be safe.

The beetle suddenly darted at the cluster of terrified boys, its horn shooting past their faces.

Darkus's jaw dropped open.

"It's trying to get me!" one of the clones shrieked, ducking.

"It's dive-bombing!" shouted another.

"Cover your eyes!" Darkus shouted. "Or it'll . . . er . . . pop your eyeballs," he continued, bluffing. "This type of beetle is called, um, an Eye-Gouger!"

The beetle swooped over the cowering boys' heads like a miniature fighter plane, hissing in their ears before circling back to Darkus. As Darkus felt the insect land back on his shoulder, he did his best to hide his surprise and delight from the boys groveling before him. He felt powerful with the majestic beetle on his shoulder. It was a new feeling, and he liked it.

"You're a nut job!" Daniel Dowie shouted, uncovering his eyes and stumbling backward. "Freakin' beetle boy!"

"Whatever you say." Darkus smiled, beginning to enjoy himself. "But the Eye-Gouger and me, we're a team, see. And if you come near me again, we'll find out where you live, and my friend here will crawl through your letter box in the middle of the night and pop your eyes while you're sleeping."

"We ain't afraid of you, cockroach breath," Robby called out from behind Daniel Dowie. "Talkin' to creepy-crawly insects 'cause you got no friends. You even look like a beetle—dirty-beady-bug-eyed loser."

Darkus looked at his shoulder. The beetle was looking up at him, its mandibles waggling. Darkus nodded as if he understood.

"Yes, Eye-Gouger, Robby *has* got juicy-looking eyes," he said loudly. "You're right!"

The boys turned on their heels and bolted down the road. "BEETLE FREAK!" shouted Robby as he disappeared around the corner.

Darkus snorted—half amused, half relieved—and turned away. The traffic was back to its usual ebb and flow. Pickering had gone, and the people washing their clothes had returned to the warmth of the Laundromat.

"Thanks," he said to the insect. "You just saved me from getting my head kicked in." He reached up and hesitatingly stroked its wing cases. They were smooth, like new plastic. As he stroked the beetle and looked into its blackberry eyes, he felt they connected somehow, like kindred spirits.

Darkus shook his head. He was being weird. You couldn't be kindred spirits with a beetle . . . could you?

He crouched down and placed the beetle on the flattened soup box.

"There you go, little fella, you're free to go home now."

The beetle didn't move.

"What's the matter?" He gave it a little shove. "Go on."

The beetle looked up at him.

"Come on, I can't hang around here waiting for you to find your way home," Darkus said, standing up. "I've got homework to do."

The beetle flew up and landed back on Darkus's shoulder.

"What did you do that for?" Darkus frowned. "Do you want to come home with me?"

The beetle opened its mouth like it had before, as if it was trying to smile at him.

Darkus shrugged. "Well, if you're going to come home with me, you'll need a name, because I'm not calling you Eye-Gouger." He looked at the soup box squashed under his feet. "Baxter's a pretty good name for a beetle. How about we call you Baxter?"

The beetle bowed its horn. Darkus blinked, wondering if he was imagining things. "I'm going to take that to mean yes."

The beetle opened its mouth, smiling.

Darkus felt a spot of rain hit his head and suddenly became aware that Mr. Patel was standing in the doorway of his shop, watching him have a conversation with an insect. He waved awkwardly, shook his head, and crossed the road.

Maybe he was losing his marbles. After all, talking to a beetle? It's not like it could understand him.

CHAPTER FOUR

The Entomology Vaults

*D*arkus took out his key and opened Uncle Max's front door, climbing the three flights of stairs to the attic.

"This is my room, Baxter," he said, turning on the light and walking to the photo hanging on the wall. "That's my dad. You'll like him. He's always telling me not to squash insects." He stared at the picture in silence for a moment. "He says you should never take a life, no matter how small. He won't even let me kill the slugs in the backyard."

The beetle's wing sheaths flickered open and closed rapidly. The insect seemed oddly overexcited, and Darkus moved away, in case the giant two-dimensional human face was frightening the beetle.

"I sleep there"—he pointed at the hammock—"and that's it, really. It's small, but it's better than living up somebody's trouser leg."

He sat down on the floor, putting the beetle on the makeshift table and leaning in to study it closely. It was pretty hairy in places, and its armor-plated underbelly reminded Darkus of a crab's. Its front legs had hinged kneecaps, but its back legs were chunkier and stretched out almost in a straight line.

The beetle suffered the inspection, staring back at him, unblinking.

Darkus had never been afraid of insects, but it hadn't occurred to him that you might have one as a pet. He wondered if Uncle Max would let him keep the beetle. It was pretty cool, and he'd liked how he felt when Baxter was sitting on his shoulder.

"C'mon." He scooped up the beetle. "Let's go down to the kitchen and find out what you eat."

"I'm home." Uncle Max's voice came up the stairs.

"In the kitchen," Darkus called back, picking Baxter up off the table.

"Good news," Uncle Max cried as he burst into the room. "I've got us an appointment at the museum." He stopped speaking when he saw what Darkus was holding in his hands. "What's that?"

"It's a beetle." Darkus lifted it up. "Isn't it cool?"

Uncle Max stared at the insect and then at Darkus. "Where did you get it?"

"In the street. It climbed onto my hand." Darkus pulled his hands into his chest protectively, surprised by the tone of his uncle's voice. "I tried to let it go, but it won't leave me alone. It seems to like me."

"Here? Outside, in the street?" Uncle Max's shoulders dropped, and he seemed to relax a bit.

"Yes. Just crawling around, all on its own." Darkus looked at the floor; he felt bad not telling his uncle the whole truth.

"How strange." Uncle Max's voice sounded distant, as if he was thinking about something troubling.

"What did you say about the museum?" Darkus asked, changing the subject.

"Ah, yes!" Uncle Max's finger shot up in the air. "Tomorrow, my lad, you and I are going to take a look inside that blasted vault."

"Really?" Darkus's heart leapt. "What about school?"

"Hang school." Uncle Max swiped the air in front of his face. "Barty's more important."

"Yes." Darkus nodded. "He is."

Uncle Max narrowed his eyes, looking at the insect Darkus was clutching to his chest. "I wonder who the beetle belongs to," he said.

"Perhaps it doesn't belong to anyone."

"There'll almost certainly be an owner, my lad. A rhinoceros beetle, like that one . . ."

"A rhinoceros beetle?" Darkus put the beetle back down on the table and looked at his uncle.

"That's the common name for a horned beauty like that chap." Uncle Max leaned over. "I must say, he is a handsome specimen—and you can tell he *is* a he because females don't have the tusk." He pointed with his little finger. "He's not a native Londoner. He's probably from the Amazon or the Far East. You'd pay a pretty penny to buy him in a pet shop, and even then"—Uncle Max's forehead creased—"I'm not sure it's legal to trade this species."

"Can I keep him?" Darkus asked, pleading with his eyes.

"Someone might be out looking for him."

"Please?"

"If anyone comes knocking saying they've lost a rhinoceros beetle, you'll have to give him back."

"I know. I will, I promise." Darkus held his breath, hoping.

"Um, well . . ."

"Please say yes."

There was a long pause, and Darkus thought he might burst.

"I suppose he can stay with us for now." Uncle Max's frown melted as Darkus's somber face was transformed by a smile. "I suppose a pet would be good company for you while I'm at the university." He sighed. "Have you already given him a name?"

Darkus nodded. "Baxter, like the soup."

"I like the sound of that." Uncle Max nodded his approval. "It's a good name for a beetle."

"I've never had a pet before." Darkus gazed happily at Baxter. "Thank you."

"That's all right, lad." Uncle Max threw his hands up in defeat. "I can hardly say no, when I know Barty would say yes."

Darkus looked up, surprised. "He would?"

"Of course! A handsome hexapod like this? He'd be bonkers about it!"

Darkus frowned. His dad cared greatly about the environment, recycling everything and using minimal energy. He watched birds in the spring and grew vegetables for their dinner table, often lecturing him on the benefits of spiders, but not once—ever—could Darkus remember him talking about liking beetles. "What do you mean?"

"Oh, sorry—a hexapod is a creature with six legs."

"No, I mean what you said about Dad being bonkers about Baxter."

"Well, it's obvious. Barty's obsessed with beetles." Uncle Max seemed perplexed by the confusion on Darkus's face. "And Baxter, well, I haven't seen a finer specimen. So it's only natural that he would be crazy about . . ." His voice petered out.

"Dad's obsessed with beetles?" Darkus felt odd inside as he watched his uncle realize this was something he didn't know.

"Doesn't he ever take you insect hunting?" Uncle Max asked weakly.

"No." Darkus shook his head and searched his memory for any time that his dad had talked to him about insects. "He tells me I shouldn't kill spiders, though."

"Oh, well, um . . . I suppose it was a long time ago. Perhaps he grew out of it. We were kids, after all." Uncle Max looked deeply uncomfortable. "And he's right, you shouldn't kill spiders."

As he and his uncle stared at each other across the table, it dawned on Darkus that he'd stumbled upon some kind of secret, and he didn't know what to say. He couldn't think why liking beetles would be something Dad should keep from him, and the fact that his dad had secrets stung inside.

Uncle Max slid his chair back from the table and disappeared out of the room without saying a word. Darkus took a deep breath and blinked back tears. He'd had the best day in ages—making friends with Virginia and Bertolt, and then finding Baxter—and now suddenly he felt horrible again.

Uncle Max was back, clutching an old red book with a gold stag beetle embossed on the cover. "If you're going to look after Baxter properly, you'll need this." He slid it across the table.

Darkus opened the cover. It was a fragile old book and some of the pages were loose. The title page said *The Beetle Collector's Handbook.* In the top right-hand corner, in a child's handwriting, was written Bartholomew Cuttle, age 9.

Flicking through the pages, Darkus saw that the book listed the various families of beetle and had color pictures on pages protected by tissue paper. He found an illustration of a rhinoceros beetle and looked up at Uncle Max.

"Dad loves beetles?"

Uncle Max nodded. "Ever since he was a boy he's been fascinated by them."

Darkus looked at the rhinoceros beetle sitting quietly on the table. "I am, too."

"Barty became something of an expert. He worked in the field for a while."

"You can become an expert on beetles?" Darkus had never heard of such a job.

Uncle Max laughed and nodded.

"Then that's what I'm going to do." Darkus closed the book and hugged it to his chest.

Uncle Max ran his hand along the top of Darkus's stubbly head. "You may look like your mother, but you are just like Barty."

"But I don't understand. Why didn't he tell me?"

"That's not for me to say, lad. It was all a long time ago, before you were born. You'll have to ask your father about it when we find him." Uncle Max leaned down and opened the cupboard below the sink, lifting out a rectangular fish tank. "Now, when I was young, I was crazy about terrapins. I had two, Howard and Carter, adorable fellows, and this"—he set the aquarium down on the table—"was their home." He scratched at a crust of algae with his thumb. "It needs a bit of a clean, but it might make a good home for a beetle."

"For Baxter?" Darkus stood up.

"Yes." Uncle Max smiled.

Darkus carefully placed the red book in the tank and wrapped his arms around it, lifting it against his chest. "Thank you. We'll wash it right away, won't we, Baxter?"

"Careful, it's heavy."

"I've got it." Darkus shuffled toward the door. "C'mon, Baxter."

Baxter's wings rattled like helicopter blades as he lifted off the kitchen table and landed neatly on Darkus's shoulder.

Uncle Max's jaw dropped open. "Good lord!"

"I know!" Darkus said from the hall. "He looks too heavy to fly, doesn't he?"

The door closed, leaving Uncle Max standing in the middle of the kitchen, stunned. He rubbed his hands over his face and sat down, his mind reeling.

He'd seen a beetle respond to a human command once before, many years ago in Bartholomew's laboratory, and he'd done his best to forget it had ever happened.

He shook his head. He must have imagined it; what with all the talk about Barty and his past, he was getting jumpy. Barty had promised Esme he'd never go back to the abominable work he'd done for the Fabre Project.

But Esme was dead. And if his brother had returned to his research, what did that mean?

Was it connected to his sudden disappearance?

Max looked up at the ceiling. None of this made any sense. If Darkus's rhinoceros beetle had anything to do with the Fabre Project, how did it come to be on Nelson Parade? And the project had been shut down for over ten years now. Professor Appleyard was retired, for goodness' sake.

He was imagining things. The beetle couldn't have been responding to Darkus. It was just following him out of the room.

But even that, Max knew, went against the behavioral patterns of an insect.

The next morning, dressed in his green sweater and jeans, Darkus scrambled into the passenger seat of his uncle's car, carefully placing his backpack at his feet.

"The car's a bit of a clunker, I'm afraid." Uncle Max turned the key in the ignition for a fourth time. "But once she's cleared her throat, she fires up like a Ferrari."

On the fifth attempt, the engine roared to life, and the mint-green Renault 4 bunny-hopped forward.

"Whoops!" Uncle Max chuckled. "Hand brake!" He released the hand brake and stamped on the clutch, grinding through the gears as he pulled out into the road. "I've persuaded Eddie to let us into the vaults," he said, leaning over the steering wheel to check that the road was clear before accelerating across a junction.

Darkus knew Eddie from visits during the school holidays. He was the security guard on duty when Dad had disappeared. He always had a smile for Darkus, and a bag of sweets in his pocket.

"Margaret is going to meet us and unlock the room Barty disappeared from." Uncle Max looked at Darkus. "You remember Margaret, don't you?"

Darkus nodded. Margaret was his father's very bosomy, overly perfumed secretary.

"Marvelous girl." He chuckled. "She used to have a bit of a thing for me when I was a younger man."

"Eeurk!" Darkus grimaced.

"Now, we'll need to keep our heads down," Uncle Max continued, ignoring Darkus, "because the museum, or rather Mr. Langley, the museum director, wasn't overly keen to let us have a look in those vaults."

"We're sneaking in?"

"Let's just say this is not an official visit." Uncle Max grinned. "But there's nothing to worry about—we archaeologists are always venturing into places uninvited. I flatter myself when I say I'm pretty good at it."

"Why won't Mr. Langley let us in?"

"I'm not sure." Uncle Max frowned. "He waffled on about the police having done a thorough search and the rooms having restricted access. To be honest, I stopped listening when I realized he wasn't going to say yes. Eddie and Margaret were much more helpful."

They parked a couple of streets away from the museum and walked in through the main entrance, like any family on a day trip. Eddie was waiting for them beside a café on the ground floor. He was standing in his uniform in front of a door marked NO ENTRY.

"Hello, Edward, how are you?" Uncle Max asked, shaking his hand.

"I'm very well, thank you, Professor." Eddie grinned at Darkus and rubbed his hand across his head. "What happened to your hair, son? Had a fight with a lawnmower?"

"Hi, Eddie." Darkus smiled shyly. "Something like that, yeah."

"You look like a hedgehog," Eddie said, offering him a hard candy from a bag in his pocket.

"Thanks." Darkus took the sweet. "I mean, for doing this. Letting us see the vault."

"No bother, son." Eddie shook his head. "Terrible strange business. Glad to be able to help."

They followed him through the door and down a flight of stairs into the belly of the building, where Bartholomew Cuttle's personal secretary, Margaret Dingle, was waiting for them.

Uncle Max lifted his safari hat. "Good of you to help with this, Maggie."

"Not at all, Max." Margaret blushed. "You know I'd do anything for Barty." She grabbed Darkus's shoulders. "Now, young man, I'm sure you're too old for a hug, but that's not going to stop me." She smothered him with her mauve cardigan and then grabbed his chin. "Let me look at you. How are you holding up?"

"I'm fine," Darkus reassured her, untangling himself. "Uncle Max is looking after me great."

"Are you feeding the child properly, Max? He looks thin . . . and what have you done to his hair?"

"He's always been thin," Uncle Max huffed. "Now, stop fussing over the poor boy and let's have a look at this room my brother magically disappeared from."

"This is the one Bartholomew was in." Margaret pulled a set of keys from her handbag and walked to the third of six gray metal doors.

"Are these rooms private?" Uncle Max asked, following her.

"The collection is open to researchers and academics, but only by appointment with the director of the museum. Occasionally, we'll exhibit parts of it to the public, but it's too big for one exhibition."

Above the door was a wooden plaque with the words THE CUTTER COLEOPTERA COLLECTION engraved in gold.

Uncle Max pointed at the plaque. "Would that be Lucretia Cutter?" he asked, his face draining of color.

"Mm-hmm," Margaret nodded, unlocking the door. "She's a great patron of the museum. She sponsors the Coleoptera collection. The Natural History Museum has the largest collection in the world, and it costs a lot to take care of it."

Darkus had never heard of Lucretia Cutter, but he could see from the expression on his uncle's face that she was bad news.

"What does *co-le-op-ter-a* mean?" Darkus asked, sounding out the unfamiliar word.

"It means *sheath wing*," Uncle Max replied. "It's the Latin name for beetles because beetles have two sets of wings, you see. The elytra—the hard protective sheath wings—and the soft ones underneath that they use for flying."

Darkus thought back to Baxter flying at the clones and remembered his surprisingly wide see-through amber wings. You'd never guess he kept them folded away, hidden under his elytra. The new word felt like a discovered secret, and Darkus was keen to use it as soon as possible.

"Hang on a minute—beetles?" he said. "Dad went missing in a room full of *beetles*?"

Uncle Max raised one eyebrow. "Precisely so, lad."

Margaret held the door open, and Darkus pushed inside, desperate to see the room his father had disappeared from five weeks ago.

The collection room was empty and bare. It had at its center an enormous wooden table, which was bare except for an impressive microscope. Along the left- and right-hand walls were floor-to-ceiling wooden cabinets made up of hundreds of slender drawers with brass handles. There was no way out of this room other than the door behind him, and there was nothing in the room but drawers and a table. The hope he'd harbored—that he and Uncle Max would find something the police hadn't spotted—evaporated as he looked around the spotless room.

His heart sank. He couldn't help but feel disappointed.

Outside the door, he heard Margaret whispering to Uncle Max: "Oh, Max—they're talking about advertising for a new Director of Science."

"Are they, now?" Uncle Max cleared his throat angrily. "Well, that's going to be embarrassing when we find Barty, isn't it?" He paused and lowered his voice. "Don't say anything in front of the lad—no need to upset him."

Darkus went rigid. He was sick of being treated like a child.

Annoyed by their secrecy, he went over to one of the wooden cabinets and pulled a drawer open. His irritation changed to wonder when he saw rows and rows of dead stag beetles pinned to a white board under a pane of glass, each with a neat red label below it. He'd read his dad's beetle book from cover to cover the night before, but he would have recognized these beetles anyway, because of their antler-like jaws. He opened another drawer, and another—they were all full of beetles. He looked around the room again. If every one of these drawers was filled with a hundred different types of beetle . . . his brain went blank when he tried to do the math.

"There's thousands!" he whispered.

He slid off his backpack, unzipped it, and pulled out a massive jam jar with a perforated lid. Uncle Max had said that Baxter couldn't sit on Darkus's shoulder when he was out of the house, in case the beetle upset people. Darkus had complained that he wanted to take Baxter out for walks, so, as a compromise, Uncle Max had found the jam jar at the back of a kitchen cupboard, and while Darkus washed it, Uncle Max had made perforations in the lid with a screwdriver and hammer.

Darkus placed the jar on the table now and tapped the glass. Baxter didn't move. Thinking he might not like being in the jar, Darkus unscrewed the lid, reached in, and picked up the rhinoceros beetle, putting him on his shoulder. Baxter was unusually still— even his antennae were motionless—but he didn't protest. Delving back into the backpack, Darkus pulled out his beetle book and flicked it open, turning over the pages until he reached the chapter on rhinoceros beetles. He found the Latin word he was looking for: *Chalcosoma*.

He walked along the wall of drawers until he saw the word on a label below a brass handle, and he pulled out the drawer.

"Whoa!" Darkus found he was looking down at rows of black and brown rhinoceros beetles. Some were big, some small, some mottled, some plain, some with five horns, some with none—but one thing was obvious: Baxter was bigger than all of them.

"Baxter, you're a giant! Look at this one." He pushed his finger against the glass. "It's like a mini version of you."

Baxter hissed at him quietly and picked his way down Darkus's shoulder, away from the dead beetles.

"What's the matter?" Darkus said. But even as he spoke, he realized that for Baxter, this room was a graveyard.

Uncle Max followed Margaret into the room.

"You brought the beetle?" Uncle Max said, stopping and staring at Baxter.

Darkus stepped backward, startled by the sharpness of his uncle's voice.

"I—I . . ." Darkus didn't want to admit he'd brought Baxter for support, in case he got upset. "I didn't think it would matter." He cupped his hand over Baxter. "I'll put him back in his jar."

"I think that would be best." Uncle Max gave Margaret an apologetic look. "You're not allowed to bring live animals into the collection vaults, Darkus."

"I didn't realize. Sorry." Darkus held Baxter in his cupped hands and looked at Margaret. "The police report said there were specimen trays open in this room. Are these specimen trays?" He nodded at the drawer of dead rhinoceros beetles.

Margaret nodded. "That's right. Some of these drawers house the beetles from Darwin's personal collection."

"Which ones were open?" Darkus asked, taking Baxter over to the jam jar. "I want to see the beetles Dad was looking at."

Margaret pointed. "The third column along, in the middle section— you'll see three trays marked with blue stickers. They were open when I came down here with the police."

Darkus tried to put Baxter back into his jar, but the beetle didn't seem to want to go. He kept crawling up his wrist and slipping out of his grasp. Uncle Max pulled open the top drawer labeled with a blue sticker. Darkus leaned over to look, and Baxter dropped onto the table.

"Some of the beetles are missing," Uncle Max announced. "There should be a row of darkling beetles here and here. There's nothing but labels."

Darkus drew closer, forgetting Baxter for a moment.

Margaret frowned. "That's odd."

Uncle Max pulled open another blue-stickered drawer. "This one is completely empty. And so is this one."

"Perhaps the police took them away?" Darkus suggested.

Margaret shook her head. "They didn't take any beetles."

Darkus looked down at the empty drawers. "And there's no glass, either."

"You're right!" Uncle Max nodded. "Why might that be, Margaret?"

"I—I don't know." She blinked. "There should be." Her voice trembled.

"It's okay, Maggie. Is there anything else you can tell us about how the room looked?" Uncle Max asked softly.

She pointed toward the seat behind the microscope. "Bartholomew's papers and coffee were there, on the table next to the microscope." She bit her lip in an effort to hold back tears. "The cup was still full."

Darkus went and sat down on the chair, placing his hands on either side of the microscope and looking into it. Nothing. He looked up just in time to see Baxter drop off the table onto the floor. He glanced up at Uncle Max, who had his arm around Margaret's shoulders, comforting her, and quickly ducked under the table.

"Baxter," he whispered, crawling toward the beetle. "Come here." The beetle ignored him, scurrying over to a wide mesh grate, two feet high, underneath the cabinets.

Darkus pulled his body forward quickly and quietly. All he could hear was Margaret's muffled sobs.

"No! Baxter!" he whispered as the beetle clambered through the grate and disappeared. He scrambled up onto his knees and poked his fingers through a hole in the mesh, but he couldn't reach the beetle. He pressed his cheek to the floor and tried to see what Baxter was doing; it was pitch-black, and the beetle was invisible in the darkness.

Darkus stood up. "Um, Margaret?" he said, looking up to the ceiling and around the room.

She lifted her blotchy face from Uncle Max's jacket lapel. "Yes?"

"What are these grates for, by the floor?"

"That's the climate-control system. It keeps the room at the right temperature to preserve the beetles," Margaret explained between sniffs.

"Does it lead anywhere?"

Margaret looked confused. "What do you mean?"

"I mean, if you took the grate off and, um, maybe crawled under there . . ."

"No, dear." Margaret shook her head. "There's a room with an air-conditioning machine that keeps all the collection rooms at the right temperature, and the shaft behind those cabinets leads to that machine and delivers cooled air into this room."

"What are you thinking, Darkus?" Uncle Max asked, moving away from Margaret and coming to look at the grates.

"Nothing. I . . ." He didn't want his uncle to get angry about Baxter's having run away. "Well, I felt the cold air on my cheek and wondered where it came from. That's all."

"Hmmm." Uncle Max stroked his chin as he looked at the grate. "Good thinking, lad, and you're right. Those grates *are* a way out of this room, but if Barty went down that air-conditioning shaft, then someone would've had to force him, or carry him—and that's too small a space for two men to crawl through, especially if one is struggling or unconscious." He sighed and returned to the puzzle of the empty specimen drawers.

Darkus's pulse quickened. It hadn't occurred to him that the grates might be a way out of the collection room. He dropped back down to his knees, suddenly excited. Uncle Max was right: The gap beneath the cabinets was small, much too small for two men to crawl through. But it was big enough for one. If he unscrewed the grate and took it off, Darkus was sure he could wriggle through the vent. There wasn't enough space to crawl on hands and knees, but if he lay on his belly, he would be able to propel himself forward using his elbows and toes.

He tugged at the grate front, and it rattled but didn't want to come off. He peered into the darkness beyond until his eyes could make out the air-conditioning shaft opposite. If Baxter didn't come back, he'd have to take the grate off and crawl after him.

He unscrewed one of the grate fasteners with his fingers, wishing he'd brought Uncle Max's screwdriver. And then he spotted a solid black shadow shuffling backward, dragging something.

Darkus licked around the widest part of his hand to make it slippery, and pushed it through the grate mesh, reaching in until his upper arm stopped him from moving any farther. He laid his hand flat on the floor.

"C'mon, Baxter," he whispered. "Get on my hand."

The beetle slowly crawled backward, gradually backing onto Darkus's palm. He had something gold hooked over his horn.

Gently cupping his hand around the beetle, Darkus carefully pulled his arm back out of the grate and sat up cross-legged on the floor. He uncurled his fingers and cried out as he recognized the gold half-moon glasses hanging off Baxter's horn.

"What's the matter, lad?"

Darkus got to his feet, clutching the glasses in his right hand and hiding Baxter behind his back with his left. "I found Dad's glasses—there, behind the grate."

"What were they doing down there?" Uncle Max wondered. He took the glasses from Darkus, studied them, and then looked at Margaret.

"I don't know!" Her bottom lip wobbled. "The police said they searched the grates. They didn't find anything."

"The glasses were quite far in," Darkus said.

"Well done, Darkus." Uncle Max winked at him. "You've found a clue." He looked at Margaret. "Did Barty come down here often? For work?"

"No," she replied. "Actually, his being in this room was strange. He avoided anything to do with the beetles. I thought perhaps he was phobic—you know, frightened of them."

Uncle Max snorted. "Barty's not frightened of beetles."

"I guess Bartholomew would have been wearing his glasses to look at samples." She sounded uncertain. "Perhaps they fell through the grate when . . . when . . . oh dear." Her voice quivered and she began to cry. "Sorry."

Darkus looked away, embarrassed by her sudden gush of emotion.

Uncle Max patted Margaret's arm gently. "There, there, Maggie, don't go upsetting yourself."

Darkus stepped over to the table and dropped Baxter into the jam jar. The beetle went in without protesting this time, but as Darkus screwed the lid on, he started to flick his elytra open, bashing them against the glass and hissing loudly as he'd done to Robby.

"What's the matter?" Darkus whispered, almost dropping the jar as it jerked out of his hands. But Baxter kept flailing about and hissing.

"What's wrong with the insect?" Uncle Max asked over Margaret's shoulder.

"I don't know." Darkus scratched his head. "He didn't seem to mind being in the jar earlier. Should I let him out?"

"Darkus, you can't go letting live insects loose in here. What if Baxter damages the collection? Keep him in the jar."

Darkus picked up the jar and hugged it to his chest, hoping Baxter would calm down, but now he was ramming the glass with his horn over and over again.

"Shhhh, shhhh. It's all right."

But the beetle kept on head-butting the glass, stopping only to hiss.

Darkus looked in the direction in which Baxter's horn was pointing and found he was looking at the door. Something moving above the door caught his eye. It was a lemon-yellow ladybug the size of a two-pence coin, speckled with black spots.

Darkus pointed. "I thought you said live insects weren't allowed in here."

Uncle Max and Margaret looked up. The ladybug paused and then took off, disappearing into the corridor.

"That's strange," Margaret murmured. "I saw a big yellow ladybug in here on the day Bartholomew disappeared. I had forgotten it in all the excitement."

Darkus looked at Uncle Max. Beetles seemed to be everywhere. Had that always been the case and he'd just never noticed, or did the yellow ladybug mean something?

Uncle Max was staring at Baxter, who was now sitting quietly in his jar. He stroked his chin and looked down the corridor, after the lemon ladybug.

"I think it might be time to leave," he said, his eyes flickering about the room as if he expected someone to jump out at him.

"What? But don't we want to find out how Dad's glasses got into the grate?" Darkus asked.

"We came to have a look around, and I think we've done that. So let's thank Margaret for letting us see the room and head out into the museum—maybe take a look at a few dinosaurs? Yes?" Uncle Max grabbed Darkus's backpack and threw it at him. "You're going to have to put Baxter away, lad, and keep him hidden. Hop to it."

Darkus lifted Baxter's jar into the bag. Something was going on that he'd missed. Uncle Max looked worried now—in fact, worse than worried—and he was ushering Margaret in the direction of the door.

"Can I take one more look at the rhinoceros beetles?" Darkus asked, crossing the room to get his red book.

"No. It's time to go," Uncle Max said firmly, looking him in the eye. *"Right now."*

"Okay." Darkus nodded, wondering if it was the yellow ladybug that had made his uncle so desperate to leave.

"No one can enter these rooms without an appointment, right?" Uncle Max said to Margaret.

She nodded. "Well, no one except the sponsor."

"That's what I was afraid of," Uncle Max muttered, handing Darkus the reading glasses. "You'd better keep a tight hold of these. You found them, after all, and Barty's going to need them when he gets home." He herded Darkus through the door.

"Shouldn't we tell the police about the glasses, Max?" Margaret asked as he pushed Darkus past her, into the corridor.

"I don't think so." Uncle Max shook his head and pulled a reassuring face. "If anything really useful crops up, I'll let them know."

"Oh, okay." Margaret closed the vault door and took out her keys to lock it.

"Well, it was very kind of you to let us see the room, but we must be getting on, Maggie." Uncle Max moved backward, down the hall.

"Wait." Margaret took a folder from her shoulder bag. "I don't know if this will help, but these are the papers Barty had in the vault with him. The police scanned them and returned them to me, assuming they were museum business. The top letter is addressed to the museum, but the rest of the notes are in Barty's handwriting, and I don't recognize the subject matter—perhaps a personal project? I thought you should have them."

"Thank you, Maggie." Uncle Max took the file and tucked it under his arm. "That's very thoughtful."

Darkus looked at the folder. It said *Fabre Project* on it. At the back of his mind, he knew that he'd seen those words before, but he couldn't put his finger on where.

"It really *is* lovely to see you, Maggie." Uncle Max covered Margaret's hand with his own. "Thank you for letting us into the vault. It means a lot to Darkus, and to me." He paused. "Perhaps you'd like to have dinner some evening?"

Margaret flushed with pleasure and gave a little nod as she stared down at Uncle Max's hand on hers. "You'll let me know if you hear anything?" she whispered.

"Of course!" Uncle Max kissed her hand. Darkus was unimpressed. "Onward!" Uncle Max pointed, and Darkus followed his order, disappearing down the corridor before there was more kissing.

Eddie let them out through the same door, and they stopped briefly to say good-bye. Then Uncle Max hurried Darkus past the dinosaur exhibition and toward the exit.

"What's the rush?" Darkus said.

"Just a hunch, lad, but I'd rather not wait around to see if I'm right," Uncle Max replied, not explaining himself.

Darkus rolled his eyes and tried to keep up.

As they rushed through Hintze Hall, past the giant *Diplodocus* skeleton and toward the open doors of the main entrance, there was a terrific screeching sound, and Darkus saw a stunning black car drive up the pedestrianized driveway. People dived out of the way, grabbing on to their children and pulling them to safety.

Darkus cried out as Uncle Max suddenly dragged him backward

through the nearest doorway into what turned out to be a bathroom for the disabled. "What are you doing?" he shouted, alarmed.

"Shhhhhhhhhhh." Uncle Max calmly put his finger to his lips. He opened the door a sliver and peered through the gap into the entrance hall of the museum.

Two sparkling black canes appeared, and then a woman's head. Jet-black hair, gold lips, and then her body came lurching into view, leaning on the canes. She wore a white laboratory coat over a long black dress, and every jarring movement of her body screamed out how angry she was.

"Where is he?" she shouted at the unfortunate young man behind the information desk.

"Who?" he quivered.

"The sniveling director of this rotting institution." She lifted a hand from its cane, which hung from a loop around her wrist, and smashed it down onto the counter. "He's let someone into *my* vault!"

"Ah, Madame Cutter!" came a terrified voice, accompanied by the pattering of hurried footsteps. "To what do we owe this honor?"

"Shut up!" she barked. "Take me downstairs *immediately*. There's someone in my vault."

"I can assure you, Madame Cutter, that cannot be true. No one can enter the Coleoptera vaults without an appointment. We do not permit the public to enter the collection rooms."

"Don't tell me what's true and what isn't," she snarled. "TAKE ME DOWNSTAIRS, *NOW!*"

"Of course! Of course! Forgive me." A trembling bald man came into view, and Darkus saw it was Mr. Langley, Dad's boss and the director of the museum. He was sweating so much that Darkus could see it dripping off his nose. He looked at Uncle Max, who still had his finger pressed against his lips.

"Follow me." Mr. Langley gestured. Madame Cutter stalked past him. "Of course, you know the way . . . I'll follow you, shall I?"

Darkus pushed his eye to the crack in the door and saw a chauffeur, a short Chinese woman, following several paces behind Madame Cutter. Behind them, Mr. Langley was tripping over his own feet.

"Who was that?" Darkus asked.

Uncle Max drew in a long breath. "That is Lucretia Cutter. And she is bad news."

"The Cutter Co-le-op-ter-a Collection woman?"

"The very one."

"So *we* were the ones in her vault?"

"That was us." Uncle Max nodded.

"But how did she know we were in there?" Darkus asked. "I didn't see any cameras, unless . . ."

"How indeed?" Uncle Max replied, poking his head out of the bathroom door. When he was certain Lucretia Cutter had gone, he motioned for Darkus to follow him. "Business as usual," he said, straightening his safari hat and giving his nephew a reassuring smile.

They walked calmly out of the museum as if nothing had happened. As they passed Madame Cutter's car, Darkus couldn't help but stare at it. It was iridescent black, and where the light bounced off its body it shimmered green and purple. It was a classic shape that looked like it had driven right out of one of his comics; the windows were tinted like cars in the movies. Darkus thought he saw the outline of a girl's face pressed against the back window. He stopped walking, but Uncle Max grabbed his arm, pulling him away.

"Keep moving," he whispered softly.

Once they were around the corner and heading away from the museum, Uncle Max relaxed the pace. "Are you okay?" he asked.

Darkus nodded. "I think so."

"Marvelous." Uncle Max pulled out his car keys. "I must say, it was a good job you spotted that yellow ladybug, or we would be in all sorts of hot water right now."

Darkus thought back to the yellow ladybug and Baxter's peculiar behavior in the jam jar. It wasn't he who had spotted the ladybug, it was Baxter. The beetle had been trying to warn him. Why? Did the ladybug have something to do with the Lucretia Cutter woman? It was also Baxter who'd found Dad's reading glasses . . .

Darkus frowned as he played through everything that had happened in that room. It wouldn't have been odd if a dog had barked at the ladybug or found the glasses, but a beetle? He'd never heard of a beetle—or any insect—warning humans of danger. He wondered, not for the first time, about where Baxter had really come from before he'd ended up in the trouser leg of the ogre next door.

Uncle Max opened the car, slid into the driving seat, and reached over to open the passenger door for Darkus. As Darkus got in, he took off his backpack and unzipped it to check on Baxter. The beetle appeared to be sleeping. It was hard to tell when he was asleep because he didn't have eyelids, but his legs were very still and Darkus took that as a sign that he was resting.

Uncle Max slotted the key into the ignition, and the car started on the first try. He clapped his hands together in glee. "That couldn't have gone any better, really, could it?"

"Starting the car?" Darkus asked. "Or in the museum?"

"All of it! We found Barty's glasses, drew the villain out from her lair . . ."

"Villain?"

"We may not know how Barty disappeared, lad, or where he is, but you can bet your britches that viper of a woman has something to do with it." He waggled his eyebrows. "And to top it all off, I've got a dinner date with the lovely Maggie!"

CHAPTER FIVE

Furniture Forest

*D*arkus couldn't return to school because Uncle Max had told them he was sick, with a high temperature. On the way home, they stopped at a pet shop and Uncle Max bought him a bag of oakwood mulch for Baxter's tank. Back at the flat, Darkus carried the newly cleaned aquarium to the yard behind Uncle Max's flat. Placing it on the concrete steps that led down to the overgrown scrub that had once been a lawn, he filled it halfway up with the mulch. Then he gathered pieces of bark from around the yard to lay on top. In the center of the tank, he leaned three strips of bark against one another to create an earthy nook, trying to make a beetle habitat like the ones he'd read about in his red book.

"How come I didn't know that Dad loves beetles?" Darkus wondered out loud as he arranged leaves and sticks around the edge of Baxter's tank. "It's weird. I know that he likes custard creams, and cats, and cycling." He turned and looked at Baxter, who was crawling along the concrete step beside him. "Don't you think it's weird?" He paused as if listening for Baxter's response, then shook himself. "I'll tell you what *is* weird. Talking to beetles. *That's* weird."

He picked up the mug of milk Uncle Max had brought down for him before he'd gone to work, and drained it. After Mum died, Dad had lost interest in everything, and there were times when Darkus thought he didn't care about anything anymore, not even him. So perhaps it wasn't so strange that he'd stopped being interested in beetles.

Darkus looked down at Baxter.

"Insect hunting sounds fun, huh?" He put down the empty cup. "When we find Dad, I'm going to make him take us."

Baxter marched up to Darkus's mug and rammed it with his horn. The mug rocked.

"Hey! What's that cup ever done to you?"

Baxter butted it again, knocking it over. Darkus watched, fascinated, as the beetle jammed his horn under the cup and raised it, clattering it against the wall of the tank.

"What'd you do that for?" Darkus righted the mug.

Baxter moved his horn slowly from left to right and then headbutted the mug again, knocking it back onto its side. He spread his elytra and lifted into the air, tugging at the handle of the mug with his claws.

"You want me to pick it up?" Darkus offered. "Is that right?"

Baxter flew into the tank and looked up expectantly.

"In there? With you?" Darkus placed the mug beside Baxter. The beetle set about pushing the mug into the wigwam of bark Darkus had made, then reversed in and out several times.

"What's that," Darkus scoffed, "a bedroom?"

Baxter reared up, lifting his thorax and front legs, waggling them at Darkus—as if delighted at being understood.

"It *is* a bedroom!" Darkus laughed. "Since when did beetles need bedrooms?"

Baxter tilted his head cockily, as if to say, *You know nothing.*

Darkus was about to argue, then chuckled and clapped his hand to his forehead. He was not going to quarrel with an insect! Sometimes he really thought he *was* communicating with the beetle, even though that was impossible. He instinctively knew what Baxter wanted, or at least he felt like he did. If Darkus paid close attention, the beetle's movements made sense to him, and at times he was sure Baxter was trying to tell him things, like in the museum with the yellow ladybug.

He wondered what Uncle Max would say if he told him—although perhaps that wasn't a good idea. Uncle Max already behaved like he didn't trust Baxter, which Darkus thought was unfair. Baxter was just a beetle, after all, and it wasn't his fault he was cleverer and more special than ordinary beetles.

Dad would have made him prove it. He was forever telling Darkus to be scientific in his approach to things. "Life is a mystery, son, and science the tool for understanding it," was Dad's stock response to every puzzle, even when that puzzle was something as ordinary as trying to find his other shoe. Darkus used to groan when Dad used the phrase, but right now he would have given anything to hear it.

"Of course!" Darkus sat up straight. "I should do a scientific experiment to see if Baxter really can understand me. That's what Dad would do."

He looked around in the dirt at the bottom of the steps. If he was going to prove that he and Baxter could understand each other, he needed to find another ordinary beetle and set up a control test.

Using a stick, he scratched around in the flower bed beside the steps. He didn't find any beetles there, so he lifted a stone and found a collection of wood lice having a meeting. "You'll have to do," he said, picking one off the stone and watching it roll into a tight ball in his palm. "Don't be frightened. I'm not going to eat you."

He picked up Baxter in his other hand, placing him and the wood louse toward the back of one of the concrete steps. "Now, when I let you both go," he said, slowly and clearly, "I want you to stay exactly where you are. Okay . . . go!"

Neither creature moved.

Darkus stared at the wood louse, willing it to take a step forward.

Nothing happened.

"Okay, this time," he said, picking up both insects again, "when I put you down, I want you to crawl to the edge of the step and then stop."

Again he placed the insects at the back of the step. For a second neither of them moved, but then Baxter started crawling forward.

"Yes. C'mon, Baxter." Darkus felt a rush of pleasure as the beetle moved toward him. Then the wood louse scurried forward. Both insects stopped when they got to the edge of the step, and Darkus scratched his head. So far, he was proving nothing.

The wood louse turned and crawled away along the edge of the step. "Ha! I asked you to stop when you got to the edge of the step, not crawl sideways," Darkus said triumphantly to it, just as Baxter fell face-first over the edge of the step, landing on his back with his legs waggling in the air.

"Oh! Are you okay, Baxter?" He picked up the rhinoceros beetle and returned him to his tank, feeling deflated. "You're pretty clumsy, did you know that?"

Deciding to give up on the experiments, he peeled the banana that Uncle Max had brought with his milk, broke off a lump, and placed it in the tank beside Baxter. Dad's beetle book said that rhinoceros beetles eat fruit and tree sap, and he'd discovered that Baxter was particularly fond of bananas. As he watched the beetle scramble onto the banana, he wondered for the millionth time that day where his dad could be, what his disappearance had to do with beetles, and what Lucretia Cutter—that strange, angry woman on canes—had to do with his father.

His thoughts were interrupted by sounds of banging and shouting from the other side of the backyard wall. The neighbors were fighting again.

"You traitorous snake, open this door!" There was a loud bang. "If you don't open it, I'll—I'll break it down."

"I'd like to see you try, you weak little weasel." Humphrey roared with laughter.

"The council is coming at the end of the week."

"Well, you'd better get a move on and start clearing the yard, then, hadn't you?"

"It's your rancid pit of a bedroom that's the real problem."

"I'll clean up my room once you've cleared the yard."

"Just KILL THOSE BLASTED BEETLES, you SLOB!"

Darkus leapt to his feet.

Beetles? There were *more* beetles next door?

He looked at the rhinoceros beetle happily eating banana in his tank. It had never occurred to him that there may be more beetles where he'd come from. What if they were special, too, like Baxter?

He ran down to the dilapidated shed at the end of the yard, stepping up onto the rotting windowsill and then pulling himself onto the mossy roof before scrambling along to the wall and lying flat along the top of it. He couldn't help but let out a low whistle of surprise as he looked down into the yard on the other side.

It was crammed full of furniture.

Uncle Max had told him the neighbors were hoarders, but he'd never seen anything like this before. The yard was piled high with junk.

It looked as if a mob of brawling furniture had been frozen with a ray gun. Table and chair legs stuck out, their feet like clenched fists about to land a punch. A brave hat stand was making a break for it at the south side of the yard, held back by tendrils of bindweed.

Wardrobes cowered beneath tarpaulin. Naked lamp stands were bound together with rope. Bedsprings pinged out of mattresses, and a giant bathtub reared up in the middle of the yard, a pink scooter dangling helplessly from its taps.

"Cool!" Darkus breathed out, immediately wanting to explore.

Near the building itself, a towering sycamore tree reached up past the window where the shouting was coming from. There were enough leaves on the sycamore tree to hide Darkus, and if he had to run, there were plenty of hiding places in the furniture. The sky was bloated with charcoal-colored clouds, and daylight was fading. The darkness would provide even more cover.

He glanced back at the flat; Uncle Max wouldn't be back from work till after six. Without another thought, Darkus dropped down into the forest of furniture, determined to climb the sycamore tree and get a peek into that room.

As his feet touched a tabletop, there was a loud splintering sound, and he launched himself sideways, swinging on the arm of a vertical sofa, sliding down its upright seat, and landing on a pile of faded cushions that farted up a cloud of mildew.

Darkus froze, listening.

"*Humphrey*, do you hear me?"

"Pardon?" Humphrey made a noise like a cat coughing up a hair ball. "You need to speak up a bit."

"YOU KNOW VERY WELL WHAT I SAID, YOU BRAIN-DEAD WARTHOG. OPEN UP THIS DOOR IMMEDIATELY."

"Now, that's not very nice, is it?" Humphrey replied in a sugary voice. "Calling me a warthog!"

Darkus let out a sigh of relief; they hadn't heard him. He crawled off, along the back of a wooden cupboard, in the direction of the voices. Beside a stack of side tables was a narrow gap. He squeezed his legs into it, his feet finding the ground, and standing, sidled along until the gap widened and met a bookshelf filled with boxes of cassette tapes, comics, and rotting toys.

A memory came to him, of being little and nestling between two stacked armchairs. He'd gone to an auction with his mum and dad and crawled into the furniture when they weren't looking. He heard their alarmed voices calling out for him and saw again the relief on both their faces when he'd poked his head out of the furniture and waved.

Sadness washed through his body. He shook his head to dissolve the memory and squatted down, slithering forward through an avenue of chair legs, pulling himself over an aggressive thistle, gritting his teeth as it tore at his sweater.

He came out in a cupboard-size clearing. Stretched overhead was a tarpaulin, blocking out the daylight and protecting a tall grandfather clock that would forever say it was a quarter to nine. He pulled open the door in its body, and it came away in his hand. Inside was a rust-speckled pendulum and a mess of shredded paper. The pointy nose of a mouse peeped out, and then two beady black eyes looked up at him.

"Sorry," Darkus whispered, placing the door back in its frame.

You could build a brilliant den in the middle of all this furniture, he thought, stepping through a curtain of ivy hanging from a wardrobe rail. *No one would ever know you were here.* He wondered if Virginia and Bertolt liked dens. Building one was more fun if you had people to do it with.

As he went, Darkus opened drawers, cupboards, and boxes, finding tongs, an ornate hand mirror, and even a set of false teeth. He left everything as he found it, keeping the location of the sycamore tree in his head. Sliding over a desk and under a bed frame, he came nose to nose with a fox. They stared at each other, neither of them moving. The fox blinked, unbothered, and walked away through the middle of a stack of empty picture frames.

"I'M WARNING YOU, HUMPHREY GAMBLE, THIS IS YOUR LAST CHANCE."

"Oh no! Boo-hoo! I'm *so* scared!"

"EITHER YOU OPEN THIS DOOR, OR I'M COMING IN!"

The voices were closer now.

Darkus saw a black front door with a silver number 73 screwed to it. He turned the handle. Behind it was a kitchen dresser. He scrambled up the dresser, using the shelves like rungs on a ladder, and found that from the top he could see across the yard. The tree was three yards away. Darkus plotted a path through the furniture that would lead him straight there. Dropping back down into the maze, he wormed his way forward until he arrived under a foldaway table opposite the sycamore tree.

Beyond the tree, a tangle of bicycles obscured the back wall of the shop. He thought about his own bicycle. It was in the shed at home, sitting unused outside his empty house, south of the river in Crystal Palace. It felt like a lifetime since he had been there, and happy. The familiar tide of sadness rose in his chest as he felt homesick for the time before Dad had disappeared. Unwanted tears sprang into his eyes.

Angrily, he pushed his feelings aside, scrambling out into the open and sprinting to the tree. He jumped up, catching hold of the lowest branch, swung his legs up, and climbed swiftly up the tree. When he arrived on the branch opposite the window, his heart was pounding in his chest.

At first, he couldn't make sense of what he was looking at.

The wooden window frame was empty of glass, which explained how he'd heard the two men quarreling. And all over the wood and surrounding brickwork, unnoticeable from the ground, were hundreds of red ladybugs. There were so many of them scurrying around the window frame that it looked like it was moving.

Darkus smiled. These ladybugs made him feel different from the giant yellow one he'd seen that morning, which had been wrong somehow.

He peered through the window. Inside, sitting with his enormous backside wedged up against the door, was the fat one, Humphrey, wearing only a pair of boxer shorts and an undershirt. He had a white bucket beside him and was scooping up a handful of pink stuff from it, pouring it into his mouth and then licking his fingers clean.

But it wasn't Humphrey that made Darkus stare.

At first glance, it looked like there was a mountain in the room, sitting on the flowery carpet and reaching up to the ceiling. Darkus thought it was some kind of model until he looked closely at the mossy hillside and realized it was a huge pile of moldy teacups. The gaps between the cups were filled with grass, mushrooms, and the tiny plants he'd seen growing out of cracks in walls. There were dandelions sprouting out of the side facing the window, and near the peak a butterfly bush grew, with purple flowers hanging down like bunches of grapes.

He gazed at the impossible thing, his eyes jumping between cup rims and handles, and suddenly he noticed that between the cups—and inside them—were flickering antennae and serrated legs. He remembered Baxter's delight at getting a mug inside his tank and realized that these cups were all *full of beetles*.

He spotted two stags peeping out of a chipped teacup, and then a rhinoceros beetle, smaller than Baxter, with copper-colored elytra, backing into a coffee mug. A flash of emerald green drew his attention to a cluster of glamorous jewel beetles, which he recognized from an illustration in his red book. When he saw the trail of giraffe-necked weevils climbing awkwardly up a path between the mugs, looking like a row of clowns dressed in red and black, he clamped his hand over his mouth to suppress a cry of delight and almost fell out of the tree.

Darkus's heart soared to see so many species. The beetle mountain was the most alien and beautiful thing he'd ever seen.

There was a bang on the door. "I'm warning you, Humphrey," Pickering's voice came from the other side, "this is your *last* chance."

Darkus saw Humphrey lick his lips and grin. He was obviously enjoying winding up his cousin.

"I'M COUNTING TO THREE," Pickering barked, "AND THEN I'M COMING IN. ONE . . ."

Humphrey guffawed into his chubby fingers.

"TWO . . ."

Humphrey leaned back. "You'll never do it," he crowed.

"THREEEEEEE!"

There was a loud crash as the blade of an ax ripped through the wooden door just above Humphrey's head.

"Spawn of Satan!" Humphrey sprang forward onto all fours, his belly swinging from side to side as he crawled away.

Shocked, Darkus startled as the door flew open, and lost his balance again, grabbing on to the branch to stop himself from falling.

Pickering stood in the doorway with the ax raised above his head. He advanced menacingly toward his cousin. "I warned you, Humphrey," he said with an unnerving smile, "but you wouldn't listen."

"Now, Pickering, old boy, no need for violence, eh?" Humphrey was on his knees.

"You just wouldn't listen." Pickering's eyes were wide and unblinking.

"A joke, Pickers . . . surely you can take a joke?" Humphrey gave a weak laugh.

"A joke? A JOKE?" Pickering pointed at the mountain. "You think *that* is a joke?"

"It's just a bunch of dirty cups," Humphrey spluttered. "I was going to wash them up, honest I was."

"You disgust me, Humphrey Gamble." Pickering shook his head. "I can't believe we're related. Look at those tea stains splattered up the walls—and what's that?" He pointed. "Fungal spores!" His chest heaved, and Darkus thought he was going to be sick. "There's creepy-crawlies all over the floor."

Darkus looked down and realized that what he'd thought was a flowery carpet was actually a threadbare rug covered in beetles.

"This room is a health hazard!" Pickering's voice was getting higher. "Now can you see why I *had* to write to the council?"

"You did it to get rid of me," Humphrey said matter-of-factly.

"Well, yes," Pickering admitted. "But can you blame me? You're a pig, letting your room get like this. How long have you been throwing your dirty cups into the corner?"

Humphrey shrugged and muttered, "Since we moved in."

Pickering turned toward the mountain of crockery. "You've even smashed the glass in the window . . ."

Humphrey's eyes followed Pickering.

To Darkus's horror, he suddenly found both men staring right at him.

Quick as lightning, Pickering darted over to the window, reached out, and grabbed Darkus by the scruff of his sweater. Darkus's horror was eclipsed by fear as he found himself dangling in midair. He grabbed at the window frame with his fingertips, letting out a strangled scream, and the ladybugs took off, a cloud of red and black. There was no one to help him. Uncle Max was out.

"BAXTER!" he cried as he was hauled through the window and thrown down onto the floor, scattering beetles in every direction.

CHAPTER SIX

Darkus and Goliath

W ell, well, look at what I've found." Pickering stood over Darkus. "It's a spying boy." His face twisted as he scrutinized Darkus. "I've seen you before, haven't I?" He nodded slowly. "Yesterday, in the street, you were watching me. Why?"

"What boy?" Humphrey said, still on his knees. "What street?"

Darkus tried to protest, but all the air had been smacked out of him when he'd hit the floor, and his body was screaming for oxygen. His lungs felt like they were going to burst.

"What are you doing spying through our window?"

"I—I . . ." Darkus gasped, finally able to breathe.

"Cat got your tongue?" Pickering sneered.

Darkus's head was throbbing, and as the burning in his lungs subsided, it was replaced by a searing pain in his lower back. The beetles were no longer on the floor; they were retreating into their cups. Darkus looked around, desperately hoping he hadn't squashed any of them.

Realizing Pickering's anger was no longer directed at him, Humphrey climbed to his feet and came to stand beside his skeletal cousin. "Speak up, or we'll chop you up and eat you." He smacked his lips.

Pickering grabbed Darkus's chin. "I know what you're doing, you nasty little skinhead. Don't you think that I don't." His fingers locked around Darkus's jaw. "You were sniffing around here the other night, weren't you? You're a thief!"

"What? No!" Darkus tried to shake his head. "I'm sorry—about looking through your window, I mean—I was just . . ."

"You were casing the joint." Pickering tightened his grip.

"What?" Humphrey spluttered.

"I didn't tell you this, Humphrey, but last week, when you were out, I heard noises in here. I came in and scared away intruders."

"Really?" Humphrey looked around in surprise. There was nothing much in the bedroom except for the mountain of cups and a dirty pink armchair the size of a small sofa that wasn't worth stealing.

"Two of them. Big ugly men, dressed in black, poking around in that rotting pile of filth." Pickering glared at the mountain, his nostrils flaring in disgust. "They were wearing face masks and rubber gloves because it's so *dirty* in here!" Pickering let go of Darkus and advanced toward his cousin, tightening his grip on the ax. "I *hate* living with you, Humphrey. Do you know that? I wake up every morning hoping that you've died in the night."

"And you saw this boy with the thieves?" Humphrey said hurriedly. He pointed at Darkus, trying to divert Pickering's attention. "He was one of the robbers?"

"I couldn't see their faces"—Pickering stopped to think—"but the two I chased away were men. This one must have been hiding."

"And now he's come back to finish what they started," Humphrey said.

"I'm *not* a thief!" Darkus exclaimed.

"Really?" Pickering turned. "Then explain to me why you were on my property, up my tree, looking in my window with your thieving little black eyes." He charged back across the room and leaned over Darkus. "It's my antiques you're after, isn't it? You're planning to steal my antiques!"

"I've never seen your antiques!" Darkus protested, scrambling backward until his shoulders came up against the wall.

"You expect me to believe that, after you've just sneaked through a yard full of them?" He grabbed Darkus's face. "You lying little toe rag."

Darkus squirmed as the man's nails sank deep into his cheeks.

"Now, what am I going to do with you?" Pickering said.

"I know." Humphrey stepped forward eagerly. "Let me bake him into a pie. That'll teach him."

"Don't be ridiculous," Pickering said, letting Darkus drop to the floor. "We need to tie him up."

Crouching down, Humphrey sniffed around Darkus like an excited dog. "I'd have to skin you before I could put you in a pie," he grinned, "because human skin is pretty chewy."

Darkus went cold. He desperately hoped the fat man was just trying to frighten him.

Pickering dropped his ax, left the room, and returned with a length of rope and a kitchen chair. "Sit on this," he ordered.

"What are you going to do to me?" Darkus asked nervously.

Pickering pushed him down onto the chair and tied him to it.

"Kidnapping is illegal, you know."

"So is stealing." Pickering turned to Humphrey. "Pass me your cranberry sauce."

Humphrey waddled over to the white bucket beside the door. "Are we going to eat him?"

"First, we'll make him talk," Pickering said to Humphrey. "Then, once you've got rid of that"—his eye twitched as he looked at the filthy mass of insect life taking up most of the room—"that . . . *thing*, you can do what you like with him."

Humphrey clapped, happily.

"Now"—Pickering stood in front of Darkus with his arms crossed—"you're going to tell me about the gang you work for, and when they plan to rob me."

"You're being ridiculous, Pickers." Humphrey's face split into a huge grin. "No one in their right mind would steal that pile of rotting junk out there."

Pickering reached down and picked the ax up off the floor.

"What I mean is," Humphrey said hurriedly, "it's more likely he's a spy from the council, gathering evidence so they can evict us."

Pickering's eyes shot wide open and then narrowed as he considered this possibility. "Then we definitely can't let him go."

"That's why I thought we should bake him into a pie," Humphrey said helpfully.

"I'll let you have him, once you've gotten rid of the insects," Pickering said, offering his hand to his cousin.

"Deal." Humphrey grinned, shaking it.

"I'm not from the council, or a gang, or a thief!" Darkus cried. "I'm just a kid. I heard you arguing and I saw the beetles and—"

"That's what you *would* say," Pickering replied, cutting him off. "We're not idiots, you know." He looked at Humphrey. "Well, *I'm* not." He picked up a giant T-shirt from the floor and ripped a strip from it.

"Hey, that's my shirt!" Humphrey protested.

"Really? It looks like a dirty old rag," said Pickering, resting his ax against the armchair and tying the gag over Darkus's mouth.

Darkus pulled his head back, trying to resist, but the horrid rag closed over his mouth, smelling like a musty dead animal. It made him think of maggots, and he retched.

"Now, give me that tub."

Humphrey did as he was told.

Darkus wriggled, the skin on his wrists burning as he tried to get free from the ropes that held him tight. He had to get away. Uncle Max was right—these men were dangerous.

Pickering cupped his hands, scooping up a load of cranberry sauce, and splattering it down on Darkus's head. It was cold and sticky, making him shiver as it dripped slowly down his back.

"Hey, don't waste it," Humphrey protested. "That's good stuff."

"I'll get you some more." Pickering reached down for another handful. "Now, you listen to me, boy. This stuff"—he held his hands under Darkus's nose—"is cranberry sauce, and it can't have escaped your notice that right behind you is a monstrous hive of creepy-crawlies, full of millions of disgusting beasties that bite and sting and burrow and scratch, and do you know what they love to eat most of all in the whole wide world?" Pickering smeared a handful of sauce across Darkus's face. "Cranberry sauce."

Darkus shuddered as the cold sauce oozed down his neck and chest. Pickering pushed up the sleeves of his green sweater and rubbed sauce down his arms.

"Now, if you don't tell me who sent you to spy on us"—he was nose to nose with Darkus—"I'm going to let those creepy-crawlies eat you alive."

Darkus stared at Pickering. He supposed it made sense that these beetles would like cranberry sauce, especially as Humphrey kept a bucket of it in his room. Baxter liked sweet fruits, too. But thanks to his beetle handbook, Darkus knew something Pickering didn't: A lot of beetles are vegetarian.

"First, they'll munch through the cranberry sauce, and then they'll burrow under your skin." Pickering lifted another handful of the pink gloop. "Next, they'll drink your blood, and dine on your muscles until only your puny bones are left." He pulled up Darkus's trouser legs and splattered the sauce onto his shins. "And there are even some nasty critters in there that eat bones." Pickering was obviously enjoying himself. "So this is your last chance." He pulled down the gag. "What do you have to say for yourself?"

"I'm from next door," Darkus insisted. *"I live next door!"*

"LIAR!" Pickering replaced the gag angrily. "The professor who lives next door doesn't have children."

Darkus struggled against the ropes, but it was no use.

"Maybe you'll feel like talking after the beetles have stripped all the skin from your body." Pickering gave a horrible simpering laugh.

"I wanted to do that," Humphrey sulked.

"Look! Here comes a big black ugly one with a giant horn. Oh dear, he looks hungry."

Darkus looked down and almost wept with relief to see Baxter crawling across the floor toward him. The beetle—*his* beetle—had heard him call. He didn't need a control test to know that Baxter understood him. He immediately felt braver, and the fear that fluttered around his chest calmed down.

"I'm hungry," Humphrey complained, staring at Darkus.

A loud knock sounded on the front door downstairs.

"Who on earth could that be?" Pickering stood up straight and looked over his shoulder like a startled meerkat.

"I dunno." Humphrey shrugged.

Pickering grabbed his cousin's doughy arm and walked him out into the hall. "I'm not done with you yet," he growled at Darkus, slamming the door shut.

Darkus immediately tried to reach the knots holding his wrists together, but his fingers couldn't get a grip on the rope. A familiar weight pressed down on his shoulder, as Baxter landed and then crawled to the back of his neck where his gag was tied. He felt the beetle slide his horn up between the gag and his skin, pulling at the cloth. He was *sawing* at it!

After a few seconds, the gag slipped down and Darkus spat it out, gladly pulling in a lungful of clean air. "Baxter! Boy, am I glad to see you!" he whispered. "Can you help with the ropes, too?"

Baxter turned to the mountain of cups and rubbed his hind leg against his elytra, making a series of strange chirping noises. Darkus hadn't heard Baxter make a noise like that before. He realized it must be what his book called *stridulation*.

A sighing sound, like sugar pouring into a jar, filled the room as the beetles emerged from their mountain and scuttled toward him.

Pickering and Humphrey were still outside the door, arguing.

"We can't let anyone in, in case they find the boy." Pickering sounded agitated.

"What if it's the police?" Humphrey asked.

"The police?" Pickering squealed. "Why would it be the police?"

"Er . . . that thing the boy said, about kidnapping being illegal?"

"But we've only just done it. How would they know he was here?"

"I dunno."

"You go down and answer the door."

"Why me? What will I say?"

"Something stupid, probably!" Pickering made a frustrated strangled sound.

The persistent knocking came again.

"All right, we'll both go," Pickering declared, and Darkus heard them clomping down the stairs.

He felt a ticklish sensation as beetles started crawling up his legs. He sucked in his breath, unsure of how he felt about being covered in beetles, but soon they were climbing up his back, clambering around his neck, and scurrying on his scalp. Shivers rippled up and down his spine as tiny clawed feet walked across his skin. Darkus let out a sigh as he realized he didn't mind them being on him at all. They were heavy, like being buried in sand, but the feeling of so many beetles was quite nice. He tried not to laugh as they tickled him, and to keep still. He didn't want to squash anyone.

With his eyes closed, covered head to toe in beetles, he thought about his dad. *You're not going to believe this when I tell you,* he said to him silently.

In seconds, he could move his left arm. He tested the ropes—yes! Both his hands were free. He tried his feet and the cords fell away; the beetles had chewed, burrowed, and cut all the way through them.

Darkus got up, carefully, splattering a blob of cranberry sauce onto the floor, and crouched down to thank the beetles who'd rescued him. He was delighted to see the gaggle of red giraffe-necked weevils among the horde, and the flashy jewel beetles, too. But the most impressive beetle on the floor, by far, was a gigantic Goliath beetle, easily recognized by its black-and-white zebralike markings. It stood quite still, its antennae barely twitching, and Darkus wondered if it was very old.

No illustration in any book could capture how awesome these beetles were.

Darkus touched his face. It wasn't even tacky. The beetles had freed him *and* given him a wash! "Thank you!" he whispered. "You're all amazing!"

Outside, the streetlight flickered on, casting a yellow glow into the room. It must be nearly six o'clock. Uncle Max would be home soon.

Darkus heard voices downstairs. Pickering and Humphrey must have opened the door.

And suddenly, the beetles were withdrawing quickly, like a departing shadow, back into the mountain of cups. Something seemed to have spooked them. Only the Goliath beetle moved slowly.

Darkus ran silently to the window and looked down into the street. The sleek black car from outside the museum was parked across the road.

A shock of fear gripped his stomach. Lucretia Cutter was here! But why?

He looked over his shoulder at the mountain, and the realization hit him. It was full of spectacular beetles. Lucretia Cutter must be interested in beetles, or she wouldn't sponsor the Natural History Museum's collection. And that unsettling yellow ladybug he'd seen this morning had something to do with her, too. He was certain of it, and Uncle Max clearly thought so.

Lucretia Cutter could only be here for one reason. For the beetles. But how did she know they were even here? He remembered what

Pickering had said about the two men dressed in black wearing face masks and rubber gloves. Did they work for Lucretia Cutter?

Darkus crouched down with his back against the giant pink armchair and powered his heels into the floor as he pushed against it with all his strength, budging it jerkily across the floor. It was a heavy piece of furniture and wider than the door frame. He wedged it up against the closed door, under the handle, and then he turned back to the mountain.

"Listen," he said urgently, "you're all in *terrible* danger. Lucretia Cutter is here. She's bad news. I don't know what she wants, but"—he thought about all the beetles in drawers with pins through them—"I think if she sees you, she'll want to kill you. Do you understand? You mustn't let her get in here!" He scooped up Baxter. "We have to go, but we'll be back. I promise."

Darkus ran to the window ledge, throwing Baxter into the air as he jumped out toward the sycamore tree. He caught hold of the first branch, dropped down to the one below, and swung to the ground, landing in a crouch as Baxter glided down and settled on his shoulder.

CHAPTER SEVEN
The Visit

Humphrey blundered down the stairs with Pickering right behind him and wrenched the front door open.

"Good lord! You smell terrible!" said a disdainful female voice. "And you're not even dressed!"

Humphrey snorted as if he'd been slapped and stared at the stunning woman on the doorstep. She had gold lips, and her skin shimmered like polished marble. Her black bobbed hair framed a large pair of sunglasses that wrapped around her face like a visor. He wondered if she was a movie star.

He felt Pickering buffeting against his backside, trying to see who was at the door.

"Am I addressing Mr. Pickering Risk and Mr. Humphrey Gamble?" the woman asked, sneering.

"Indeed!" Pickering squeezed past and bowed low. "Pickering Aloysius Risk, Esquire, at your service. How may I help you?"

The woman, who was leaning on two black canes and wearing a white lab coat, reached into her pocket and withdrew a clenched fist decorated with a dazzling array of diamond rings. The cousins stared, mesmerized, as she lowered her hand and five black fingernails sprang out like flick knives, revealing three dead beetles in her palm. One was red, one was green, and one was gold.

"Recognize these?" A painted eyebrow arched above her sunglasses.

Humphrey stared uncomprehendingly at her hand. "Have you come about the boy?" he asked idiotically.

"What boy?"

With a yell, Pickering pushed Humphrey aside and slammed the door.

"What's the matter with you?" Humphrey asked.

"What's the matter with me? What's the matter with *you*?" Pickering panted, his back against the door. "Do you want to go to prison? Don't tell her anything, especially not about the boy." His eyes whirled. "She must be from the council."

"She doesn't look like she's from the council. Did you see her car across the road?" Humphrey whistled. "Now, that's what I call a passion wagon!"

"She *has* to be from the council . . ."

"I think she liked what she saw." Humphrey beat his chest like a gorilla.

". . . otherwise how do you explain those beetles?"

"What beetles?"

"The ones in her hand!"

"The sweets?"

"They were beetles, not sweets—and those weren't just any beetles." Pickering clapped his hand to his forehead. "They're the same three beetles I pulled from my hair and posted to the council three weeks ago, to show them how squalid you are: red, green, and gold."

"We could open the door and find out," Humphrey suggested, sniffing his armpits and checking his breath.

"No." Pickering shook his head vehemently. "We have to get rid of her."

"I can hear you!" The woman's voice stabbed through the door like a knife.

Pickering yelped and leapt forward.

Humphrey made a decision. It wasn't every day a pretty lady knocked on his door, and he wanted to keep talking to her. So he lifted Pickering out of the way and reopened the door.

"My most gigantic apologies," he said, bowing. "Ignore my cousin; he's not right in the head." He crossed his eyes and stuck out his tongue to demonstrate Pickering's craziness. "Mr. Humphrey Winston Gamble at your service." He offered his clammy hand.

"Who are you?" Pickering demanded. "What do you want?"

"My name is Lucretia Cutter." The woman lifted her chin as if she expected the cousins to have heard of her. Humphrey stared blankly back at her, then looked at Pickering, who obviously hadn't heard of her, either.

"Look, you have something that I want," she said.

"You bet I have." Humphrey sucked in his gut and puffed out his chest.

"I'm prepared to pay you," Lucretia Cutter said, "handsomely."

"Go on," Pickering said.

"There have been reports of exotic beetles in this part of the city."

Pickering's eyes narrowed. "I haven't seen any beetles."

She held out the three beetles again. "Really? Because I believe you sent these to the health and safety department of the council."

"There are no beetles here," Pickering insisted.

"Mr. Risk, I'm not from the council. I'm a coleopterist."

"What have feet got to do with anything?" Humphrey asked.

"Not a chiropodist, a coleopterist," she hissed. "A collector and studier of beetles. I've been tracking a group of rare arthropods that escaped from my laboratory several years ago." She held up the lifeless bodies again. "These beetles have DNA that matches the missing ones. I believe I've finally found their habitat, and it's here." She leaned forward hungrily. "Isn't it?"

Humphrey nodded, grinning. "Do you want to see my bedroom?"

Pickering pulled him backward into the hallway. "Stop nodding like a fool," he hissed. "This could be a trap."

"Mr. Risk, please, this is not a trap. It's a simple business transaction." She held out a glossy black rectangle. "Here's my card."

Humphrey and Pickering both lurched for it, but Humphrey grabbed it first, and Pickering had to stop himself from knocking into Lucretia Cutter by grabbing the door frame. The tip of his nose halted a fraction of an inch from a sparkling black brooch pinned to the lapel of her lab coat and tethered by a fine platinum chain.

"It's alive!" Pickering squealed as the brooch slowly traveled across Lucretia Cutter's coat.

"It's a stag beetle encrusted with black diamonds. Black diamonds are rare, but stags are even rarer now." Lucretia Cutter ran a finger over the glistening black stones and the beetle stopped moving. "It's my take on a Maquech, and it's priceless."

"Maqu . . . what?"

"Maquech. Bejeweled beetles, a living brooch from Mexico. Isn't it stunning?"

"Oh—it's, um, lovely." Pickering wrinkled his nose.

"It's a pity the exotic beetles aren't on your premises"—she cocked her head and curled her gilded top lip—"because I pay by the insect."

"You want to *buy* them?" Pickering asked, stunned.

"Yes."

"All of them?" Humphrey couldn't believe what he was hearing.

"Yes, all of them."

"But there's thousands . . ." Humphrey marveled.

"Are there? How interesting." Lucretia Cutter tipped her head back, exposing her perfect neck. "They must have bred." She sighed and then swooped close to Humphrey. "Are they exhibiting any unusual behavior?"

"Um, er . . ." he stammered.

She thrust her canes through the door frame and swung herself forward. "Why don't you show me?"

"No!" Pickering shrieked, barring her path. "There's nothing for you to see here."

The image of a boy tied to a chair and covered with cranberry sauce flashed into Humphrey's head, and he joined Pickering to block the hallway.

Lucretia Cutter reared up threateningly, suddenly seeming impossibly tall.

"LET ME IN!"

"I'm sorry. You have to leave now. Bye-bye," Pickering shouted in a voice filled with terror. "Thank you for your visit."

"Suit yourself," Lucretia Cutter said angrily, backing out of the doorway. "You have my card. I'll give you a week to think about it."

As she turned back to her car, two men dressed in black got out. One crossed the road to provide an escort for Lucretia Cutter; the other held the car door open.

Pickering stared at them. "They look like the two men I chased out of your room last week!"

Darkus scrambled back through the forest of furniture as fast as he could. Baxter clung on tightly to his shoulder as he threw himself over the wall and bolted up the stairs to Uncle Max's living room, falling to his knees in front of the window.

The car was still there.

Darkus lifted the latch and slid the window open. He heard a subdued pop. The chauffeur he'd seen earlier, at the museum, was opening a rear car door. A doll-like girl stepped out, wearing a sleeveless black dress with a stiffened hood that framed silver curls piled high on her head. The dress was pulled tightly in at the waist, the skirt exploding out like a parachute, hanging just above her knees. She was wearing white leather gloves, a belt, and ballet pumps, and a white triangular handbag swung from her elbow as she crossed the road to the newspaper store. As she walked, she held her left arm up like a teapot spout and swung her hips from side to side.

Forgetting the window was wide open, Darkus snorted with laughter, and the girl looked up. He froze, a broad grin plastered on his face. The girl raised her gloved hand to her lips and blew him a kiss before flouncing through Mr. Patel's shop door. Darkus felt himself grow hot. "What did she do that for?" he wondered crossly, leaning out of the window, but the girl was inside the shop now.

He could hear murmuring from Humphrey and Pickering's doorstep, but he couldn't make out anything they were saying. He leaned out as far as he dared to see if it made any difference.

A silvery laugh startled him. The girl was back, standing in the middle of the road, sucking a lollipop. Looking up at him, she took a small white card from her handbag, waved it at him, and let it drop to the ground, returning to the car without a backward glance.

"Wait!" Humphrey's voice boomed. "What would you do with all those beetles?"

Darkus glanced down. Lucretia Cutter was looking back over her shoulder at the cousins, a cruel smile twisting her gold lips. "Kill them, Mr. Gamble. Kill them all. And once they're dead, I'll stick pins in the special ones and add them to my *personal* collection."

Leaning forward over her canes, she swung away, ignoring the hand of her bodyguard. Her elbows stuck up at right angles like the legs of a praying mantis, her black skirt snaking behind her like the body of a centipede. *I wonder what's wrong with her legs,* he thought, giving an involuntary shiver as he watched her move, a feeling of dread like a cold mist settling over his stomach.

"What do you think she's doing here, Baxter?" Darkus looked over his shoulder. Baxter was on the coffee table, his elytra flickering.

"What are you doing? Are you hiding?" He picked up Baxter, holding him to his chest and stroking his elytra. "Don't worry. I won't let her hurt you."

He stared down into the street. The room Dad had disappeared from had that woman's name above the door. Uncle Max had called her a villain. Now she was here for the beetles. Well, she couldn't have them. Darkus vowed silently that he would stop her—and the men living next door—from hurting the amazing insects. He was certain that's what Dad would do.

Tomorrow, at school, he'd tell Virginia and Bertolt about the museum and the beetles, and ask them to help him.

The engine roared, and Darkus watched as Lucretia Cutter's vehicle crawled down the street like a mechanical scarab.

CHAPTER EIGHT
The Oath

"Where are we going?" Bertolt asked nervously as Darkus pulled himself up onto the shed roof.

"You'll see," Darkus said. "Virginia, give him a leg up."

Bertolt scrambled up onto the roof of the shed, squealing when his shoe got stuck in the gutter.

"This way," Darkus said, running lightly along the wall and pulling himself up. He sat on the top, dangling his legs, and offered Bertolt his hand.

He'd spent the day at school pretending to feel ill. Uncle Max had said he could have a second day off, to make their story more believable, but Darkus had wanted to go back. He was desperate to see Bertolt and

Virginia. His only worry was being spotted by Pickering and Humphrey on his way to school. So he'd borrowed Uncle Max's beanie with a pom-pom on top and a long scarf from the coat stand in the hall, and covered his head and face. He checked that the coast was clear before slipping out onto the street, and did his best impression of one of the clones, hunching his shoulders and strutting to school.

At the end of school, he invited Virginia and Bertolt to come back to Uncle Max's, keeping the reasons as mysterious as he could. He was worried that if he told them the truth they'd laugh at him—or, worse, pity him—for making up such a crazy story. He needed them to see for themselves, and then perhaps they'd help him.

"I can't believe you persuaded me to do this," Bertolt grumbled, slowly pulling himself along the roof on his bottom, trying not to look down.

Darkus grabbed his arm and hiked him up onto the wall. He pointed down into the yard next door. "Take a look at that."

Bertolt's mouth dropped open.

"What is it?" Virginia asked, pulling herself up on the other side of Darkus. "Holy guacamole! Would you look at that!"

"I call it Furniture Forest," Darkus said grandly.

"What are you, a poet?" Virginia laughed, throwing her legs over the wall. "C'mon, what are you waiting for?"

"Virginia!" Bertolt said. "That's trespassing!"

"Whoops!" said Virginia, smiling at Bertolt as she let go of the wall and dropped onto the top of a wardrobe.

"Follow me." Darkus swung himself so that his feet hit the vertical sofa, and he slid down the cushion, disappearing into the warren.

He waited under the table for Virginia and Bertolt, who soon scrambled in and sat with him in a huddle. "I'm not sure this is a good idea," Bertolt whispered, looking around nervously. "We don't know who lives here."

"I do," Darkus said.

"Are they friendly?" Bertolt asked hopefully.

"Not exactly." Darkus changed the subject. "Look, I've brought you here because I need your help."

"Is it to do with your dad?" Virginia asked.

Darkus nodded.

"I knew it!"

"Some stuff has happened, and I don't know what it all means yet, but I think my dad's disappearance has something to do with this." He slid the backpack off his back and pulled out Baxter's jam jar.

"What is that?!" Bertolt exclaimed, leaning forward.

"Whoa! Where did you get a rhinoceros beetle that big?" Virginia knelt and grabbed the jar from Darkus, lifting it up to eye level. "He's magnificent!"

"How do you know that?"

"Know what?" Virginia tapped the glass jar lightly with her fingertip.

"That Baxter is a rhinoceros beetle?" Darkus was impressed.

"I know lots of things." Virginia smiled. "But I also have three brothers, and Sean is big into bugs. He's got two stick insects, a tarantula, and a whole shelf of DVDs about insects. He'd suck a bucketful of lemons to get his hands on a beetle this big."

Darkus took the jar back from her and unscrewed the lid. "I found him the day before yesterday." He tipped the jar gently. "Everybody, meet Baxter," he said as the rhinoceros beetle crawled out of the jar and onto his hand. "Baxter, this is Bertolt and this is Virginia."

"Does it bite?" Bertolt asked, transfixed.

"Don't be an idiot." Virginia shoved him. "Rhinoceros beetles eat fruit and tree sap."

"Well, I don't know that, do I?" Bertolt huffed. He looked at Darkus. "I don't understand. What has the beetle got to do with your dad's disappearance?"

"Yesterday I went to the museum and saw the room he disappeared from."

"No way!" Virginia's eyes grew wide. "Did you find any clues?"

"The police already did a thorough search." Bertolt looked over his glasses at her disapprovingly.

"Actually, yes, I did." Darkus stroked his finger along Baxter's thorax. "Or rather, Baxter did."

"The *beetle* found a clue?" Virginia looked skeptical.

Darkus described how he'd found Baxter, and then told them about the trip to the museum.

"I wasn't ill yesterday," Darkus said. "Uncle Max made that up." He described the collection room full of beetles, the mystery of the empty drawers, finding his father's glasses, and the arrival of Lucretia Cutter.

"It turns out the room Dad disappeared from is the Cutter Coleoptera Collection room."

"You saw her?" Bertolt asked, amazed. "The actual Lucretia Cutter?"

Darkus nodded. "I saw her twice, but I'll get to that bit in a minute."

"Twice!" Bertolt squeaked.

"Who's Lucretia Cutter?" Virginia asked.

"I don't know." Darkus shrugged. "She's rich, I know that; she's got the most amazing car, and she's big into beetles. Uncle Max thinks she's got something to do with Dad's disappearance."

"You've never heard of Lucretia Cutter?" Bertolt asked, astonished.

Darkus and Virginia shook their heads.

"The House of Cutter is one of the biggest fashion brands in the world. Lucretia Cutter is known as the Mad Scientist of Fashion," Bertolt said. "She's a genius, and a powerful businesswoman."

They stared blankly back at him.

"You must have seen the winged scarab logo on handbags and stuff." He drew a circle in the air with his fingers.

"How come you know about fashion?" Darkus asked, surprised.

"My mum reads the magazines." Bertolt blushed.

"So what has this fashion designer got to do with beetles?" Virginia wondered. "Or your dad, for that matter?"

"Last season, she made a suit of armor from spider silk for the ghost of Joan of Arc," Bertolt said. "Maybe she wants to make a dress out of the beetles."

"Gruesome!" Virginia pulled a face. "A dress made of insects."

"I can't believe you saw her," Bertolt said to Darkus. "She's hardly ever seen out, not since her accident. She doesn't even attend her own shows."

"Accident?"

"She was in a terrible car crash about a year ago." Bertolt's high-pitched voice dipped into a dramatic whisper. "The papers said she would never walk again."

"She had canes when I saw her," Darkus said. "She moved weirdly, but she can walk."

"They say she almost died," Bertolt added.

"Yeah, well, you can't always believe the papers," Darkus said bitterly. "Anyway, Uncle Max says she's bad news."

Bertolt looked dismayed. "Why?"

"I'm not sure. I'm guessing she must know Dad, because Uncle Max told me Dad used to be a beetle expert. But, listen, there's more."

Darkus went on to describe hearing the neighbors arguing, discovering Furniture Forest, climbing the tree, and finding the mountain of cups full of beetles, then being captured. Bertolt looked nervous as he told of his escape and Lucretia Cutter's visit, and seeing the girl get out of the car and drop her card. Darkus left out the bit about her blowing him a kiss. It was too embarrassing, and he knew Virginia would tease him.

"And if you don't believe me"—he pulled a white rectangular card out of his pocket and held it out—"this is it."

Bertolt took the card and read: "*Novak Cutter, Actress. Towering Heights, Regent's Park, London.*" He looked up. "That's a fancy address."

"Hang on." Virginia held her hands up. "This is getting crazy. You're telling me that Baxter flew in and helped you, like some kind of superbeetle? And made the other beetles gnaw through the ropes so you could escape?"

"Yes." Darkus frowned; he could tell Virginia didn't believe him. "Look, I need your help. I feel like I'm doing a dot-to-dot puzzle, only there's a whole load of dots with no numbers, and I can't figure out how they're connected."

"Okay, I get that there's lots going on, but a beetle with superpowers?" Virginia pursed her lips and raised her eyebrows. "You're kidding me!"

"I know it sounds like I made it up, but this is not a joke." Darkus shook his head. "I can't talk to anyone else about it. Uncle Max is a bit weird about Baxter already, and he'd kill me if he knew what happened last night. He might make me give Baxter away." He looked from Virginia to Bertolt. "I need you to believe me. That's why I brought you here, to show you."

"Show us what?" Virginia asked.

"Baxter"—Darkus held out his hand as far as possible—"time to do your stuff. Fly to my shoulder."

The beetle's elytra lifted and his soft wings unfurled, vibrating as he jumped into the air, flew the short distance to Darkus's shoulder, and landed, turning around and settling in his favorite spot.

Bertolt's and Virginia's faces were a picture of shock.

"How did you do that?" Bertolt squeaked, astonished.

Darkus shrugged. "I didn't do anything."

"Do it again," Virginia said, her low voice insistent. "No, get Baxter to do something else. Do something harder."

"Baxter," Darkus whispered, "fly up, do a loop"—his finger traced the movement in the air—"then land on Virginia's hand." He reached over and took her hand, opening it and holding it palm up. "Okay? Go!"

Baxter leapt into the air, zooming upside down in a circle before coming to land on Virginia's palm.

"AHHHHHHHH! NO WAY!" she shrieked with delight.

"SHHHHHHHHHHHH!" Darkus scolded.

"And you say there are more of these beetles up there?" Bertolt pointed at the Emporium.

"They're not all like Baxter," Darkus said, "but yes, there are hundreds, maybe even thousands, of different beetles up there."

"This is amazing!" Virginia said, staring down at the rhinoceros beetle on her hand.

"Now do you believe me?" Darkus asked, enjoying himself.

"You betcha!" Virginia looked at him, an excited sparkle in her eyes. She held out her hand in front of Darkus's shoulder so Baxter could clamber back.

"So will you help me?"

Virginia nodded.

Darkus looked at Bertolt. "And you?"

He pushed his glasses up on his nose and swallowed nervously. "I'll do my best."

"So, what's your plan?" Virginia asked.

"Lucretia Cutter wants the beetles up in that room," Darkus said, "and if she gets her hands on them, she'll kill them. I heard her say so." Baxter's elytra flickered open and then closed. "It's okay, Baxter, we're not going to let that happen." He looked at Virginia. "I don't know much about those beetles, but if any of them are like Baxter, then they're special and should be studied, not killed." Darkus felt himself getting angry. "We need to find out more about those beetles. Where did they come from? And why does Lucretia Cutter want them? And, most important, we need to find out how she knows my dad, and if there's any link between these beetles and whatever Dad was working on." An image of a folder under his uncle's arm flashed into his head. "I think it might be something called the Fabre Project."

"I wish you could hear how crazy you sound right now." Virginia chuckled.

"This is NOT FUNNY!" Darkus found himself shouting.

"Shhhhhhhhhhhh!" Bertolt looked alarmed.

"Whoa! Calm down. I get it." Virginia held her hands up. "We're on a beetle preservation mission, fighting against an evil tycoon from the fashion industry, who may, or may not, have kidnapped your dad for some reason to do with beetles that we don't know yet." She smiled. "I'm in! I was just saying it sounds crazy." She leaned back and grinned. "But crazy is cool."

Bertolt reached over and put his hand on Darkus's arm. "I'll do everything I can to help you find your dad, Darkus," he said earnestly.

"Thanks." Darkus felt suddenly deflated. His head had been spinning ever since he'd visited the museum, and now that he'd finally emptied the contents of it to Virginia and Bertolt, he could hear how strange he sounded. "Sorry for shouting."

"Ah, that's okay." Virginia gently punched his arm.

"I don't really have a plan," he admitted. "But I can't let Lucretia Cutter go in there and murder all those beetles."

"Let's make an oath." Virginia held her hand out.

"An oath?"

"I, Virginia Wallace, solemnly do swear to help Darkus Cuttle in his mission to find his father and save the beetles."

Bertolt put his hand flat on top of Virginia's.

"I, Bertolt Roberts, solemnly do swear to help Darkus Cuttle in his mission to find his father and save the beetles."

Darkus did the same.

"I, Darkus Cuttle, solemnly do swear that I will not rest until I've found my dad and the beetles are safe."

Baxter zoomed down and landed on the back of Darkus's hand.

They looked at one another and then at the rhinoceros beetle.

"There," Virginia said. "We've made an oath. Now it's gotta happen."

CHAPTER NINE

Base Camp

They decided the first thing to do was build a camp in Furniture Forest so they could keep a closer eye on the Emporium. Virginia wanted to go up the sycamore tree and see the beetles, but Darkus thought they should wait until Humphrey and Pickering were out, and Bertolt had strongly agreed.

"As there's three of us on this adventure," Bertolt said, "shouldn't we have a name, like the Fabulous Four, or the Famous Five?"

"No!" Virginia screwed up her face. "We are not having a name!"

"But we could be called the Three Beetle-a-teers," Bertolt said, "like the Musketeers, but with beetles."

"What are you? Seven? Names are lame."

Bertolt wasn't listening. "Or we could be a gang called the Beetle Boys." He paused. "And Girl."

"Can I tape his mouth up?" Virginia asked. "He's getting on my nerves."

Darkus laughed.

"How about the Bug Detectives?" Bertolt tilted his head, looking hopeful.

"I'd rather eat my own leg than be in a gang called the Bug Detectives." Virginia shook her head and changed the subject. "Where are we going to build the camp?"

"It needs to be a place far away enough from the Emporium that we can make a bit of noise and not be discovered, but with a clear view so we can see into all the windows," Darkus reasoned.

"That's going to be in the back left-hand corner," Bertolt said. "The sycamore tree obscures the view from the right."

"We need to make proper paths through the furniture," Darkus said, "so we can move around quickly and disappear if we need to."

"Can we make booby traps?" Bertolt asked. "In case someone tries to follow us in here?"

"That sounds good." Darkus nodded enthusiastically.

"What about explosions?" Bertolt's nostrils flared at the thought. "In the booby traps, I mean."

"Er, I think most of this furniture is flammable," Darkus replied with a frown.

"Of course." Bertolt scratched his head. "Perhaps just a few firecrackers."

"C'mon, then." Virginia moved onto her hands and knees, crawling away through a backless cupboard. "Let's get moving."

The three of them set about worming their way around Furniture Forest, mapping its alleyways and dead ends, quietly moving things to clear paths and create a labyrinth only they knew the secrets of. They signaled to one another in silence as they moved chairs, lifted boxes, and slid shelves around, creating hidden doorways, wider tunnels, and paths to nowhere.

At the southern corner of the yard, as far away from the Emporium as possible, they constructed a room against the yard walls, using tall pieces of furniture and sheets of tarpaulin for the roof. They dragged in the grandfather clock, complete with resident mouse, and used the black door with the silver 73 to make the entrance.

"We should call this place Base Camp," Bertolt suggested as he pushed a circular coffee table into the middle of the floor. "That's what you call the camp on a mountainside, just before you get to the top."

Darkus was rearranging shelves in a metal unit to make a wall. "Base Camp." He tried out the name. "That's good."

"Look at all this amazing stuff I've found." Virginia came through the door with an armful of goodies, which she unloaded onto the sofa. "A telescope for spying, an oil lamp, some string—always useful—a mirror, and a car battery."

"This is nice." Bertolt picked up the brass telescope and peered down it. "We could use it to see into the Emporium."

"They don't call him Einstein for nothing," Virginia teased.

"I wonder if Pickering and Humphrey got into the bedroom last night," Darkus said. He'd been worrying about the beetles all day. "That armchair is really heavy and I wedged it under the handle so they couldn't turn it."

"We could take the telescope and see." Virginia grabbed it out of Bertolt's hands.

Darkus nodded, looking about. "We've pretty much got the camp built now."

Bertolt shrugged. "Okay."

They made their way through their newly constructed tunnels to a lookout post in line with what appeared to be Humphrey and Pickering's kitchen window, up on the second floor.

"Ooo, look at that!" Bertolt pointed at a languishing crystal chandelier poking out of a suitcase. "Can we bring that to Base Camp on our way back?"

Virginia had climbed up on top of a tall chest of drawers and poked the telescope out through a hole in the tarpaulin. "I can see one of them in the kitchen," she whispered. "He's putting his coat on." She turned. "Do you think he's going out?"

"We could go around the front and check," Darkus suggested.

Virginia shimmied back down the chest of drawers. "Go, go, go, or we'll miss him."

The three of them scrambled over to a ladder they'd strapped to the wall. Scaling it and dropping down the other side, they ran through Uncle Max's flat and out into the street. Looking up and down, they could see no sign of the neighbors, so they bolted across the road and burst into the empty Laundromat, throwing themselves on the ground behind the row of machines in the window.

"There he is!" Darkus said, breathless, pointing across the street. "That's the skinny one. His name's Pickering."

Virginia and Bertolt peered over the top of a washing machine as a tall bony man, dressed in a tatty raincoat, emerged from the door beside the boarded-up shop and scurried away up the street. Darkus suddenly remembered that in a moment of blind panic he'd told Pickering he lived next door. He hoped Pickering still believed he was lying, or had forgotten what he'd said. He was about to tell Virginia and Bertolt when the gray door opened again. He grabbed them and pulled them down behind the machine.

"That's the other one," he whispered. "That's Humphrey."

"He's ginormous!" Bertolt gasped, peeping through a gap in the machines.

Humphrey plodded off in the opposite direction to Pickering.

"I know," Darkus agreed. "He's the one who said he wanted to put me in a pie."

"Wait!" Virginia looked at him. "If they're both out, surely now is a good time to meet the beetles and see the mountain?"

Bertolt swallowed. "Um, isn't that breaking and entering?"

"Only if we break something," Darkus said, grinning at Virginia.

"We're not going to steal anything—and if we're quick, we can be out of there before they get back," Virginia said, trying to reassure Bertolt.

"It's dangerous," Bertolt pointed out.

"Danger is my middle name."

"No it isn't," Bertolt muttered, fidgeting nervously with a loose thread hanging from his blazer cuff. "It's Winifred."

"C'mon, Bertolt," Darkus cajoled. "I swear, you've never seen anything like this before, and it might help my dad."

Bertolt gave the tiniest of nods with the unhappiest of faces.

CHAPTER TEN
Beetle Mountain

"That's the window." Darkus pointed up through the branches of the sycamore tree. "We need to climb up to the branch opposite and jump in." He looked at his shoulder. "Baxter, you can fly up."

"I'm still not sure about this." Bertolt clutched Virginia. "I'm not very good with heights."

"Don't you want to see?"

Bertolt nodded reluctantly. "Yes, but . . ."

"What's the worst that could happen? We get in there and it turns out that there are only a handful of ordinary beetles in a teacup?"

"No." Bertolt looked somber. "We fall and break our necks, or get caught and end up in prison."

"If we get caught, we'll tell the police we were trying to rescue Darkus. They kidnapped him, remember? We'll be heroes."

"What if *we* get kidnapped?"

"Look, they're out—and if they come back, we can be out of the window and down here in seconds," Darkus said, reassuring him, swinging up into the tree and leaning back down to offer Virginia a helping hand. She scoffed at him, wrapping her hands around the lowest branch and walking her feet up the trunk until she could flip into a sitting position beside him.

They looked down at Bertolt, who was jumping up and down, trying and failing to reach the branch. Virginia and Darkus both leaned down, each grabbing hold of one of his hands, and pulled him up beside them.

"Thanks." Bertolt pushed his glasses up on his nose and gave them an apologetic smile.

Darkus went ahead, climbing up to the branch opposite Humphrey's room and launching his body in through the window. The beetles were hidden away inside their mountain, with only the odd hind leg or antenna visible, and he was relieved to see the pink armchair was still wedged against the door.

"Hello," Darkus whispered, picking himself up off the floor. "I'm back."

Baxter landed gently on his shoulder. He could hear quiet scufflings and chitterings as the other beetles began emerging from their mountain.

"Move over." Virginia was crouching on the window ledge. "This window is swarming with ladybugs."

"I might just stay here." Bertolt was still clinging on to the branch.

"Come on." Virginia reached out, and Bertolt hurled himself into her arms, knocking them both through the window onto the floor.

"Sorry," Bertolt whispered. "I'm at a height disadvantage when it comes to trees."

"It's dark in here." Virginia looked about.

"There isn't a light," Darkus replied, pointing up at the bulb-less fixture dangling from the ceiling. "I wish I'd brought my flashlight."

A gentle buzzing noise answered him, and thousands of tiny flickering yellow lights floated up to the ceiling.

"Wow!" Darkus looked up.

"Peenywallies!" Virginia gasped.

"Peeny what?" Darkus asked.

"Fireflies," Virginia said, her eyes shining. "Our very own starlight."

"Fireflies!" Bertolt echoed. "Now, *they're* beautiful!"

"Welcome to Beetle Mountain." Darkus proudly stepped over to the towering mound, enjoying the expressions on Virginia's and Bertolt's faces as hundreds of beetles poked their heads out of their cups. Baxter flew up and landed on the butterfly bush.

"Those are *big* beetles!" Virginia moved to take a closer look.

"Freeze!" Darkus pointed. "Look down."

The floor in front of her feet might have looked like carpet, but it was, Darkus knew, a live tapestry of beetles weaving in and out of one another.

"What do I do?" she asked Darkus.

Darkus knelt down. "Please, would you let my friend through?" he asked politely.

The beetles at Virginia's feet drew back, parting to create a path.

"Amazing!" She laughed with delight, stepping up gingerly beside him.

Darkus pointed out the beetles in the cups, discovering that some of them housed beetle larvae, too. He spotted traces of cranberry sauce in several cups, and was mesmerized by the turquoise and caramel mold growths springing up between the various pieces of crockery. He resisted the urge to poke them but noticed that different types of beetle furnished their cups with different things, like twigs, or water, or even an old sock!

"My brother Sean is going to die when I tell him about this," Virginia said, peering into the cups. "Look! An *elderberry beetle*!" She pointed at a black beetle with absurdly long antennae and elytra that had a rim of bright gold. "These are a seriously endangered species. Oh, and there's a stag beetle—and an oil beetle! This room should be a conservation zone."

"Um, guys . . ." Bertolt's voice had shot up an octave. "HELP!" he squeaked.

"Relax. We'll hear the front door open if they come back," Darkus said.

"No, look!" Bertolt rolled his eyes up to the ceiling. "Beetle!"

"I know." Virginia smiled up at the fireflies. "Aren't they stunning?"

"NO!" Bertolt wailed. "On my head!"

"Wowsers! What *is* that?" Virginia exclaimed. "It's enormous!"

"Is it?" Bertolt looked like he might faint.

Resting on his white-blond curls was the enormous zebra-striped beetle.

"It's all right." Darkus smiled. "It's a Goliath. I met him yesterday. He won't hurt you."

"Get it off me," Bertolt pleaded.

Gently, Darkus held his hand against Bertolt's forehead, and the huge beetle crawled onto it. Bertolt slumped against the wall with his eyes closed, sighing with relief, until he opened them again and found a cluster of mint-green lavender beetles feeding off a tea splatter right in front of his nose. He sprang back with a shriek.

Virginia tutted. "Stop being so jumpy or you'll squash someone. C'mon, surely you're smart enough to see how amazing these guys are."

Bertolt looked down, shamefaced. "Sorry."

"Oh! Look! Dung beetles!" Virginia pointed.

"Oh no! Yuck!" Bertolt grimaced. "Look what they're pushing!"

Darkus saw a brown, cricket ball–sized lump roll out of a hole in the skirting board, steered by two bronze beetles. One beetle was working heroically hard, walking in a kind of handstand and pushing the ball with his hind legs, while the other was pretending to help but really sitting on top, getting a free ride.

"Do you think it's human poo?" Bertolt asked.

"What other kinds of poo do you think they have around here?" Virginia chuckled at Bertolt's horror. "Oh, come on, we all do it, and if beetles didn't get rid of it we'd probably all be wading around in it."

She looked around the room, taking in the dirty armchair, the ax, and the wooden chair with ropes wound around its legs. "Everything you said was true!" she said to Darkus.

"I thought you said you believed me."

"I did—sort of." She shook her head in wonder. "But this is bonkers."

"I know." He nodded. "These beetles are like no beetles I've ever seen before." He gently placed the Goliath beetle on the mountain. "And they need our help. They're in danger."

Baxter dropped down from the butterfly bush and crawled to the Goliath beetle, his antennae flicking in silent conversation.

"But"—Virginia shook her head—"beetles don't have a hive mentality. They don't behave the way you're talking about, working together."

"Maybe these ones do." He looked at his friends. "Something important is happening in this room. I don't know what it is, exactly, but I know we have to protect these beetles. It's what Dad would do."

"Are you going to tell your uncle about this place?" Bertolt asked.

"I don't know." Darkus frowned. "Not yet."

"I think you should," Bertolt said quietly.

A loud bang sounded downstairs, and they looked at one another in alarm.

Bloodcurdling laughter echoed up the stairwell. "What *do* you look like?" Humphrey roared.

"*Me?*" Pickering snapped. "Take a look in a mirror and you'll see that satin highlights your talent for sweating like a warthog."

"Your tie looks like a monkey spewed bananas on it!" Humphrey snorted.

The cousins were back.

Goose bumps popped up all over Darkus's body. "Time to get out of here," he whispered urgently. "We don't want to get caught." He held his hand out to Baxter, who flew straight to it.

They ran to the window. Virginia clambered onto the window ledge, leaning out and catching hold of the branch. She swung down and dropped to the ground.

"What if I can't reach?" Bertolt clung to the window frame in fear.

"You'll be fine," Darkus said. "Just give yourself a good push off."

Bertolt screwed up his courage, closed his eyes, and flung himself off the window ledge with his arms thrown wide like a flying squirrel. He overshot the first branch, screaming as he hit the second and grabbing on to it for dear life.

Virginia was up the tree in a shot, grabbing on to Bertolt and helping him down to the ground.

"Back to Base Camp." She pushed him. "Quick!"

"Hey!"

"You made a noise like an air-raid siren just now, so get on your knees and get under that table, fast, before we're seen."

Bertolt crawled into the tunnel. A firefly appeared before him, lighting the way.

Darkus was shinnying down the tree, Baxter on his shoulder, when a window opened one floor down from Beetle Mountain. The cousins were in the kitchen. He froze.

Pickering's head poked out. "I definitely heard something."

"No you didn't," came Humphrey's voice.

"Yes I did." Pickering scanned the yard. "There's someone out there."

Darkus held his breath. *Don't look up . . .*

"It was probably a fox." Humphrey's head popped out of the window beside Pickering's. "Can't see anything—except a yard full of rubbish."

"It's *not* rubbish!" Pickering shouted, slamming the window shut.

Darkus dropped to the ground and crawled, as fast as he could, into Furniture Forest. Bertolt and Virginia were waiting for him just inside.

"C'mon, let's get back to Base Camp," he said.

"Wait! Where does that door go?" Virginia pointed to a shabby wooden door on the other side of the tree, partly obscured by a stack of furniture.

"I don't know," Darkus admitted, out of breath. "I've never noticed it before."

"It could be a way into the boarded-up shop."

"Then we don't want to go through it." Bertolt looked at Darkus, clearly hoping he'd agree. "Do we? Because we'd be in their building, and they're back home now."

"It's probably locked," said Darkus.

"It might not be." Virginia cocked her head. "If we are going to protect those beetles, we need to identify all possible escape routes out of the building, in case Lucretia Cutter shows up."

Darkus nodded. "Okay, let's take a look."

Before anyone could protest, he was dashing back across the yard, Baxter still on his shoulder. When he reached the door, he twisted the handle and pulled. The swollen wood popped out of the door frame with a grunt. Darkus held his thumbs up and slipped inside.

Bertolt groaned as Darkus disappeared.

"You stay here," Virginia said, wriggling past him. "Be our lookout."

"Okay!" Bertolt said, looking relieved.

"If you see them coming, create a diversion so we can get out." Virginia peeked out from under the table.

"Wait." Bertolt blinked frantically. "What kind of diversion?"

"Do something noisy." She pointed. "Push that stack of chairs over." She launched herself after Darkus.

Bertolt looked up at the firefly hovering above his head. "I'm the lookout," he said.

Virginia found herself standing on a black-and-white-checked lino-leum floor at the entrance to a dingy kitchenette. To her right was a neglected bathroom. In the floor in front of it was a manhole cover.

I wonder if that goes to the sewers, she thought, remembering the dung beetles.

She stepped over the manhole cover into the kitchen.

A butler's sink sat below a dark window, the light blocked by furni-ture outside. Opposite was a built-in cupboard with a threadbare floral apron hanging from the hook on the door.

"Darkus," she called out in a whisper, "where are you?"

"Here." His voice came from an archway to the left. "Come and look at this."

He was in the middle of the shop floor, surrounded by a mess of sewing-machine parts. A powder-blue sign—FANNY FLOOTER'S KNITTING AND STITCHING EMPORIUM—lay beside a shattered display case that held a cobweb-covered ball of yellow wool. On the wall behind the cash register, in enormous dripping red letters, was the word *PIES*. Scrawled underneath, in spidery black marker, were the words *MAKE YOU FAT!*

There was evidence of insect life everywhere. Chair legs had been eaten away until they looked like burnt matchsticks. Dark exoskeletons scurried in and out of nooks and crannies, glistening in the half light as they trundled about their business.

Darkus looked past Virginia. "Where's Bertolt?"

"Being our lookout. We don't want to get caught in here."

Darkus nodded. "If we could get that open"—he pointed to the shop door—"we'd have an escape route into the street." He went over to the door, pulled back the bolts, and tried it, but it was locked. "Don't suppose you can pick locks?"

She shook her head.

Darkus rose up on tiptoe and ran his fingers along the top of the door frame. He stopped and grinned, pulling a key out of the dust and cobwebs.

"Dad keeps a spare key above the door for forgetful days," he said, slotting the dusty key into the lock and turning it. The lock opened.

"Yes!" he whispered, yanking the door open an inch, stopping it before it hit the gold bell hanging from the ceiling.

Virginia held up her hand to give him a high five. It took an awkward second before Darkus realized what she was doing and lifted his own hand to meet hers. Closing and locking the door, he pocketed the key and followed Virginia back into the kitchen.

Opening the cupboard with the apron on the door, she whispered to him, "Look at this." Inside was a staircase. Leaning their heads into the stairwell, they heard Pickering's and Humphrey's voices.

"*I* have Lucretia Cutter's card, and the beetles are *mine*," Humphrey shouted. "They're in my room; therefore they belong to me."

There was an almighty crash of crockery.

"It leads up to their kitchen!" Virginia mouthed.

"You've forgotten something." Pickering's voice was dripping with acid. "We can't get your door open, and unless I'm mistaken, there's a boy tied up and gagged in there. I wonder what the police would say if someone told them about that?"

"But *you* did that!"

"Ah, but he's in *your* room, and he'll remember you wanting to bake him into a pie. I'm *sure* the police would be interested—that's murder, that is."

Humphrey growled.

"All I'm suggesting is that we work together," Pickering said. "You've tried to break the door down, but it won't budge, and my ax is in there, which means the only way in is through the window. So unless you want to continue sleeping on the hall floor, you're going to need my help getting in." Pickering sounded triumphant. "If I get in and dispose of the boy, then we BOTH do the deal with Lucretia Cutter. What do you say?"

There was a pause.

"Deal," Humphrey said reluctantly. "As long as I get to bake him into a pie."

Virginia closed the cupboard door. "Let's get out of here."

CHAPTER ELEVEN
Newton

"Where have you been?" Uncle Max called down the stairs. "I was beginning to worry."

Darkus beckoned Virginia and Bertolt into the flat. "Um, nowhere much," he replied, climbing the stairs to the living room.

"Nowhere, eh?" Uncle Max appeared in the doorway. "That's often a very interesting place . . ." He stopped, seeing Virginia and Bertolt. "Oh! Hello! I'm Darkus's uncle, Professor Maximilian Cuttle." He held out his hand. "Pleased to meet you."

"Bertolt Roberts." Bertolt shook Uncle Max's hand.

"Virginia Wallace." Virginia waved. "We've, um, we've come to help Darkus with his homework, because he's new and a bit behind."

Darkus shot Virginia a look.

"Well, that is nice." Uncle Max stepped back, smiling.

"Why did you say that?" Darkus said to Virginia under his breath as they filed past Uncle Max into the living room.

"You want to tell him what we've really been doing?"

Darkus shook his head.

Virginia gave him a knowing smile. "Thought not."

"Come in. Come in. Oh, and I see Baxter's with you, too. Darkus, you didn't take the beetle to school, did you?"

"Of course not."

"Good." Uncle Max clapped his hands together. "Well now, isn't this lovely, having guests." He beamed. "Eh, Darkus?"

Darkus smiled awkwardly and nodded.

Virginia dropped to her knees in front of a ship made from balsa wood trapped inside a glass bottle. "You've got some cool stuff," she said to Uncle Max.

"Why, thank you, Virginia, that's very kind of you." Uncle Max looked delighted. "Most of these old things I've found on my travels." He waved at the assortment of curiosities scattered around the living room. "It's a hodgepodge collection, but I like it. It reminds me where I've been."

Bertolt sat down cross-legged on the floor beside a purple hookah pipe. "Look! I'm the caterpillar from *Alice in Wonderland*!" He pretended to suck on the pipe and blow out a smoke ring.

Virginia laughed and Darkus smiled at Uncle Max. But Uncle Max wasn't looking at him; he was frowning and edging his way toward

Bertolt, peering down into his mass of white-blond curls. "Don't move, lad," he said. "There appears to be a rather large bug in your hair."

"Not again!" Bertolt wailed, dropping the pipe. "Why do they like my hair so much?"

"Don't panic," Darkus said, leaning forward. "It's a firefly!"

"A big one," Virginia added, "with a belly like a burning coal."

"A firefly?" Bertolt looked up, trying to see. "Oh, I don't mind them. They're beautiful!"

"Shall I pick it out?" Uncle Max asked.

But there was no need. The firefly rose up out of Bertolt's hair, bathing his face in a golden light. Hesitantly, Bertolt held out his hand for the beetle to land. The firefly was long and thin. Its copper wing casings had gold edges and a white vertical stripe down the middle. It had a tiny face and stubby mandibles that looked like a mustache.

"You wouldn't know he's a firefly when you look down at him, because the light comes from his belly," Virginia said loftily. "It's only when he's flying that you can see it. It's called bioluminescence."

"He's brilliant, Bertolt," Darkus said happily. "Now we've *both* got beetles!"

"I've got a beetle?" Bertolt's eyes grew big. "How can you tell?"

"Look at him," Darkus said. "See how his mouth is held open? He's trying to smile at you. Baxter looks at me like that sometimes. It's cute."

"Hello," Bertolt whispered to the firefly. "My name's Bertolt. What's yours?"

The firefly sat still, staring up at him, smiling.

"Would you mind if I called you Newton?" Bertolt said. "He's my favorite scientist. He discovered that light was made of colors."

The firefly skipped up into the air, flashing his belly.

"Does everyone around here have a pet beetle?" Uncle Max asked, huffing.

"I don't," Virginia sulked. "I wish I did."

"Why don't you get a puppy, or a rabbit?"

"They're not as cool," Virginia replied as if Uncle Max had asked a dumb question.

But he was staring at the firefly, and Darkus could see he was concerned. "What's wrong, Uncle Max?"

"Nothing, I just don't understand where all these beetles are coming from." Uncle Max scratched his head. "They're bigger than normal beetles, and they seem, well . . . it's as if . . ."

"Yes?" Darkus leaned forward.

"Hmm, I don't know. I'm probably imagining things." Uncle Max shook his head. "Getting funny in the brain. Must be my age." He sighed. "And look, in all the excitement, I've forgotten my manners. What a terrible host! What can I get you to drink?" Uncle Max looked from Virginia to Bertolt. "Coffee? Mint tea? Does anyone fancy a licorice stick?"

"A mint tea would be lovely, Professor Cuttle," Bertolt said politely. "Thank you."

"Could I have some orange juice?" Virginia asked.

"Orange juice—right, of course. Um, we're right out of that.

Perhaps I should nip down to Mr. Patel's and get some bits and bobs. What goes well with orange juice?"

"Biscuits," Virginia replied. "Custard creams, or bourbons."

Darkus and Bertolt nodded.

"Marvelous. Well, don't let me stop you from getting on with your homework. I'll pop out for supplies and deliver the refreshments forthwith." Uncle Max backed out of the door, beaming at everyone.

"He's nice," Virginia said when she was sure he'd gone. "I've never seen a grown-up so pleased about a kid bringing friends home." She laughed.

Darkus felt his cheeks grow hot and changed the subject. "Why the demands for orange juice and biscuits?"

"Well, I don't know about you, but I don't like mint tea or licorice sticks." Virginia raised an eyebrow. "I prefer orange juice and biscuits. Anyway, I thought we needed to talk in private. So let's do it quickly before he comes back." She put her hands on her hips. "First thing I want to know is how Bertolt got himself a beetle." She stared at him. "Did you catch it?"

"No!" Bertolt looked horrified. "The firefly was in the tunnel after we left Beetle Mountain. It followed us. When you ran into the shop I talked to it a bit, because"—Bertolt looked at the floor—"I didn't like being on my own in the dark. Talking to the firefly made me feel braver." He turned to Darkus. "I lost it when you came back. I thought it had flown away, but it must have hidden in my hair."

"Perhaps Newton chose Bertolt, like Baxter chose me," Darkus said.

Virginia flared her nostrils, scowling at the idea.

"Darkus," Bertolt blinked, "how do you talk to Baxter?"

"I don't know. I just do."

"Can you teach me to understand Newton like you understand Baxter?"

"I'm not sure." Darkus looked at his beetle crawling across the coffee table and frowned. "I haven't really thought about *how* I do it."

"What is it that lets you understand what he's telling you?"

"Can I hold Newton?" Darkus asked.

"Of course." Bertolt offered Darkus his cupped hand.

Darkus gently lifted Newton, placing the beetle on his palm and lifting him to eye level. "Hello there, Newton, nice to meet you."

The firefly fluttered up and flashed his belly at Darkus.

"Why, thank you." Darkus nodded to the beetle, looking closely at his face and thorax. "Bertolt, I think he uses his belly to communicate. Watch what he's doing with it." He turned back to the beetle. "Can you flash once for yes and twice for no?" he asked.

The firefly flashed once.

Virginia and Bertolt gasped.

"That's amazing!" Bertolt squealed, barely able to contain his excitement.

"Baxter talks to me with his body," Darkus said. "He shakes or nods his horn, flicks his antennae, or waves his legs. If you look really closely and carefully at what the beetles are doing, you'll understand them."

Bertolt was impressed. He held out his hand to take Newton back.

"I found a stairway in the Emporium," Virginia said, keen to talk about something else, "that leads from the shop to the flat upstairs, and Darkus found a key to the Emporium shop door."

"We heard them talking," Darkus added. "They think I'm still tied up in Humphrey's bedroom. They plan to climb in the window, get rid of me, and then sell the beetles to Lucretia Cutter. I wonder what they'll do when they find that I'm not there?" He smiled.

"They're so stupid they'll probably think the beetles ate you!" Virginia laughed. She looked at the wall of book-stuffed shelves between Uncle Max's flat and the neighbors'. "It's weird to think that all those beetles are on the other side of that wall. I mean, how did they get there in the first place?" She turned to Darkus, looking thoughtful. "If Lucretia Cutter *has* got something to do with your dad's disappearance, and the connection between her and your dad *is* to do with beetles, don't you think it's weird that there's a mountain of superbeetles living next door to *you*?"

Darkus frowned. He hadn't thought about it before, but it did seem an unlikely coincidence. "But I've only lived here a couple of weeks," he pointed out. "The beetles must've been living next door for ages; look at the size of the mountain."

"How long's your uncle lived here?" Bertolt asked.

"Oh, years; since before I was born."

"Could the beetles have anything to do with him?" Bertolt asked.

"I don't know." Darkus shrugged. "He does behave strangely when he's around Baxter."

"We should ask him," Virginia said.

"How do we do that without telling him we broke in next door?" Darkus asked.

"I don't know, but you should definitely ask him more about Lucretia Cutter. If your uncle thinks she has something to do with your dad's kidnapping, that means they must know each other."

"He dodges my questions about her. I think there's something important he's not telling me. Like, in the museum, he told Margaret not to tell me they were going to give Dad's job to someone else. He thinks if he tells me the truth I won't be able to handle it."

"That's stupid," Virginia scoffed. "It's much worse not knowing."

"Tell me about it." Darkus sighed.

"Then let's try again, all of us, together. We'll do it when your uncle brings in the orange juice."

As if on cue, they heard Uncle Max's key in the door downstairs. Five minutes later, he entered, carrying a tray of orange juice, biscuits, and a mint tea for Bertolt. He laid it on the coffee table.

"Thank you, Professor Cuttle," Virginia said, picking up a glass of juice and flashing him an innocent smile. "Darkus was just telling us about his dad disappearing, and how you and he are going to solve the mystery. It sounds ever so exciting."

"Well, I wouldn't say—"

"Bertolt and I would like to help. Wouldn't we, Bertolt?"

"Oh yes!" Bertolt nodded enthusiastically as he reached for a biscuit.

"That's very kind of you, but—"

"We heard all about the visit to the museum," Virginia said, talking over Uncle Max, "and about Darkus finding the reading glasses, and how that lady on the canes turned up, and it turns out Bertolt knows all about her—don't you, Bertolt?"

"Lucretia Cutter." Bertolt nodded again. "She's in all the magazines—they call her the Mad Scientist of Fashion."

"Do they, now?" Uncle Max looked like there was a bad smell in the room. "Well, I suppose if the cap fits . . ."

"But we were wondering . . . how did *you* know who she was?" Virginia asked.

"I beg your pardon?"

"I don't mean to be rude or nothing, Professor Cuttle, sir, but I wouldn't think you were the kind of man who'd have an eye on the fashion runways and magazines."

"Virginia!" Bertolt scolded.

"So, I was wondering," Virginia continued, "when you saw Lucretia Cutter in the museum, how did you recognize her?"

Uncle Max's mouth fell open. He closed it.

"Yes." Darkus leaned in. "How?"

"Do you know her?" Virginia persisted, taking a bite of biscuit as she waited for him to answer.

Uncle Max looked at the three children and, with a great sigh, sat down on the couch. "Well, actually, yes. I did know her, once."

"Was that before she was famous?" Virginia shot Darkus a triumphant sideways look.

"Yes, yes, it was." Uncle Max pulled at his earlobe and looked into the distance.

"How did you meet her?" Darkus asked.

"Through Barty," Uncle Max admitted. "He introduced us at a party."

"But how does Dad know Lucretia Cutter?" Darkus asked.

"They met at university."

"Dad went to university with Lucretia Cutter?"

"In a way." Uncle Max shook his head. "It was a long time ago, Darkus. Your father hasn't spoken to that woman for over fifteen years."

"Then why did she turn up at the museum?" Darkus asked. "And why is her name above the room that Dad disappeared from?"

"Darkus, if I knew the answers to those questions . . . I would have told you already."

"What Darkus's dad and Lucretia Cutter did at university . . ." Virginia said, "was it to do with beetles?"

Uncle Max blinked as he thought about his answer. "Barty's specialist field was beetles, but Lucretia Cutter was a different kind of scientist, a geneticist. I think her interest in beetles came from knowing Barty. His passion for beetles was infectious—once he started talking about them, you couldn't help but become fascinated, too."

"What about you?" Virginia asked, leaning forward and taking another biscuit. "Did *you* ever have anything to do with beetles?"

"No." Uncle Max shook his head.

"You've never had any beetles here in the flat, then?" Darkus asked.

"I . . . er, um . . ." Uncle Max looked terribly uncomfortable. "Oh, look! We need more biscuits." He jumped up and hurried out of the room.

"You're right, Darkus. There's something he's not telling us," Virginia whispered. "There are loads of biscuits left."

"He didn't explain the connection between your dad and Lucretia Cutter very well," Bertolt said. "It must be more than just meeting at university and chatting about beetles."

"Yes, we need to find out more." Virginia nodded.

"And I know exactly how to do it." Darkus stood up, putting his hand into his trouser pocket and pulling out a white rectangular card. "I'll ask Novak Cutter."

"You're going to go to Towering Heights?" Virginia's eyebrows shot up.

Darkus nodded. "Saturday morning."

"Darkus!" Bertolt gasped. "That could be dangerous, and she may not even know anything."

"Yes"—Virginia cocked her head—"but then again, she *might*. And I'll bet she can tell us other stuff that will help the beetles—like why her mum *really* wants them." She looked at Darkus. "You can't trust her, though. She's the enemy's daughter. She'll probably lie to you— she may even hand you over to her mother."

"I'm not frightened of her," Darkus said, bristling. "If Lucretia Cutter is behind Dad's disappearance, then I want to know."

Thursday and Friday, after school, Darkus, Bertolt, and Virginia worked on Base Camp. They drew a map of Furniture Forest and taped it to the back of a wardrobe, marking each booby trap they'd built around the perimeter to warn them if hostile forces approached, and hooked up an alarm system made of bottle tops threaded on strings, which jangled when a trap was set off.

The days quickly passed in a flurry of scavenging, building, and planning. Newton had made a permanent home in Bertolt's hair, and a trail of fireflies—Newton's friends and family—had followed the beetle out of the Emporium and into Base Camp.

When Saturday morning arrived, Bertolt and Virginia met outside the Emporium.

"You're wearing a bow tie!"

"Don't you like it?" Bertolt looked at his chest.

"It's a bit formal, isn't it?"

"It goes with my vest."

Bertolt looked over his glasses disapprovingly at her clothes.

Virginia looked down at her red tracksuit. It was worn and baggy at the knees, a hand-me-down from her sister Serena. She pushed Bertolt toward the Emporium doorway. "Come on, hurry up and open the door before someone sees us."

They let themselves in with the key, creeping through the shop and out the other side to Furniture Forest. Once in the tunnels, they followed the already familiar path to Base Camp. Its higgledy-piggledy walls glowed and sparkled as thousands of fireflies greeted them by illuminating the dangling chandelier crystals that Bertolt had stitched to the tarpaulin ceiling.

Virginia lifted the oil lamp down from the shelves, placing it on the table and lighting the wick. Bertolt settled down at his workbench—an ironing board propped up on crates—and Virginia sat down on the sofa with Darkus's book on beetles.

"This book is really interesting," she said. "But do you think Darkus has read all of it?"

"I don't know. Why?" Bertolt was working on a new booby trap. The grandfather clock's pendulum was to be installed in the tunnel beyond the foldaway table and rigged to swing down and clobber anyone following the person who'd triggered it.

"Well, there's a bit here . . ." Virginia paused.

"What?" Bertolt put down his screwdriver.

"It's about the average life span of a beetle." Virginia frowned. "It's not very long."

Bertolt looked up at Newton and the cloud of fireflies flickering and fizzing above his head. "I don't want to know," he said, picking up his screwdriver again.

Virginia sighed, putting the book down, and went over to the collage of newspaper articles and magazine cuttings they'd taped to the wardrobe above the map. They were all about Lucretia Cutter. She stared at a photo of Novak and her mother on a red carpet. "I wonder how Darkus is doing. He should be at Towering Heights by now."

"I still think we should have gone with him," Bertolt said.

"Me too," Virginia agreed, "but he didn't want us to."

Darkus got off the bus at Regent's Park and walked alongside the railings. To his left, trees and parkland stretched up toward the entrance of London Zoo. On the opposite side of the road were grand detached white houses, some with names and some with numbers. He walked along until he came to a tall imposing town house with TOWERING HEIGHTS written over the gates, and he suddenly realized that he'd no idea what he was going to say to Novak Cutter.

There was a wall in front of the property, about the same height as Darkus. Beyond it, the house was surrounded by a copper beech hedge at least eight feet tall. There was an intercom on the gatepost to let people in. Through the gate, a white gravel driveway veered to the left of the house. The front yard, to the right, was paved black and white, like a man-size chessboard, and a glossy black door was framed by enormous flowerpots bursting with red lilies.

Darkus paced up and down, talking to himself, trying to think of a good way to ask Novak Cutter if her mum had kidnapped his dad. All sorts of ridiculous sentences came out of his mouth. He cursed himself for not practicing on Virginia and Bertolt.

He crossed over the road and looked through the bars of the gate. He couldn't even think of something to say into the intercom.

This was not good. He'd have to go back to Base Camp and ask Virginia and Bertolt what to do. He took two steps toward the bus stop and froze. Ahead, and coming straight toward him, were Pickering and Humphrey, dressed in ridiculous yellow and purple suits. Without thinking, Darkus pulled himself up onto the wall and dropped down the other side into the copper beech hedge surrounding Towering Heights. He could hear the cousins arguing.

"You'd better not ruin this for me, Humphrey."

"Shut it, Pickers, or I'll change my mind about bringing you."

"We had a deal. I got your door open, didn't I?"

Darkus held his breath as the voices approached. His neck was being scratched by the shrubbery, but he didn't dare move. He heard the buzz of the intercom and the two men saying their names. The black door opened silently, and a butler with dark slicked-back hair and a mournful face came out. He walked stiffly and steadily to the gate.

"We have an appointment to see Lucretia Cutter," Humphrey shouted.

"Monsieur Gamble and Monsieur Risk, yes, I know," the butler replied in a French accent. Now that he was closer, Darkus could see that he had dark circles under his gray eyes.

"That's right." Humphrey puffed up his chest and Pickering nodded eagerly. The butler opened the gate by keying in a number, and the cousins followed him through the front door, which closed behind them.

Darkus wriggled out of the other side of the copper beech hedge, covered in scratches. He stood facing the house. Coming here alone had been a mistake. He needed to get back to Base Camp.

He ran to the gate, but it was closed. He tugged at the bars in frustration; he'd either have to climb it or go back through the hedge, getting even more scratched. He was halfway up the gate when he heard the door behind him open, and a voice. "You! Boy." Darkus froze. It was a French accent: The butler had come back. "Come down." Darkus did as he was told but didn't turn around. "Her ladyship will see you now."

Darkus looked over his shoulder. "*Me?*"

"Yes, *you.*"

"But I don't have an appointment." He stammered.

"You don't need one. You're being invited in." The butler's face was a blank; his sad eyes didn't blink. "Come on, boy. Don't you know you shouldn't keep a lady waiting?"

Darkus dragged his feet toward the door of Lucretia Cutter's house, his heart hammering against his rib cage.

CHAPTER TWELVE
Towering Heights

The butler escorted Darkus into Towering Heights. It was a cathedral of white, punctuated by polished steel, glossy black fixtures, and red fabric. It reminded Darkus of a modern art gallery. He was led to a sweeping staircase with a bloodred carpet and ebony banister, and they climbed up two flights of stairs to the third floor, passing landings displaying globular sculptures of glass and aluminum.

The butler pointed at a door on the landing ahead of him, and Darkus stepped up to it as the butler melted backward and disappeared. Darkus knocked on the door, his heart in his mouth. There was no response, so he gently pushed and the door swung open.

"Hello?" The room was dark.

"I knew you'd come," a voice said from the darkness.

"You did?" Darkus strained to see who was speaking.

A spotlight flickered on, lighting a Persian rug in the center of the room.

"I could tell from the first time our eyes met that you'd follow me to the ends of the earth."

Novak Cutter stepped into the spotlight.

She was wearing a white floor-length dress, her platinum curls sculpted around her face and an ostrich feather boa draped over her shoulders. She placed the back of her delicate hand on her forehead, letting the feather boa slide to the floor.

Relieved, Darkus came forward into the room and picked it up. He opened his mouth to speak.

"No," she whispered, covering his mouth with her hand. "Don't say it. There can never be anything between us. I'm promised to another."

"*What?*"

"Don't pretend you don't love me." Novak clutched her hands to her chest as if her heart were trying to fly away.

"Sorry, but"—Darkus dropped the boa and stepped backward—"y-y-you've got the wrong—"

"You heartless beast." She looked straight at him. "Your eyes"—she reached out her arms—"they call out to me."

"They do?" Darkus shuffled backward toward the door. "It's not on purpose."

"You can't leave." Novak collapsed to her knees and began to weep.

"Um, please don't cry." Darkus looked about nervously. "I'm sure you're very nice . . . but, er, I don't know you."

"I'm Novak Cutter," she sobbed.

"I know your name."

"You picked up my card?"

Darkus nodded and wondered whether now would be a good time to bring up the beetles.

"And you came here." Novak eyes sparkled with tears. "Why?" she whispered.

"This may sound strange . . ."

"You don't need to explain," she said, shuffling closer. "You've come to set me free from this prison."

"Are you a prisoner?" Darkus looked about in alarm. The room was dark, the curtains closed. He couldn't see if there were bars on the windows.

"Let's run away together, to Africa. We'll hunt lions and sleep out under the stars," Novak said in a dreamy voice, moving closer, still on her knees.

"Why are you talking all crazy?"

"Oh, my darling!" She threw her arms around Darkus's legs. "You love me. I know you do!"

Flustered, Darkus tried to step out of her grasp, lost his balance, and fell to the floor.

"Let go! What are you doing?"

"Say you love me!" she cried out, clinging to his ankles.

"No. I won't. Stop it!" Darkus shouted crossly. "I *don't* love you."

He tried to crawl away. "I was going to ask for your help, but you're obviously bonkers."

"There's no need to be rude," Novak said sharply, letting go of him. She got up and brushed herself off. "You could have at least had the decency to *pretend* you loved me."

"But I *don't* love you!"

"I heard you the first time." She turned away. "There's no need to rub it in."

Darkus had never been so confused.

"When I saw you across the street, looking all lovesick—"

"I *wasn't* lovesick."

"I thought you'd come to see me because I blew you that kiss. I even put on my best dress." She smoothed down the satin of her skirt. "I saw you hide in the hedge when those weird men came. I thought it ever so romantic. That's why I sent Gerard to let you in."

"Gerard?"

"Our butler," said Novak. "I thought you'd come to tell me that you loved me." She picked up her feather boa.

"That's not why I'm here . . ."

"Obviously."

"It's your mum, you see; she wants to buy these beetles from my neighbors and—"

"She doesn't see children—doesn't even like them." Novak walked to the door. "But I'll let Gerard know that it's her you want to see."

"No, wait," Darkus called after her. "It's *you* I came to see."

Novak gave an exasperated sigh and spun round. "Make your mind up."

Darkus got to his feet. "I need your help."

"Really?" Novak said sarcastically.

"Yes." Darkus stepped toward her. "Please listen. My dad has"—he chose his words carefully—"disappeared, and I think the reason might be to do with these beetles I found living next door to me, and your mother wants to buy them, and—"

"Beetles? Yuck!" Novak wrinkled her tiny nose. "Nasty, dirty, creepy-crawly things."

"These beetles are special, and if they have anything to do with my dad's disappearance, I've got to protect them." Darkus could see he was losing her attention. "I was hoping you might be able to find out more about them, or even persuade your mother to leave the beetles alone."

Novak let out a mean peal of laughter. "Open your eyes, boy."

"I have a name."

"What is it?"

"Darkus."

"Well then, Darkus"—Novak sashayed over to the light switch—"look around you." The walls, previously hidden in shadow, were suddenly brightly illuminated.

Darkus pivoted. He was in an oak-paneled library filled with leather-bound books and solid wooden furniture. An imposing portrait hung above the fireplace, a studded leather armchair beside it. On the mantelpiece was a lump of amber. At its heart was a beetle with horns; it looked like a miniature bull.

Novak followed his eyes. "That's *Onthophagus taurus*."

"A what?"

"It's a species of dung beetle that can pull a load over a thousand times its own body weight"—Novak sounded bored—"which is like you pulling six London buses. It's the strongest insect in the world."

"He's magnificent," Darkus replied. "It's a shame he's dead."

"Mater caught it on one of her beetle safaris in Africa. She had it dipped in resin and made into a trophy."

"Who is Mater?"

"Don't you go to school?" Novak sneered. "*Mater* is Latin for Mother. Lucretia Cutter doesn't like to be referred to as Mother, unless it is in the Latin form."

"You don't call her Mum?"

"No," Novak replied, making it clear that was the end of the conversation.

Darkus changed the subject. "She goes on beetle safaris?" He wondered if a beetle safari was like an insect hunt.

"Once a year," Novak said. "She always comes back with new species for her personal collection."

"Is that the one at the Natural History Museum?" Darkus asked.

"Ha! No. She sponsors that one; she doesn't own it. As the sponsor, she can control who gets to see it and find out what their research is about. *This* is where she keeps her private collection."

"Who's that?" Darkus pointed at the portrait.

"That is *Sir Charles Darwin* by Gracen and Gracen. It's made of the thorax and wing casings of scarab beetles." Novak sounded like she was reading from a textbook. "In those drawers"—she pointed to a deep cabinet that stretched along the only wall without books—"is the Carson Coleoptera Collection from 1903, containing beetles from East Asia."

Darkus pulled open one of the thin wooden drawers. Inside, hundreds of brightly colored beetles were lined up next to one another. Each had a pin stuck through its right elytron, like the specimen trays in the museum.

"The carpet and curtains"—Novak was relishing her TV voice-over persona and speaking in an exaggerated singsong tone—"are made of silk from worms, and stained red by the blood of the cochineal bug, which isn't a beetle, although many people think that it is."

Darkus looked around. This room, with its heavy red curtains and brown leather armchairs, was grander than the room at the museum, but really it was the same—a room filled with dead beetles.

"Each leather-bound volume in this, the personal library of Lucretia Cutter"—Novak was dancing around the room now—"is part of a rare scientific collection of books mapping the history of beetle evolution."

"So many dead beetles," Darkus said quietly.

"Yeah, it gives me the creeps," Novak said in her normal voice. "But I would rather they were dead than alive."

"How can you say that?" Darkus asked, surprised. "Beetles are amazing."

Novak screwed up her face. "No. They are all creepy and crawly and gross."

"You aren't looking at them properly."

"I see quite enough of beetles every day, thank you very much."

"Dead ones?"

"Of course dead ones, stupid." Novak sighed, exasperated.

"But I don't understand. Why'd you bring me here if you don't like it?"

"Because all the rooms above this floor are out of bounds to visitors, and Mater is downstairs with guests. This was the only room I could use without her knowing."

"If she already has all these beetles, why does she want more?"

"I don't know." Novak shrugged. "Mater is a serious collector. She's obsessed. I have a lesson every day about insects. She says it's important for my future that I know all about them. That's how I know their Latin names."

"What's she going to do with my beetles? Is she going to stick pins in them and put them in drawers?"

"Don't know. Probably." Novak gave a curt nod. "Unless it's for work."

"She's a beetle killer?"

"You really are stupid," Novak giggled.

Darkus smiled. "Thanks."

"Mater owns Cutter Couture. You know, with the scarab logo?"

Darkus nodded. "Bertolt told me about it, but what's fashion got to do with beetles?"

"Who's Bertolt?"

"My friend."

"Oh." Novak sniffed. "Cutter Couture is the biggest fashion brand in the world. It makes designer clothes and things, and the secret ingredients of *all* Mater's products come from insects. But that's boring. The best bit is that she's started putting her money into films. She's a movie producer now, and I'm going to be a huge movie star. I've already done my first film, and I've been nominated for an award."

"Really?"

"Don't I look like a star?" Novak turned away, looked over her shoulder, and gave him a dazzling Hollywood smile. She held the well-practiced pose for an alarming length of time.

"I suppose." Darkus scratched his head and looked around the room. "But I don't understand what this has to do with my beetles."

"Who cares? Beetles are boring." Novak walked over to the window. "Darkus is a good name for a love interest. I don't suppose you're a stable boy. Stable boys always rescue fair maidens in the stories, and then they turn out to be princes."

"No. I go to school, like all boys." Darkus snorted.

"Are you sure you don't want to kiss me?" Novak said, hiding her face behind a curtain and peeping out.

"Yes."

"Not even just a little bit?"

"Look, you're really nice and everything, but—"

"Oh, you're so dull!" Novak slapped her hands down on her dress in frustration. "Why are you still here?"

Darkus persevered. "Those weird men you saw—they're the ones with all the beetles in their house. They've come here to sell the insects to your mother."

"It must be an unusual infestation," Novak said, surprised. "Mater's not in the pest control business."

"She visited them," Darkus said, "that day you saw me in the window—"

"I wondered why we were on that horrible street."

"—and you dropped your card for me."

"You make it sound as if *I* were in love with *you*." Novak bristled. "I'm not. I'm *practicing* being in love. There's a difference." She clenched her fists. "It's important for my acting, and you don't even have the decency to play along!" She stamped away and threw herself into the enormous armchair. "You obviously don't think I'm a bit pretty, 'cause all you want to talk about is icky bugs."

"Please don't get upset." Darkus approached her chair. "I'm just looking for my dad."

"Well, I don't know where he is."

"The thing is, these beetles . . . I think they're somehow linked to my dad's disappearance. They're different from normal beetles—they're special—and that's why I want to protect them. One of them, Baxter, is my best friend."

"Your best friend is a beetle?" Novak scoffed.

"Yes. Would you like to meet him?" Darkus knelt down at her feet, took off his backpack, and pulled out Baxter's jam jar.

"It's alive!" Novak shrank back into the chair. "Oh no! I don't like it. Get it away from me."

Darkus unscrewed the lid, putting Baxter on the flat of his hand. "He's harmless."

Baxter lifted his elytra and flew straight back into the jar.

"It flew," Novak said, amazed. "I've never seen a beetle fly before." She leaned forward.

"Usually, he sits on my hand quite happily," Darkus said, puzzled.

"Perhaps he doesn't like me," Novak said mournfully.

"It's probably this room." Darkus looked around. "It's full of dead beetles. You wouldn't like to be in a room full of dead people, would you?"

Novak shook her head.

"It's all right, Baxter. Novak is a friend." Darkus turned the jar on its side and put his hand out. Baxter didn't move. "Come out and say hello, and then you can go straight back into the jar and I'll put you safely away in my bag. I promise."

Novak laughed as Darkus talked to the beetle but stopped when Baxter walked forward and stepped onto his hand.

"Beetles can't understand humans," she said, astonished.

"That's right," Darkus said, bringing his hand before Novak. "Ordinary beetles can't, but I told you—these aren't ordinary beetles." Darkus ran his finger over Baxter's glistening wing cases. "Say hello to Baxter."

"Don't be silly."

"Pretend you're in a movie, and Baxter is a handsome soldier returning from battle."

"But he's a beetle." Novak was appalled. "A big spiky gross one."

"Call yourself an actor?"

Novak pouted. "All right, give me a moment." She sank back into the chair, closed her eyes, and took a deep breath. Opening her eyes again, she sat up and, lowering her head and looking through fluttering eyelashes, said in an American accent: "What a pleasure it is to make your acquaintance, Corporal Baxter. I have heard many great things about your bravery in battle."

Baxter lowered his horn.

"He bowed!" Novak looked at Darkus in surprise.

"He's returning your greeting." Darkus smiled.

"Will he fly for me, do you think?" Novak asked, excited.

"I don't see why not." Darkus whispered to the beetle, waving his index finger in a pattern in the air. Baxter spread his wings and jumped into flight, making a noisy circuit of the room, the vibration of his wings throbbing like a distant engine.

Novak laughed with delight. "Can I touch him?"

"I'm sure he won't mind." Darkus grinned as the beetle landed on his hand.

Novak reached out and gave Baxter's thorax a gentle stroke before touching the tip of his horn. "Ouch! It's like a needle!" she exclaimed, holding out her hand in front of Darkus's. "Can I hold him?"

Baxter was already crawling onto Novak's palm.

"I think he likes you."

"Really?" Novak smiled at Darkus. "Gosh, he's heavy, isn't he?"

Lifting his elytra, Baxter opened his flying wings and jumped into the air. He zoomed in a figure eight around Darkus and Novak, returning to her outstretched hand.

"He does like me!" laughed Novak happily.

Darkus held the jar on its side and Baxter crawled in. "So, you see, my best friend *is* a beetle," he said, putting the jar into his backpack. "Now do you believe that I need your help?"

"Yes, but *I* can't help you. I mean, what can I do?"

"Do you know if your mother knows my dad? His name is Bartholomew Cuttle. He works at the National History Museum."

Novak shrugged. "She does know people at the museum, but I don't know who they are. I've never heard that name before, and I'd remember it, because it sounds like mine." She looked at him curiously. "Is Cuttle your surname too?"

Darkus nodded. "Cutter. Cuttle." He sounded the names out. "Your name sounds sharper."

"Cutter's not Mater's real name. Did you know that?"

Darkus shook his head. "What's her real name?"

"Lucy Johnstone. Isn't that a nice, friendly-sounding name? She changed her name to Lucretia Cutter before I was born, when she set up her business. 'Cutter' is what they call a tailor who invents patterns for clothes. It's good for a fashion designer, but I think Lucy Johnstone is much prettier."

"Well, whether your mother knows my dad or not, I still need to find out why she wants those beetles, and what she plans to do with them."

"Is Mater your enemy?" Novak asked, frowning.

Darkus felt his cheeks grow hot as he tried to answer. "I don't know. Maybe if you explained to her why she shouldn't kill the beetles . . ."

Novak shook her head. "Nothing stops her from getting what she wants. Look at how amazing Baxter is. If she knew he were here, she'd make him into a trophy, just like poor *Onthophagus taurus*."

A chill traveled down Darkus's spine as he realized the danger he was putting Baxter in, bringing him into this house.

"I should go." He pulled his backpack on. "Look, I understand why you can't help us, but I'll be your friend for life if you can help me and Baxter get out of here without being seen."

"I've never had a friend." Novak sounded the word out like it was new to her.

"You must have school friends."

"I don't go to school." She shook her head. "I have a tutor, Ms. Boyle."

"Well, I'm your friend now, and Baxter is your friend, too," Darkus said, "and if you help me get out of here, we'll have a secret as well, which makes us even better friends."

"A secret? Oh yes, I like that." Novak leapt to her feet. "Friends are better than love interests."

"Much."

"If Mater knew we were friends, she would forbid it." Novak's eyes were shining.

"Why?"

"She says I don't need friends because everyone will want to be my friend when I'm famous."

"That's not friendship."

"Do you think being famous is silly?"

"A person ought to be famous for doing something really good or really difficult, like climbing Mount Everest or landing on Mars," replied Darkus. "If you were a famous explorer, I'd think you were amazing."

"How about a spy?" Novak asked, looking mischievous.

"A spy?"

"You want to find out what Mater and your neighbors are planning?"

Darkus nodded.

"Well, only a world-famous spy can help you, then." She shot him a look loaded with mystery, walked to the bookshelf, and pulled on a large red book. The section of shelves that made up that part of the wall slid backward.

"You have secret passages in your house?" Darkus's jaw dropped open.

"They aren't secret if you know they're there," Novak said, stepping into the gap between the shelves.

CHAPTER THIRTEEN
The White Room

"The passages are for the servants," Novak explained as the library shelves silently returned to their original position. "Towering Heights has eight floors, all with hidden doors and passages. My room's on the sixth floor, and it has a passage that leads out from the back of my wardrobe."

Darkus felt a thrill of excitement as he followed Novak down the narrow corridor. The servants' passages were gray and functional, lit by floor lights, and a stark contrast to the front of the house.

They came to a brass gate with a handle. It was an old-fashioned lift, the kind Darkus had seen in movies.

"Get in."

He obeyed, and Novak leaned across him, pulling the gate closed. The lift whirred and lurched downward.

"Where are we going?" Darkus asked.

"The White Room. It's Mater's office and where she meets people. That's where your friends will be."

"They're not my friends," Darkus said. "They're my enemies."

"You are so lucky to have real enemies," Novak sighed. "I have to make mine up."

"They mustn't see me."

"Don't worry." Novak fluttered her eyelashes. "No one will see us."

"Good," Darkus said, feeling uncomfortable.

A delicate bell chimed, announcing they were on the first floor. He stepped out of the lift and set off after Novak, who was running silently down the corridor on the tips of her toes. She turned left and right, then suddenly stopped and pushed her fingers against the wall, making a hidden handle pop out.

Putting her finger to her lips, she whispered, "We must be very quiet. If Mater hears us, we'll be in trouble."

Darkus nodded, and they entered a room the size of a bathroom, containing nothing but a bench covered with a sheepskin throw. Novak motioned for Darkus to sit. Opposite the bench was a window into the room next door.

"It's a two-way mirror," Novak whispered, sitting down beside him. "We can see them, but they can't see us. Mater uses it to watch models, or clients, when they're having dress fittings. Look"—she pointed up at speakers in the corners of the room—"we can hear them, too."

Lucretia Cutter, instantly recognizable by her lab coat and canes, was standing in front of the mirror with her back to them.

Darkus swallowed down the confusion of fear and anger that bubbled up inside him when he looked at her. He studied the room beyond the mirror, memorizing every detail to tell Virginia and Bertolt. There wasn't much furniture, and everything was either white or transparent. To the right was a laboratory bench, like the ones at school, only much cooler. The worktop was made of the same shiny white stone as the floor, a silver gas tap rising up out of it like a swan's neck, and beside it a powerful-looking microscope. Below the bench was a row of fridges with see-through doors. Darkus could see stacks of petri dishes and racks of test tubes inside them.

A clear Perspex shelf stretched across the opposite wall, and Darkus registered the three white sculptures sitting on it: a human figure, a beetle, and the DNA double helix.

Lucretia Cutter was standing behind a sleek glass desk, which was bare except for a white telephone and a framed photograph. Facing her, in their yellow and purple suits, were Pickering and Humphrey, looking ridiculously out of place in the spotless room. Darkus couldn't help but smile at the sight of them.

Pickering was pointing at Humphrey. "His revolting habits led to the infestation. He is disgusting. I, on the other hand, wash three or four times a day."

"Shut up, or I'll mash you." Humphrey lifted his massive fist above Pickering's head.

"Silence." Lucretia Cutter's voice cut through the cousins' bickering.

"You will give over your property to me for forty-eight hours, to remove every last beetle."

Pickering and Humphrey nodded like eager puppies. "Whatever you desire," Humphrey spluttered, spraying spittle across her glass desk.

"Eurgh!" Pickering squealed.

"I'll be paying you handsomely for the beetles, and the inconvenience, so I expect you to do exactly as I ask."

"Inconvenience?" Pickering clasped his hands together. "No inconvenience at all. It will be a pleasure."

"You will move out of the building for the duration of the operation," she continued.

"What?!" the cousins cried in unison.

"Where will we go?" Humphrey asked.

"But we can help you," said Pickering.

"I won't be doing it myself, Mr. Risk. I will be sending my men, Dankish and Craven, to deal with your mound of beetles. You did say it was a mound."

The cousins nodded.

"A six-figure sum will be transferred to your bank accounts on the day you leave, and the funds will clear once the beetles have been removed from your premises and counted. Then you will be free to return. During the interim, I will make my private suite at the Empress Hotel available for you to stay in. You will not be permitted to talk about this arrangement with anyone. Do you understand? If you do, you forfeit the fee."

Pickering and Humphrey nodded again.

Lucretia Cutter walked around the desk and held out her perfectly manicured hand, her expression unreadable behind the enormous sunglasses. "Do we have a deal?"

Humphrey leapt up. "It's a deal," he said, bending down and kissing the back of her hand.

Lucretia Cutter's gold lips curled with disgust.

"W-w-wait!" Pickering got to his feet. "What about the council? They know about the infestation—they want us to clear the yard. They said—"

"The council will not bother you again, Mr. Risk. I'll make sure of that." Lucretia Cutter pulled her hand away from Humphrey. "How do you think I found out about your beetles in the first place?" She laughed, a low guttural sound. "I have people everywhere."

"Right. Yes. I see," said Pickering, clearly not seeing anything at all.

She pressed a button on the white telephone in front of her. "Gerard."

The butler entered with a tray containing two documents and two gold pens.

"Sign and date the last page." Lucretia Cutter held out her hand so that Gerard could clean it with a steaming hot towel he pulled from a cylinder in his pocket.

Darkus crept closer to the mirror. He felt vulnerable so close to the glass and had to remind himself that no one in the room could see him. But he now had a clear view of the framed photograph on her desk.

The picture was of nine smiling people in white coats, sitting in two rows. Printed in a white box at the bottom of the picture were the words *Fabre Project*.

"What's the matter?" Novak whispered, alarmed. "Are you ill? You look like you're going to be sick."

"That picture . . ." Darkus pointed.

"What about it?" Novak came to stand next to Darkus. "Oh, that. That's from when she was at university. You can hardly recognize her. She looks so different now. Look, her hair is all messy and scraped back; she's wearing glasses and she's smiling." She sighed. "She looks nice, doesn't she?"

Darkus's heart was thumping against his ribs.

"What's so interesting about it?"

"That"—Darkus cleared his throat, finding he couldn't get the words out—"is my dad."

Novak leaned forward. "Which one?"

"The one with the beard, next to your mum."

Novak stared at Darkus. "He doesn't look like you at all."

"Novak." Darkus looked her in the eye. Suddenly finding his voice, he blurted out loudly, "Someone's kidnapped my dad, and I don't know why!"

"Kidnapped?" Novak looked frightened.

A shadow fell across the mirror, and they both looked up.

Lucretia Cutter was admiring her reflection in the glass. As she turned her head from left to right, it was as if she was looking through the mirror, into the room.

Darkus froze. If there hadn't been glass between them, Lucretia Cutter would have felt his breath on her cheek.

"She can't see us," Novak whispered as though to reassure herself as much as Darkus. "She can't hear us."

In the room, Humphrey had signed the contract and was holding the paper out to Gerard. Pickering made a show of reading every word of his, then arranged his face in a thoughtful expression. "Perhaps we could discuss this over dinner?"

"There's nothing to discuss." Lucretia Cutter turned away from the mirror. "You either want to sell me the beetles or you don't."

Darkus let out a huge sigh, suddenly aware that he'd been holding his breath.

"C'mon, sign it, Pickers. It's half a million quid," Humphrey said. "That's a quarter of a million each."

"I can do the math, Humphrey, thank you." Pickering looked at Lucretia Cutter. "You must really like killing beetles, to pay such a large amount of money to do something we'd normally have to pay for ourselves."

Lucretia Cutter leaned over her desk menacingly.

"I'm a collector, Mr. Risk," she hissed. "A very wealthy collector. I've paid more money for a handbag than the figure I'm offering you for those beetles. It's entirely up to you whether you want the money or not." Leaning back on her canes, she propelled herself toward the door. "This conversation is over." She looked back at the mirror. "I have something I need to take care of."

"Get under the bench!" Novak sucked in her breath, pulling at Darkus. "She knows we're here."

"What? I thought you said . . ."

"Do as I say! *She's coming!*" Novak kicked the back of Darkus's knees, and his legs folded underneath him. *"Quick!"*

Finding himself on the floor, Darkus started to protest, then heard the heart-stopping click of the door handle. He rolled under the bench and squashed himself against the wall. There was a muffled crunch as Baxter's jar smashed inside his backpack.

Novak pulled the sheepskin rug down to hide him, then sprang away from the bench. "Mater!"

Darkus saw the ends of Lucretia Cutter's canes and the hem of her long black velvet skirt as she swirled into the room.

"What do you think you're doing?"

Darkus heard a squawk, and Novak's feet were lifted off the ground, dangling in the air.

"I'm sorry, I . . ." Novak choked.

Darkus's heart was jumping with fright. Lucretia Cutter was shockingly strong.

"You're forbidden from entering any of my rooms on this floor."

"I wanted to see the clowns!" Novak rasped.

Lucretia Cutter let go of her daughter, and Novak fell to the floor. She coughed and spluttered, gasping for air.

"You know the penalty for breaking the rules."

Novak nodded, looking down. "The cells." She bit her lip, looking frightened, and whispered, "But please, not with the bugs. I only wanted to see the clowns."

Lucretia Cutter turned away toward the mirror. "Look at those two idiots," she snarled. "They're revolting."

"They are very ugly," Novak agreed.

"Their level of the species should have been wiped out by now."

"Are you really going to give them all that money for some beetles?" Novak asked.

"Don't be ridiculous, child."

"But you said . . ." Novak's voice trailed off, and she frowned. "You made them sign contracts."

"I suppose the last will and testament of a person can look like a contract to the untrained eye." Lucretia Cutter laughed softly.

"Why would you want them to sign a will?"

"None of your business!"

Novak fell silent and kept her eyes on the floor.

"Those are *my* beetles. I made them, and I want them back." Lucretia Cutter let out a hiss. "I don't know how they escaped from my laboratory, but if those two buffoons have realized what the beetles are capable of, they could ruin everything. I can't let that happen. I'm not ready yet." She banged her canes on the floor with frustration. "I will NOT let anyone stop me. Not *them*, not *him*, *nobody!*"

"Him?" Novak said, catching Darkus's eye under the bench. "Who do you mean?"

Lucretia Cutter spun round and struck her daughter across the head with the silver handle of one of her canes. Darkus struggled not to cry out as Novak was thrown backward like a rag doll, collapsing in a heap on the floor.

"How dare you question me, you insolent girl?" Lucretia Cutter spat. Rigid with fear, Darkus stared at the girl sprawled on the floor. "You will spend two nights in the cells for your insolence—*with* the bugs."

She turned to stride out of the room. Her skirt whirled up as she went, and where he should have seen an ankle and a shoe, Darkus saw a giant black claw. He pulled back in shock, hitting his head against the wall.

Lucretia Cutter paused in the doorway.

Darkus closed his eyes and held his breath.

There was a long silence, then she stepped out of the room and the door slid shut.

Darkus waited for as long as he could bear before wriggling out from under the bench on his belly, keeping low to the ground. Novak's eyes were closed, and she wasn't moving.

"Novak?" he whispered. "Are you okay?" He touched her arm, but she didn't respond. Darkus's blood ran cold. "Please, Novak, wake up." He stroked her hair. "Please."

She groaned, and her eyes flickered open.

Darkus sighed with relief. "Are you okay?"

She blinked as she looked up at him. "Don't look at me." She covered her face with her hands. A nasty purple bruise was blossoming below her eye.

"You need a doctor."

"I'm ugly," Novak sobbed.

"You were so brave." Darkus knelt by her side. "She was so angry."

"She would have been angrier if she'd found you," Novak whispered.

He shook his head. "I shouldn't have come here," he said, the image of a black claw flashing through his mind and filling him with dread.

Novak put her hand on his and gave him a weak smile. "I'm glad you came."

"We've got to get out of here," Darkus said. "Can you get up?"

She gave a tiny nod.

"Put your arm around my shoulders."

Novak wrapped her arms around Darkus's neck, and he lifted her to her feet. They turned toward the door, and heard a sickening click as it slid open.

CHAPTER FOURTEEN
The Cry of a Seabird

*L*ucretia Cutter stood in the doorway, motionless, like the angel of death.

Novak cried out, gripping Darkus tightly. "I can explain," she gabbled. "I was making him fall in love with me, for my acting. He wanted to see the house. I thought he would be impressed by the mirror; I didn't know you were working . . ."

Lucretia Cutter wasn't listening to her daughter. She was staring at Darkus.

"I'll show him out right now, shall I?" Novak's voice was rising in pitch and volume.

Lucretia Cutter finally spoke. "I think not."

Novak gave a terrified squeak.

Darkus felt like a rabbit trapped in the sights of a hungry hawk. He stared at the ground.

"I've seen you before, boy. Haven't I?"

Darkus shook his head and kept his eyes on the floor.

"What's your name?"

"Daniel Dowie, miss," he mumbled.

Novak looked at him, and then away.

Lucretia Cutter moved her head, tipping first one ear up to the ceiling and then the other. "I see you've brought me a present, Daniel. How kind."

Darkus looked up, confused, and she smiled at him, her mouth stretching freakishly wide across her face. His heart jumped up and down so hard inside his chest that he thought she must surely be able to hear it.

"Present? No, I . . ."

"Ah, but you're wrong. Look." She lifted the end of one of her canes and pointed. "You've brought me a *Chalcosoma caucasus* for my collection."

Darkus looked, and there was Baxter, standing proudly on his shoulder. He must have climbed from his broken jar and out of the top of the backpack. The beetle was very still, his eyes fixed on Lucretia Cutter.

Darkus clenched his fists. He wasn't going to let this woman come anywhere near Baxter.

Novak suddenly launched herself at her mother, catching her off guard and pushing her backward through the doorway. "RUN! RUN!

RUN!" she screamed as she wrapped her arms around her mother's skirt, and they both fell to the ground in a tangle.

Darkus bolted out of the door, and Baxter leapt into the air, flying at his shoulder. Out of the corner of his eye Darkus saw two black claws kicking out of Lucretia Cutter's skirt.

He raced down the hallway toward the lift, praying for it to still be there.

A shocking hissing noise exploded out of the room behind him. It was like the noise Baxter had made to ward off Robby and the clones, only a hundred times louder.

The lift was there. Novak had left the gate open. Darkus hurled himself forward, clattering into the lift, slamming his hands on all the buttons.

Nothing happened.

The gate. He had to close it.

She was coming.

Lucretia Cutter was impossibly tall. Her head brushed against the ceiling as she skittered toward him at horrific speed, her arms thrown wide, an ebony cane pointed at him. Darkus froze in terror.

There was an ear-shattering crack. Splinters of wood from the back wall of the lift sprayed against his neck. Darkus stumbled forward in shock. She had shot at him!

Baxter rounded angrily, flying out of the lift, straight at her.

Lucretia Cutter swiped at the beetle with one cane, trying to hit him with the other as he circled her head.

"Arghhh!" she shrieked with rage as Baxter dragged all six of his sharp claws across her neck. Her canes fell to the floor as she lifted her left hand to cover the bleeding scratches, her right hand grabbing at the rhinoceros beetle. "I'll smash your exoskeleton like an egg," she howled as she thrashed around.

Baxter dodged about, flying at her face again and again with his horn down, hissing loudly.

Darkus grabbed the brass latticed gate and slammed it shut.

"BAXTER!" he screamed.

The lift door started to close.

"BAXTER!" he cried again.

The beetle looped up and flew back toward the lift just as the door shut and the car lurched, dropping down.

When the lift stopped and the door opened again, Darkus pulled aside the gate and fell to his knees. His breath and his heart were all he could hear. He felt sick.

What had happened to Novak?

He thought about that bloodcurdling hissing noise. Baxter was still up there with that monster of a woman. He shuddered; whatever she was, she wasn't human.

The lift had come down, so that meant the way out must be two or three floors up. He pushed himself out of the lift and into the corridor, still on his hands and knees. The corridor was utilitarian and gray, a dark floor with a lighter shade on the walls. There were strip lights overhead.

He had to keep moving.

She had shot at him with her cane! How had she done that?

Darkus was shaking. He thought about Uncle Max. "Grit and determination," he whispered.

He heard a faint rattling sound, and his pulse jump-started, throbbing in his neck and temples as he tried to see where it was coming from. There was a clunk overhead, and he looked up to see Baxter clambering through a gap between the top of the lift and the door frame.

"Baxter!" Warm relief flooded his body, and his legs found the strength to stand. He reached up, and the beetle dropped onto his hand. He pulled Baxter in against his chest, curling his shoulders forward and whispering to him. Baxter stood upright, reaching his forearms up to rest against Darkus's sweater, returning the hug.

"We need to get out of here," he whispered, putting Baxter on his shoulder, where he belonged. Leaving the gate open so Lucretia Cutter couldn't use the lift, he set off down the corridor. Either side of it, at sporadic intervals, were numbered gray doors with small square shutters. He tried a few, but all the doors were locked. He guessed these were the cells that Novak had referred to.

He needed to find a staircase and get to the ground floor. Maybe he could climb out of a window.

Turning a corner, the hallway continued. To the right was a white door. He tried it, and it opened. Cautiously peering in, Darkus saw a wall of subdued green light divided into rectangles. He felt for the light switch, and the overhead fluorescents flickered on. The room was full of tanks and aquariums, each teeming with a different species of beetle.

"Baxter, look!" Darkus stepped forward, immediately recognizing darkling beetles and Darwin's beetles, the rare chestnut-brown stag with mandibles as long as its legs, making it look like a spider in armor . . . and, in the middle of the wall of aquariums, a tank full of yellow ladybugs the size of a two-pence coin . . .

So the beetle in the museum *had* belonged to Lucretia Cutter.

The sudden light startled the beetles, and they churned, excited to see who was responsible for the disturbance, running to the walls of their tanks and clawing at them. The Darwin's beetles bashed their antlers against the glass as if trying to get at him, and a tank of vicious-looking giant tiger beetles screeched and gnashed their mandibles together threateningly.

Darkus was shocked by the howling cacophony of hisses and chirps that rose out of the aquariums as the aggressive beetles threw themselves at the walls of their prisons, clambering over one another in their frenzied desire to get at him. These beetles were totally different from the ones in the mountain; *his* beetles on Nelson Parade were peaceful and calm.

Darkus took another step forward to try and quiet the insects, but Baxter rose up off his shoulder and tugged at his sweater with his legs, pulling him away.

The tank holding the Darwin's beetles shifted forward an inch, and then another, as a multitude of giant jaws hammered against the glass in unison. If it dropped off the shelf, the glass would smash and the beetles would escape.

Darkus suddenly realized Baxter wasn't hissing back, or readying himself to attack—he was trying to tell him to run away.

The tank with the Darwin's jumped forward again.

Darkus spun around and ran out of the door, back into the corridor.

An eerie wail, like the distant call of a seabird, echoed up the hall-way. The hairs on the back of Darkus's neck lifted and he shivered. But he couldn't go back, so, taking a deep breath, he moved forward, toward the sound. He hoped fervently that he'd find a staircase before he encountered whatever was making that noise.

But as he got closer, a tone in the mournful wail vibrated like a harp string in his chest. Tears sprang into his eyes, and he started running. The sound was a man crying, and Darkus recognized that crying with every atom of his body.

"Dad!" he shouted.

The crying stopped.

"Dad?"

"Darkus?" came a stunned reply from somewhere just ahead of him.

It was the sound he'd craved for six torturous weeks. He'd dreamt about it. Now he was really hearing it, and the sound of that one word set fire to his soul.

"Dad!" Darkus cried out, running faster.

Suddenly, a door to his left opened, and a pair of arms reached out and grabbed him. A hand covered his mouth and an arm wrapped around his waist, lifting him off the floor. He tried to cry out and kick, but he wasn't strong enough. He was dragged backward into a wine cellar.

"Stop fighting me, boy. I've got to get you out of here before you get yourself killed."

Darkus went limp. He recognized the French accent. It was the butler.

Gerard let go, and Darkus pulled away. "No! I'm not leaving. My dad's here. I—"

Darkus felt something strike him hard on the back of his head. His neck flamed hot, and everything spun.

"Forgive me," he heard the butler say as the world faded away. "Madame is coming, and she must not find you."

Darkus felt something cold splash across his face. His eyes flickered open. His head was throbbing.

"Listen, boy," said the voice of the butler. "You must get up. You are beside the servants' entrance to Towering Heights, at the side of the house."

Darkus propped himself up on his elbows, confused.

"Now you must run. Do you hear me? I cannot assist you a second time."

Before Darkus could reply, the butler had shut the door, and he heard the key turn in the lock.

"No!" Darkus knelt up and beat his fists on the door. "No! Dad!" He sank down, his aching head in his hands. "Dad," he sobbed.

He felt a tickling sensation on his neck. Baxter had hidden down the back of his sweater and was climbing out. He reached around and picked up the beetle, holding him in front of his face.

"Dad's in there, Baxter, and I don't know what to do."

Baxter reared up onto his back legs and nudged Darkus's cheek with the side of his horn.

"Pssst!"

Darkus froze.

"Pssst, over here," came a loud whisper.

Darkus turned to see Virginia, hiding behind a row of flowerpots full of the same red lilies he'd seen by the front door.

"It's me!" she mouthed, looking worried. "Are you okay?"

He nodded dumbly, feeling a rush of warmth. He'd never been so glad to see a friend.

"I know you didn't want us to come, but we did anyway, and then I saw that butler lay you out on the floor like you were dead, and the gate opened for a delivery van, and I had to make sure you were . . ."

"I'm alive," Darkus said, rubbing the tender lump on the back of his head. "Just."

Virginia scurried over to him. "Great, let's get out of here. Can you walk?"

"She's got him." Darkus's voice broke.

"What?"

"Dad. She's got Dad." His shoulders started shaking, and he couldn't stop the hot tears spilling out of his eyes and rolling down his cheeks. "She's got my dad."

"Darkus." Virginia shook him. "Pull yourself together. Listen to me. Your dad needs you to be strong. *I* need you to be strong. C'mon. Please. You won't be able to rescue him if you get yourself caught." She hauled him to his feet. "Now follow me."

They reached the corner of the building. The gate was still open, and less than twenty yards away. Virginia peeped around to make sure the coast was clear.

"Okay, we're going to run, on three," she whispered. "One, two—" She stopped suddenly, pushing Darkus backward against the wall.

"GET OUT!" Lucretia Cutter screeched as Pickering and Humphrey stumbled backward out of Towering Heights.

"We didn't bring a beetle!" Pickering insisted.

"We don't know any boys!" Humphrey blustered.

Lucretia Cutter poked one of her canes into Humphrey's spongy chest. "I'm coming to get my beetles tomorrow, first thing."

"Tomorrow?" Pickering blinked. "But I thought . . ."

"TOMORROW!"

The door slammed shut.

The confused cousins stared at each other and then staggered down the path and out of the gate, squabbling.

"THREE!" Virginia sprinted toward the closing gate, and Darkus ran after her. They darted through just before it clanged shut.

CHAPTER FIFTEEN

The Sewer Solution

*D*arkus's feet thumped the pavement as he ran. Baxter flew beside him.

Virginia's long legs easily matched Darkus's, pace for pace, but eventually she called out, "Slow down!"

"We've got to tell the police," Darkus gasped. "She's got Dad."

"Darkus, stop!" Virginia ordered, coming to a halt.

He ran on for a few steps, then squatted to catch his breath.

"You can't leave Bertolt behind," Virginia added.

"What?"

"He was hiding behind the blue van. Look, he's trying to catch up."

"There's no time, we need to—"

"What we need to do is think this through before we do anything crazy. How do we know the police will help us? They haven't so far."

"She's got him in a cell!" Darkus said angrily. "We've got to get him out of there!"

"You're bleeding"—Virginia leaned over him to look—"all down the back of your neck."

"Doesn't matter." Darkus checked to see if Baxter was still flying overhead. "I'm fine. We need to rescue Dad."

"Darkus, there's a massive splinter in your neck!" Virginia put a hand on his shoulder and, without warning, whipped the shard of wood out.

"Ahh!" he cried out, and his neck began to bleed in earnest.

"You're hurt!" Bertolt wheezed, finally catching up and sinking to the ground beside Darkus.

"It must've been a splinter from the lift." Darkus put his hand up to his neck. "Lucretia Cutter shot something at me. She missed, but it smashed into the wood behind me."

"She shot at you?" said Bertolt, aghast, as Newton zoomed up out of his hair, flickering angrily.

"She didn't have a gun." Darkus thought about what had happened in Towering Heights. "She was pointing one of her canes at me."

"Bloody hell!" Virginia said.

Darkus looked at the blood on his hand. "She's a monster, and she's got Dad locked in a cell underground."

He told them about the library, and Novak, about how she took him through the secret passage to the two-way mirror, about the photograph of his father on Lucretia Cutter's desk, about how brave Novak had been when they got caught and how she'd helped him escape back to the lift, about finding the room of angry insects with the yellow ladybugs, and then about how he'd heard his father's voice.

"You saw your dad?" Bertolt was visibly upset by what he was hearing.

"I didn't see him," Darkus said quietly. "I heard him. I called out, and he heard me." He swallowed. "He called out my name, and then that stinking butler dragged me backward through a door and hit me over the head."

"That stinking butler may have saved your life," Virginia pointed out.

"What about the beetles?" Bertolt asked. "Why does she want them?"

"I still don't know," Darkus admitted. "She said something about them belonging to her and wanting them back. She wants to keep them secret. She said she *wasn't ready yet.* But I don't know what that means, and then she said she wouldn't let anyone stop her . . ." Darkus paused. "I don't know what's going on, but I think Dad may have been trying to stop Lucretia Cutter from doing whatever it is that she's planning to do."

"But what we *do* know is that she's coming for the beetles tomorrow morning," Virginia added.

"Tomorrow?!" Bertolt squeaked. "That's not much time!"

Virginia nodded. "I know."

"This is bad." He blinked. "This is very bad."

"There's something else." A horrifying image flashed into Darkus's mind, of a swirling skirt and a giant serrated claw. He shuddered.

"Lucretia Cutter . . ." He stopped, not knowing how to put into words what he'd seen. "After she hurt Novak, she turned to leave, and her skirt sort of lifted up, and it looked like . . . I mean, I think I saw . . . a claw."

"A claw?" Bertolt looked confused.

"As part of her dress?" Virginia asked.

"No, I mean, she had a big black claw, like Baxter's. It was where a foot should be. I mean, she was standing on it, like it was her leg. Like she had the legs of a beetle, but human-size." Darkus heard himself saying the words and knew it sounded crazy.

"Are you sure?" Virginia asked.

"Yes, I'm sure."

"Your mind could've been playing tricks on you, 'cause you were scared."

"Maybe it was a boot," Bertolt suggested. "A designer boot?"

Darkus shook his head. "I know what I saw." He looked back at Towering Heights. "She's a monster," he said again.

Bertolt looked at Virginia. "What are we going to do?"

"Darkus, we have to move the beetles tonight," Virginia said, "or they'll all be dead in the morning."

"I—I—" The sound of his dad calling out his name was ringing in Darkus's ears. "I've got to get Dad out of there."

"To move the beetles means moving the cups," Bertolt said. "All their babies, their eggs and larvae, are inside. They won't leave without them." His face betrayed how impossible he thought the task was. "Even if we could move Beetle Mountain in one night, where would we put it?"

Darkus felt all the energy in his body drain away. His T-shirt was stuck to his back with sweat and blood. He felt weak and his hands were shaking.

"I don't know what to do," he admitted, covering his face with his hands.

Baxter dropped down, landing on Darkus's fingertips, nuzzling the side of his horn against his forehead.

Bertolt patted his shoulder. "It's okay. Things are better than they were this morning."

"How?"

"Well, this morning you didn't know where your dad was and we had no idea when the beetles would be attacked."

"He's right"—Virginia nodded—"now we know what we're up against."

Bertolt scowled at Virginia. "The main thing is that your dad is alive." He mimed at Virginia to say something nice.

Virginia mimed back that she didn't know what to say.

"We need a plan." Darkus tapped his hands against his temples as he thought.

"Your uncle will know what to do about your dad. We should go and find him," Virginia said. "But the beetles, it's up to us. We've got to save them. We made an oath."

Darkus looked down at Baxter, now on the palm of his hand.

"If Lucretia Cutter says they're hers," Bertolt said, thinking out loud, "then perhaps she bought them through a special insect dealer."

"But then surely they'd have arrived dead, with pins in," Virginia said. "The real question is, why does she want to keep them a secret?"

"Do you think she knows about their, um, special abilities?" Bertolt looked at Darkus.

Darkus nodded. "I think that's why she wants them, and it's their abilities she wants to keep a secret."

"Because she's not ready yet . . ." Virginia stroked her chin. "This may sound crazy, but if the beetles belong to her . . . is it possible she's *making* beetles with superpowers? You said she had a room full of angry beetles in there, and a laboratory."

"How on earth do you *make* a superbeetle?" Bertolt scoffed.

Darkus blinked down at Baxter, thinking about the statues of the man, the beetle, and the double helix that were in Lucretia Cutter's white room. He remembered something Uncle Max had said. "She's experimenting with DNA."

"DNA?" Virginia frowned.

"It's the genetic code that makes up every living creature," Bertolt explained.

"I know what DNA is!" Virginia retorted.

"Uncle Max said that when Lucretia Cutter knew Dad, she was a geneticist."

Bertolt held his hand out for Newton to land. He cupped his glowing body to make a lantern. "Do you think our beetles are clever enough to have escaped from her laboratory?"

"I don't know." Darkus shrugged. "Maybe. But why would Lucretia Cutter want to make superbeetles?"

Bertolt shook his head, unable to think of an answer.

"Who cares? She's got your dad, and if he was trying to stop her from doing something, then anything we can do to put a wrench in the works has got to count for something, right?" Virginia reasoned. "Let's fight her every step of the way."

"That's it!" Darkus looked up, his eyes bright with an idea.

"It is?" Bertolt smiled, hopefully.

"Tomorrow, when Lucretia Cutter is collecting her beetles"—he lifted his hand holding Baxter—"I'll rescue Dad from Towering Heights . . ."

"You're going to *sacrifice* the beetles?" Virginia looked shocked.

"No! Of course not!" Darkus got to his feet and straightened his shoulders. "We're only just beginning to learn what the beetles can do." He thought about the angry beetles in Towering Heights and held Baxter out in front of him. "I think we should convince the beetles in the mountain to stand their ground, to fight. What do you reckon, Baxter?"

The rhinoceros beetle bowed his horn, and Darkus felt a thrill of defiance in his chest.

"Good. And if I'm right, when Lucretia Cutter arrives, there'll be a beetle army waiting for her—and that's the last thing she'll be expecting." He placed Baxter on his shoulder. "We'll show her that she can't just take what she wants."

Virginia cocked her head. "Okay, this is beginning to sound good."

"I'm glad you think so, because you're going to have to lead the beetle army."

"Me?" Virginia looked delighted. "Bring it on!"

Back at Uncle Max's, Darkus left Virginia and Bertolt in the street while he went upstairs to talk to his uncle. But he returned shaking his head. "That's weird. There's no one home . . . the radio's on, and the kitchen window's open, but there's no one there."

"Maybe he popped out to the shops?" Bertolt suggested.

"Let's go to Base Camp," Virginia said. "We've got planning to do, and we can use the telescope to see when your uncle gets back."

Darkus nodded and, because the coast was clear and they knew Pickering and Humphrey were out, they went in through the Emporium shop door. As they were crossing the shop floor, Virginia suddenly stopped dead, and Bertolt and Darkus stumbled into her back.

"I'm a genius!" she said, her eyes wide with excitement. "I've just had a brilliant idea. Follow me."

Moments later, they found themselves outside the bathroom, looking at the manhole cover Virginia had seen the first time she'd explored the shop.

"What if we moved the beetles below the city, to the sewers?" she said. "No one would ever know that they were there."

"Let's try to lift it." Darkus bent down and grabbed one of the handles.

The three of them heaved the heavy circle of metal to one side. The faint breath of sewage wafted out of the yawning black hole, making Bertolt's nose wrinkle.

Virginia pulled a key-ring flashlight from her pocket. "Look, there's a ladder in the wall." She put the flashlight between her teeth and stepped onto the embedded iron rungs. "I'm going down."

Darkus dangled his legs down the hole until there was room for him on the ladder. The shaft of light from above showed him the shadowy outlines of a cavernous brick chamber. The air was damp with the unsavory tang of ammonia and slurry clay. A perpetual dripping sound accompanied his descent, and when he reached the ground, he saw shallow puddles everywhere.

"What do you think, Baxter?" Darkus asked as he stepped off the ladder.

Baxter flew off to take a look around.

Virginia was already exploring a man-size archway on the other side of the room. Darkus set out across the floor to join her.

"Wait for me!" Bertolt called anxiously from the top of the ladder. Newton rose out of his hair and lit up the rungs for him. "Thank you, Newton," Bertolt said, steadying his shaking hands and smiling at the firefly.

Through the archway was a giant tunnel the height of five men, its brick walls covered in lichen and lime scale. Oozing along the middle of the floor was a pea-green stream. In the distance, Darkus could hear the thunderous rumble of falling water.

"This place is cool," he said.

"It's perfect," Virginia said proudly. "I wonder if there's a room like this below each shop." She peered across the tunnel to a similar archway opposite.

"Baxter seems to like it." Darkus pointed to the rhinoceros beetle, who'd left his perch on his shoulder and was climbing the tunnel wall.

"Beetles don't mind a bit of sewage, do they?" Virginia shone the flashlight back into the chamber below the ladder. Bertolt was gingerly picking his way across the floor.

"Some beetles *love* sewage." Darkus grinned, thinking of the dung beetles. "But there's no sewage in the chamber, just puddles of water. It's perfect. No one will know Beetle Mountain is here, except us."

"It's disgusting," Bertolt complained as Newton flew in loops above his head, glowing happily. "It stinks!"

"So now all we have to do is figure out how we get Beetle Mountain down here," Virginia said.

"Leave that to the beetles," Darkus replied, thinking back to how Baxter had pushed his mug up against the wall of his tank. "They might be small, but they're strong, and there are loads of them."

"Anyone who's seen Beetle Mountain will know it can't just vanish," Virginia pointed out. "How do we stop Humphrey and Pickering from going to look for it?"

"That's a good point." Darkus scratched his head. "Lucretia Cutter's offering them a lot of money. They aren't going to be happy when the beetles suddenly disappear."

"Actually"—Bertolt coughed—"I may have a solution." Virginia and Darkus looked at him. "The other day, I read that there are bee-tles that can turn furniture into sawdust . . ."

"Someone's been doing their homework!" Virginia teased.

". . . and can destroy giant trees or eat entire crops overnight," Bertolt continued.

"So?" Darkus asked.

"Well, I was thinking we could employ those talents to make this building a bit, er, unsafe." He blinked.

"How unsafe?" Darkus asked.

"Definitely too unsafe for Humphrey and Pickering to be able to live in it anymore."

Virginia whistled. "Go on."

"If a bit of Humphrey's bedroom floor were to, er, cave in, say, then everyone would assume the mugs had gotten smashed to pieces and the beetles had scattered."

Darkus laughed. "Well, that sounds like the beginning of a plan."

CHAPTER SIXTEEN
The Rat Trap

Scrambling out of the sewer, they replaced the manhole cover and snuck out the back of the Emporium. As they entered Base Camp, Darkus saw one of the strings of bottle tops was jangling.

"It's the Rat Trap!" Bertolt said as Newton flew up to join his cousins on the ceiling.

Virginia ran her finger over the map on the wardrobe. "The one by the wall?"

Bertolt nodded. "What shall we do?"

"If it's Humphrey or Pickering, we should leave them in there," Virginia said. "It'll make moving the mountain easier."

"It's probably a fox," Darkus said, seeing the frightened look on Bertolt's face.

"There's only one way to find out," Virginia said, running back out of the door and falling to her knees.

As they crept toward the Rat Trap, Bertolt whispered, "Surely Humphrey couldn't get into Furniture Forest. He's too big. It must be Pickering."

"If it is, let's tie him up and tape over his mouth," Darkus said, thinking about the time he'd spent tied to a chair. Suddenly, Baxter leapt off his shoulder and zoomed forward.

"Shhh." Virginia put her finger to her lips. They could hear a man struggling and cursing.

Baxter landed and crawled along the top of the Rat Trap, flicking his elytra in the air.

Virginia silently climbed up onto a chest of drawers and peered down into the trap. "Oops!" She clamped her hand over her mouth.

"Who is it?" Bertolt whispered.

"Hello? Is someone there?"

"It's Uncle Max!" exclaimed Darkus, scrambling up beside Virginia.

"Darkus?" Uncle Max peered up at them. "Is that you? Get me out of here."

"Oh gosh, Professor Cuttle. I'm so sorry!" Bertolt exclaimed.

"How did you get in there?" Darkus asked.

"I was trying to find you. *Ouch!* I need to talk to you about . . . *Arghhh!*" He sucked in his breath. "Blasted things are biting me!"

"We'll have you out of there in a second, Professor Cuttle," Virginia said. "Please stop struggling."

"Stop struggling?! There's a plague of rats in here!" Uncle Max looked at Darkus. "I saw you three climb over the wall the other day and thought you might have made a den over here, so I came looking for you, which in hindsight was a terrible idea. I've been stuck in here for at least an hour!"

Darkus jumped down and helped Bertolt to move aside a mirrored panel and unlock the gate that had swung shut and trapped Uncle Max.

"They're tame rats," Bertolt explained, "from a pet shop. You must have frightened them."

"*I* frightened *them*?" Uncle Max pointed to the dead rats hanging down on strings around his face. "What about these poor chaps?"

"I found them in the basement of our block of flats." Bertolt smiled apologetically. "They were already dead, from poison. I put them in there to scare an intruder."

"Well, they certainly gave me a turn," Uncle Max huffed, crawling out of the cage. "They smell awful!"

"I do apologize, Professor Cuttle," Bertolt stammered. "They weren't meant for you."

"Thank heavens!" Uncle Max sat up on his knees and smiled at the worried Bertolt. "Jolly good trap, though—not quite up to Egyptian tomb standards, but nonetheless, pretty impressive." He looked at the children's guilty faces. "So, is someone going to tell me what's going on here, or do I have to guess?"

Virginia nudged Darkus, who was staring at the floor.

"Your neck's bleeding!" Uncle Max took Darkus by his shoulders.

"It's fine. I had a splinter," Darkus replied, covering the cut on his neck with his hand.

"Er, would you like to come back to our camp for a cup of tea, Professor Cuttle?" Bertolt asked politely. "It might soothe your nerves, and we can explain everything there."

"A camp, eh?" Uncle Max straightened his safari hat. "Don't mind if I do."

They set off through the tunnels on their hands and knees, Baxter flying in front, leading the way. "This place is a rabbit warren!" Uncle Max exclaimed as they inched forward. "It's a good job archaeologists are used to confined spaces."

"I'm sorry, Professor Cuttle, but we need to be quiet," Virginia whispered. "We don't know when Pickering and Humphrey will get back."

"Apologies!" Uncle Max whispered back. "Understood."

As they all filed through the door of Base Camp, Uncle Max whistled in amazement at the throbbing glow of fireflies reflected in the chandelier crystals dangling from the ceiling.

"This is quite a setup you've got here," he remarked as Bertolt plugged an electric kettle into the car battery.

"Most of this stuff was already here," Darkus said.

"Apart from the kettle," Virginia added. "That's Bertolt's."

Uncle Max gazed up at the ceiling in wonder. "Where have all these beetles come from?"

Darkus looked at Virginia but didn't reply. Baxter settled on his shoulder.

Uncle Max saw the map on the back of the wardrobe and wandered over, inspecting the collection of images around the words *LUCRETIA CUTTER*. He touched the edge of Novak's card.

"Do you take milk or sugar?" Bertolt asked.

"Black, six sugars, thank you, Bertolt." Uncle Max turned to face Darkus, his voice suddenly serious. "I think you'd better tell me exactly what's going on here, lad. Don't you?"

Darkus, Virginia, and Bertolt looked at one another.

"And no flimflam, please." Uncle Max took his cup of tea from Bertolt and sat down on the sofa. "I want the truth."

There was an awkward silence, in which Uncle Max took a mouthful of tea.

"I've found Dad," Darkus said.

Uncle Max sprayed his tea across the table. "WHAT?!" he spluttered.

"Lucretia Cutter has him in a cell, in the basement of her house," Darkus said hurriedly.

"How can you know that?" Uncle Max was on his feet. "By Jupiter, please tell me that you haven't been there!" His face was flushed purple, and his eyes were bulging out of their sockets.

Darkus looked guiltily at Virginia and Bertolt, then nodded.

"DID SHE *SEE* YOU?"

Darkus nodded again, wondering if Uncle Max was about to have a heart attack. "She shot at me, but she missed," he said. "That's how I got the splinter."

"She shot at you?" Uncle Max paused, then dropped back down onto the sofa and picked up his tea. "Well, that's a relief."

"What?!" Bertolt spluttered. "Why is that good?"

"Because it means she doesn't know who he is," Uncle Max explained. "If Lucretia Cutter had recognized Darkus, she wouldn't have shot at him—she'd have kidnapped him and used him against Barty." Uncle Max shook his head. "I can't believe you'd be so stupid as to go into that Gorgon's house! You could have gotten yourself killed, and your father, too."

"What's a Gorgon?" Virginia whispered to Bertolt.

"A monster-woman who turns men to stone by looking at them," he replied under his breath.

Darkus felt like he'd been slapped in the face. When he'd gone to Towering Heights, he hadn't meant to put himself or Dad at risk. How could he, when he didn't even know Dad was there? Then another thought occurred to him.

"You knew she had him all along!" he gasped.

"No! At least, not until we went to the museum—and even then, I had no real evidence." Uncle Max shook his head. "Her name over the door, that yellow ladybug, and her sudden arrival—these things are not enough to accuse someone of kidnapping." He sighed. "I've been trying to find out where she's keeping him. I thought he might be in her cosmetics factory in Wapping." He blinked. "I tried her offices, and her string of warehouses on the Thames, but with no luck."

"How?" Darkus asked. "When?"

"I haven't been going to work," Uncle Max admitted, "and you may not believe this, but I do a rather convincing impersonation of a confused delivery man." He smiled. "I've got a blue jumpsuit, a badge, and a cardboard box. I wander into a building, looking lost, and start asking questions. People can be astonishingly helpful, you know." He tugged on his earlobe. "I must admit, it didn't occur to me that she'd have him at her house. The nerve! She must be very confident she won't get caught."

"But why didn't you tell me?" Darkus asked angrily.

"Darkus, I didn't have any proof that Lucretia Cutter had Barty, just a hunch. I was looking for evidence."

Darkus glared at his uncle.

"But today I thought I should pursue a different line of inquiry. Instead of trying to find out *where* Lucretia Cutter has Barty, I decided to try and find out *why* she has him, and that's why I came looking for you. I need to talk to you about your friend." He pointed at Baxter. "I need to know more about your beetles." He lifted his hands up, gesturing to the fireflies.

Darkus wasn't listening. He was so angry his whole body was shaking. "You've been keeping secrets from me."

"No, Darkus, I haven't," Uncle Max said softly. "I wanted to be sure of the facts before I told you anything that might get your hopes up. Barty is in grave danger." Darkus struggled with what he was hearing. "I'm here now, aren't I?"

Darkus nodded, his teeth clenched.

"What about you?" Uncle Max raised an eyebrow. "Haven't you been keeping a few secrets of your own?"

Darkus looked at the floor. "I didn't tell you the whole truth about how I found Baxter," he admitted. "I thought you'd make me give him back."

"Well, how about you tell me now?"

Bertolt set about making more tea while Darkus told his uncle about Baxter falling out of Humphrey's trouser leg, discovering Beetle Mountain, and being kidnapped by the neighbors and then rescued by the beetles. Virginia described Darkus taking them to Beetle Mountain, and the oath they had sworn to help him rescue his father and protect the special insects.

Uncle Max sat, listening intently.

"If I wasn't seeing this with my own eyes, I'd never believe it," he muttered, looking up at the ceiling and shaking his head. "But none of this explains why you went to Lucretia Cutter's house."

"Lucretia Cutter visited Humphrey and Pickering last week," Virginia explained, "on the night they kidnapped Darkus."

"Novak Cutter saw me looking out of the window and dropped that card." Darkus pointed at it.

"Lucretia Cutter was *here*?" Uncle Max recoiled.

Darkus nodded. "She's buying the beetles."

"Over my dead body she is," Uncle Max growled.

Virginia looked at him, surprised.

"That's why I went to her house—to find out why she wants them—but also"—Darkus paused—"also to find out whatever it is about her and Dad that you won't tell me."

Uncle Max's eyebrows shot up. "I see."

"Now it's your turn to tell the truth," Darkus said, thinking about the photograph on Lucretia Cutter's desk. "What's the Fabre Project?"

Uncle Max lifted his safari hat, smoothed down his hair, and replaced it, looking at Darkus as if measuring him in some way. "I made a solemn promise to your father, when you were born, that I would never speak of the Fabre Project to you—or anyone else, for that matter." He scratched his chin. "But then, we never knew we'd find ourselves here, did we?"

Darkus stared at his uncle. "I thought it was *you* keeping something from me—that you didn't trust me." He turned away. "But all along, Dad's been the one keeping secrets."

"Your dad trusts you, lad," Uncle Max said. "It's just . . . well, there are some things that the young shouldn't be burdened with."

"When Dad disappeared, people said terrible things about him." Darkus's voice was flat and unemotional. "But I kept his face here." He tapped a finger between his eyes. "Each time someone said that he'd run away—or, worse, that he'd killed himself—I knew they were wrong here," he touched his fist to his heart, "because *my dad* would never do that. *My dad* isn't like that." He looked up at his uncle, his vision blurred by tears. "But I don't know what my dad is really like, do I? I don't know him at all."

"Nonsense. Look at me, lad." Uncle Max took Darkus's hand. "You know your father better than anyone. But before he was your dad, he was a young man with ambition, and without the responsibility of a family. That young man was like you in many ways, and he was a great adventurer. That's something you should be proud to learn."

"An adventurer? Like you?"

"No, no. I search for secrets, dig for truths, and if I'm lucky, I'll find an interesting story, or a valuable object." Uncle Max sighed. "Your father's adventures were far greater than any of mine, and more dangerous. His adventures were in thought. He explored the very fabric of nature, experimented with possibility, and all within the confines of his own head. You can only do that sort of thing if you have a brilliant mind, and he does. Mine's rather ordinary by comparison. Your father, Darkus, is the kind of person who changes history."

"That doesn't sound like Dad." Darkus frowned. His father was gentle and liked staring out of windows; he would never describe him as an adventurer.

"That's because he stopped his adventures when you came along."

"But why?"

"Adventures are dangerous, Darkus, and villains are real." Uncle Max seemed to grow older as he spoke. "Ideas are powerful, and there are people who'll exploit even the most charitable idea for power, or money. The greedy stop at nothing to satisfy their appetites, with no thought to the devastation or destruction it causes." He sounded angry. "That's not a world in which your father wanted to raise a family."

"Dad gave it up to have me?"

"In a manner of speaking." Uncle Max rested his chin on his hands. "Barty was an entomologist, a genius with arthropods. He specialized in Coleoptera; beetles were his passion. And because of his great skill in observing and understanding insects, Professor Appleyard invited him to be one of the esteemed scientists working on the Fabre Project."

"An entomologist?"

Uncle Max nodded. "The Fabre Project had a bold mission: to see if it was possible to reverse the damage humans have done to the planet by harnessing the power of insects."

"The power of insects?" Bertolt whispered in awe. "Is that possible?"

"The sad fact is, the number of insects is in decline. As we destroy their habitats, so we destroy their species, but we desperately need them. If all the mammals on the planet were to die out, the planet would flourish—but if all the insects disappeared, everything would very soon be dead.

"Led by Professor Appleyard, the Fabre Project explored the possibility of setting up global insect farms to breed species of insect that would boost pollination, naturally control pests—cutting down the use of pesticides—provide humans with food, and deal with human and animal waste."

"The dung division." Virginia sniggered.

"Esme was part of that team. That's how your father met her."

"Mum was a scientist?" Darkus was flabbergasted.

"She was a mighty fine ecologist," Uncle Max said. He shook his head with a sad smile. "Your father was working with a geneticist to see what could be achieved by tampering with the genetic makeup of beetles."

"Lucretia Cutter," Darkus spat.

"She was plain old Dr. Lucy Johnstone back then. An odd girl, if I'm honest, but very clever and fiercely ambitious. She and Barty had a major breakthrough with their transgenic experiments on certain types of beetles."

"Transgenic?" Virginia frowned. "What does that mean?"

"It means changing the genetic structure of an organism by adding genes from another organism. They took genes from mice and successfully added them to the genes of a beetle."

"A beetle-mouse?" Virginia laughed. "I don't get it—what's so amazing about a beetle-mouse?"

"The first transgenic experiments used genes from mice . . ." Uncle Max paused for an uncomfortably long time. "But the aim—the *true* aim—was to find a transgenic process that would successfully transfer *human* genes into beetles, producing a new species of beetle capable of intelligent thought, to work collaboratively with humans and clean up the environment."

"Beetles with a human gene!" Darkus looked at Baxter perched on his shoulder.

"Did they do it?" Virginia sat up, staring at Newton bobbing about above Bertolt's head. "Did they discover the trans-thingy process?"

Uncle Max sighed, looking at Baxter. "I've seen a beetle behave like Baxter before, when your father was still working on the Fabre Project, and it was carrying his genes."

"Our beetles are transgenic!" Bertolt looked up at Newton, smiling in wonder.

Darkus studied Baxter. "Was Dad's beetle a rhinoceros beetle, too?"

"It was a Goliath beetle, and he was a majestic beast."

Darkus thought about the zebra-striped beetle he'd met on Beetle Mountain. "What happened to it?"

"Barty had Goliath frozen and donated him to the Natural History Museum's collection for future research."

Darkus blinked. He was certain that if they looked, they would find Dad's beetle gone.

"What happened to the Fabre Project?" Virginia asked.

"When they started having successful results, Lucy tried to persuade Barty to leave the project and set up their own laboratory. She believed their work would make them rich."

"She didn't want to help the planet?" Bertolt asked, dismayed.

"But she's got loads of money," Virginia said.

"Yes, she has now," Uncle Max agreed.

"Dad refused," Darkus said with certainty.

Uncle Max nodded. "Realizing what her motives were, Barty destroyed all their research and handed his resignation to Professor Appleyard, explaining what Lucy was planning. Outraged and furious, Lucy Johnstone disappeared, emerging several years later under a new name—Lucretia Cutter. Without the genetics work, the Fabre Project floundered and it was closed down."

"Darkus's dad destroyed his research!" Bertolt said.

"But he didn't—did he, Uncle Max?" Darkus stared at his uncle. "It's upstairs, in your flat." He'd remembered where he'd seen the words *Fabre Project*. "The box that ripped open, with Nefertiti's teeth in it—it was full of folders that said 'Fabre Project' on the side."

Uncle Max looked gray. "I didn't want to take it. I'm not a fan of mucking about with nature. I'm a man of the Old World, and I didn't approve of what your father was doing. I felt he was opening Pandora's box. In fact, we almost fell out about it. Barty promised your mother he'd burn the research, but he couldn't bring himself to destroy his life's work, so I agreed to keep it on the condition that he never meddle with it again. It's been sitting in my box room for years. I'd forgotten it was there, until you came to stay."

"Lucretia Cutter said that the beetles belonged to her," Virginia said.

Uncle Max frowned. "It was only a matter of time before she found a way to complete the human-beetle transgenic process on her own."

"This is serious, isn't it?" Darkus said.

"Very," Uncle Max replied gravely. "Beetles are the single most successful species of creature on this planet. They can adapt to almost any environment. The question your father was trying to answer was what happens if you genetically enhance the most adaptable creature on the planet? I thought that was the most dangerous question I had ever heard."

"But Lucretia Cutter also said that she wasn't ready yet," Darkus said, remembering what she'd said in the room with the two-way mirror, "and that she wouldn't let anyone stop her—*not them, not him, nobody* . . . I think Dad was trying to stop her."

"I've been trying to find out what she's up to, but every avenue I've explored turns up a blank. It's impossible to investigate her. No one will speak about her. They're all petrified." Uncle Max shook his head. "However, I am certain of one thing. Whatever she's up to, we have to do everything in our power to stop her."

"We've got to tell the police," Bertolt said.

"The police are astonishingly uninterested in investigating any of the leads I have provided them with."

"But why?" Bertolt asked.

"Because someone is exerting their power and making sure that Barty's disappearance is not looked into."

"Lucretia Cutter," Virginia snarled.

"And if she thought that we knew where Barty was, she'd move him immediately, and we'd *never* find him," Uncle Max said.

"So we have to tread very carefully. We can't trust anyone but one another."

Darkus looked at Virginia and Bertolt. "We have a plan to rescue Dad."

"Really?" Uncle Max smiled. "I hoped you might. Care to share it with me?"

Baxter rose up from his perch on Darkus's shoulder and hovered beside the boy's face, his elytra lifted high, his soft wings vibrating like a hummingbird's.

"We'd love to," said Darkus.

"But first, I need to go home and get two bottles of champagne," Bertolt said, climbing to his feet.

Darkus smiled at his uncle's surprised expression. "It's all part of the plan."

CHAPTER SEVENTEEN
Band of Beetle Brothers

*D*arkus put his eye to the crack in the kitchen door.

Pickering was setting the table for supper.

"Tomorrow I'll be *rich*!" Pickering said, hugging himself. He started humming and then burst into song: "Take a gold coin, spin it in the air, the next day, boom, you're a millionaire . . ."

"Singing about me again?" Humphrey spun around, clutching a white plastic bag. Tucked under his opposite armpit was Bertolt's box.

Darkus felt his pulse quicken. He silently ushered the beetles through the crack in the door. This needed to work or their whole plan would fall apart.

"Look what I found on the doorstep." Humphrey ripped open the box and lifted out two bottles of champagne. "They're from Lucretia Cutter."

He slid a bottle to Pickering. Shaking his own, he popped the cork, tipped his head back, and poured a fountain of champagne in the direction of his face. "Man, I love that woman!"

Pickering carefully filled a yellow mug with the bubbling liquid. "A toast!" He raised his cup. "To Lucretia Cutter."

Humphrey clanked his bottle against Pickering's cup. "A mighty fine woman."

He took the lids off the food containers as he pulled them out of the bag, then grabbed the bucket of cranberry sauce from the counter and sat down to eat. Snatching a duck dumpling, he dunked it in the cranberry sauce and stuffed it in his mouth.

Darkus could see Baxter was ready, in position, on the ceiling. Underneath the table was a unit of shiny, black, fat-tailed blister beetles and the scruffy diabolical ironclad beetles who looked like blobs of rust.

"Do you *have* to eat with your mouth open?" Pickering said, sitting down across from Humphrey.

Humphrey burped. "Oops, bubbles!"

"You're a pig," Pickering said with disgust. "Eating with your hands. Drinking from the bottle."

"It's Chinese takeout. That's how you're supposed to eat it," Humphrey scoffed. "Anyway, my way means there's less cleaning up."

Pickering and Humphrey glared at each other.

Darkus gave the signal to the waiting emerald-green tiger beetles, huddling under the lip of the table. They immediately raced up onto the surface, dashing over Pickering and Humphrey's food. They moved so fast Darkus couldn't see them, but he definitely noticed when they slowed down, crawling toward the edge and then grinding to a halt. "Something's wrong," Darkus hissed to the four dung beetles waiting by his feet.

"Cleaning up? You never *do* any cleaning up," Pickering snapped, spooning noodles into his mouth.

"That's because I don't make messes."

"What!" Pickering went purple. "What is that revolting *thing* in your bedroom if it isn't a ginormous mess of dirty dishes?"

Darkus saw that Baxter had dropped down from the ceiling and was hovering above the table. There *was* something wrong with the tiger beetles.

"How can you say you don't make messes?" Pickering demanded, outraged.

"Because it's the truth!" Humphrey said, eating two spring rolls at once.

Pickering angrily grabbed his mug and threw his champagne in Humphrey's face, hitting the hovering rhinoceros beetle and flinging him onto Humphrey's nose.

Shocked, Humphrey jerked backward, knocking Baxter into his noodles, his chair tottering and then crashing to the ground.

Pickering was on his feet, screeching with laughter.

"Look at you!" He cackled.

Humphrey flailed his arms and legs frantically trying to get up.

"You—you look like a—a giant *beetle*!" Pickering roared and slapped his knees with delight.

"Get in there and get them all out," Darkus hissed. The dung beetles reared up and shook their legs in the air, then took off and zoomed into the kitchen. They landed on the table and quickly loaded the tiger beetles onto their backs. The blister beetles and diabolical ironclad beetles ran up the table legs to help Baxter.

Darkus held his breath as he watched. Baxter was tangled in the noodles and couldn't get free.

Pickering turned back to his dinner. "Humphrey," he said, scratching his head. "The table is covered in beetles. I think they are trying to eat our food . . ."

"What!?" Humphrey grabbed the tabletop and heaved himself onto his knees, his nose level with the table surface.

The blister beetles pulled Baxter from the tray of noodles. The rhinoceros beetle stumbled as he tried to fly. On the third attempt he was airborne.

Pickering grabbed a frying pan and, using it like a tennis racket, hit Baxter onto the floor.

"Blasted beetles!" Humphrey roared. "Take that!" He pounded the diabolical ironclad beetles with his sledgehammer of a fist. "Got them!" He lifted his hand and looked.

The diabolical ironclad beetles ran forward to form a defensive circle, back to back with the blister beetles.

Humphrey was surprised to see them move. "They should be dead. I gave them a good beating."

"Bet they wouldn't live if we put them through your grinder," Pickering said, picking up Baxter by his horn.

Darkus was up on his feet, not knowing what to do. He couldn't let them grind Baxter.

Humphrey clapped his hands gleefully and ran to the cupboard beside the sink, pulling out a silver-and-red meat-grinding machine with a crank handle.

Pickering dropped Baxter onto his palm and swept his hand under the table, collecting all the other beetles into it and bringing his other hand over the top to make a cage.

"Ouch!" Pickering's fingers sprang open. The skin on his palm was beginning to blister. "Argh! It's burning me!"

The beetles quickly scrambled onto the rhinoceros beetle's thorax, and Baxter was up in the air, flying toward the door, with a diabolical ironclad beetle dangling from his horn.

"Argh!" Pickering ran to the sink, turned on the cold tap, and thrust his hand under the water. "It burns! It burns!"

"*That's* why they're called blister beetles," Darkus whispered, pushing the door open a fraction for Baxter and the other beetles before silently creeping away.

Darkus crept back to Humphrey's bedroom, carrying Baxter in his hands. His shoulders were littered with sleeping tiger beetles and exhausted dung beetles. A raggle-taggle posse of blister and diabolical ironclad beetles clung to the sleeves of his green sweater.

"Part one of the mission is complete," he whispered, triumphantly. "Now we have to wait and see if Bertolt's mum's sleeping pills work."

"They'll work," Bertolt said. "When they're mixed with alcohol they'd knock out an elephant."

"Help me push the armchair up against the door." Darkus said, carefully delivering his cargo of beetles to the foot of the mountain.

"What happened to the tiger beetles?" Virginia asked as they pushed.

"I think the sleeping powder must have gotten into their spiracles and knocked them out," Darkus replied. "They dropped it over the food just fine, but then it was as if they wound down like clockwork. The dung beetles had to fly them out. I think Baxter might have been affected, too—he got knocked into a plate of food and now he's acting woozy."

At Baxter's call, every beetle in the building gathered on Beetle Mountain; the surface seethed and shimmered with brightly colored insects. Darkus tried to take them all in, but there were so many different species, shapes, and colors of beetle that his mind couldn't hold on to them: dung beetles, jewel beetles, giraffe-necked weevils, Goliaths, stags, bombardiers, fireflies, lavender beetles, ladybugs, Atlases, Hercules and titan beetles, tiger beetles, rhinoceros beetles, carpet beetles, deathwatches, and tok-tokkies hammering their heads and abdomens against the cups for all they were worth. His breath caught in his throat as he recognized the true power of these beetles. Suddenly he understood why his dad thought beetles could save the planet. But right now they needed him to save them, and he wasn't about to let them down.

Uncle Max was sitting outside in the sycamore tree, with a branch wedged under his armpits, staring wide-eyed and openmouthed through the window.

"Are you okay?" Darkus waved at his uncle.

Uncle Max saluted a speechless reply.

The beetles fell silent as Darkus came to stand in front of them, between Virginia and Bertolt. A million compound eyes looked at him, waiting for him to speak.

"Lucretia Cutter is coming," he said.

The beetles hissed.

"And we cannot stop her." He paused. "But we can *fight* her!"

The beetles stamped their feet.

"And we *WILL* fight her." He took a deep breath. "Your enemy is my enemy. Lucretia Cutter has kidnapped my father and is holding him prisoner in her house. Tomorrow, when she's here, I'm going to rescue him."

The room hummed and clicked.

"But," he raised his voice over the noise, "I can only do it with your help."

There was silence, and Baxter lifted into the air, waggling his front legs and beating his soft wings in a rhythmic pattern.

"Will you help me? I need a small tactical division of beetles to get me into Towering Heights and get Dad out."

A soft drumming of horns, jaws, and legs on porcelain answered him, and a troop of bombardier beetles scurried forward. They'd be useful, Darkus knew, because of the acid they fired from their abdomens. They were joined by speedy and vicious tiger beetles, dung beetles, fire beetles (good for illumination), and a battalion of Hercules and titan beetles, all known for their strength.

Darkus knelt down.

"Thank you, my friends." He turned and pointed. "That's my uncle Max outside, in the tree." Uncle Max waved. "Follow him down to the car."

"This way," Uncle Max called as he climbed clumsily down the tree.

Darkus stood up, watching the beetles troop out through the window, and then turned back to the mountain. "Lucretia Cutter has a daughter called Novak," he said, "and she's on our side." He remembered Novak stretched out on the floor, unconscious. "She needs a friend, and we need a spy in that house, to find out what Lucretia Cutter is doing. Is there a beetle brave enough to volunteer?"

"She's getting a beetle?!" Virginia said jealously.

A group on the side of the mountain parted, and a jewel beetle, the size of a golf ball and shaped like a coffee bean, flew up to Darkus's outstretched hand. She had a neat pinlike head with delicate antennae, a perfectly rounded thorax, and iridescent rainbow-colored elytra.

"Oh my goodness, she's so pretty!" Bertolt marveled. "Novak's going to love her."

The beetle seemed to like the attention and flickered her elytra open, showing off the bright colors of her wing cases.

Virginia glared at the beetle. "Great!" she muttered. "Now everyone has a beetle except for me!"

Darkus pulled Virginia forward to stand beside him. "I won't be here when Lucretia Cutter comes, but Virginia will be by your side as you fight. She will be able to understand what the humans are doing and help command your troops. Listen to her."

Virginia smiled and waved awkwardly.

"Tonight we move Beetle Mountain downstairs to your new home, in the sewer, and make it impossible for Lucretia Cutter to follow you."

"I'm helping with that," Bertolt blurted out proudly, and an excited Newton rose up out of his hair, glowing brightly.

"Together," Darkus said, "we'll show Lucretia Cutter that our lives are not hers to control."

A high humming sound rose from the mountain, filling the air like a sustained note from a violin. A second harmonizing note joined the first, and then a third as a swarm of tiny green-and-yellow iridescent beetles hovered above the mountain surface, their wings vibrating in unison. Battalion after battalion of black stag beetles marched over the peak of the mountain, coming to a halt and beating their jaws on the crockery surface. The drumming was melodic, like a miniature steel band. The humming and drumming became insistent, crescendoing as the beetles fell into military formations. The weird and wonderful music grew louder and more frenzied as the beetles marched and the mountain reverberated with the rhythm of war.

Darkus surveyed the ranks of beetle soldiers stretched out before him, and hoped that Lucretia Cutter was not prepared for what she was about to face. Surprise was the best weapon they had. "In this battle," he said, "victory is survival." He raised his fist. "And we *will* be victorious."

The room erupted. Beetles flew into the air, looping in and out of dancing swarms, light ricocheting off their outstretched elytra and radiating from their iridescent markings.

Darkus smiled at Virginia and Bertolt. It felt amazing to be finally fighting back. There was a fire in his belly, and grit in his soul, and he wasn't the least bit frightened. Tonight he was going to get Dad back.

CHAPTER EIGHTEEN
Marvin

Downstairs, Pickering was trying to glare at Humphrey, but his eyes kept closing.

"I think it's time for bed," he said, pushing his chair backward.

"Good idea." Humphrey yawned. "Big day tomorrow."

"Yes, a glorious day . . ." Pickering slumped forward.

"Pickers, you've fallen asleep with your face in the noodles."

"No I haven't." Pickering sat up, a noodle stuck to his forehead.

Humphrey got up, and Pickering tried to stand, too. "Urgh, the room's spinning! That champagne has gone to my head."

The cousins staggered out of the kitchen and upstairs.

"It's a bit like chopping down a tree," Bertolt said to Darkus, pushing his glasses up on his nose, "except more complicated, because we want some bits to fall down and some bits to stay up."

He and Darkus were kneeling on the floor, poring over the architectural plans of the building that Uncle Max had given them. Newton bobbed around above Bertolt's head, while Baxter sat calmly on Darkus's shoulder, resting. They were surrounded by beetles, gathered about them on the floor and up the walls.

"This bit of floor first." Bertolt moved his finger to the ceiling above Pickering's bedroom. "Then this bit, and so on."

Darkus looked at the bess beetles and the Asian longhorns. "Is it clear what you and your larvae need to do?"

The beetles buzzed and clicked to show they understood.

"Good. Then you need to take your larvae up to the joists in the attic and start eating."

He watched the furniture, deathwatch, and powderpost beetles scurry after the bess beetles.

"Those of you eroding iron and metal," Bertolt said, "or breaking down cement and brick, your task is harder. So I've made something to help."

Blister beetles, bark beetles, and bombardiers shimmied forward as Bertolt pulled a cardboard box out of his bag and lifted the lid. Inside were four blue tubes with long fuses.

"Where did you learn to make bombs?" Virginia asked, looking over his shoulder.

"They're not bombs; they're explosive charges," Bertolt said, correcting her.

"What's the difference?" Darkus asked.

"Explosive charges are controlled chemical reactions in a confined space. The beetles will make a hole and wedge one of these into it. I'll trigger one from a safe distance. There's one for each floor."

"You're a total pyromaniac!" Virginia said, sounding impressed.

"Are you going to be all right? You know, with all the beetles?" Darkus asked.

"I'll be fine." Bertolt smiled. "Newton's made me see I was being silly. I'm not frightened of them anymore."

Darkus patted his arm and then froze as he saw the door handle turn.

"The door's locked!" Humphrey halfheartedly threw his weight against it. "How can that be? We got it open! Pickers, I can't get into my bedroom!"

"I don't care," Pickering muttered, concentrating on putting one foot in front of the other as he pushed himself upstairs to his own bedroom on the next floor.

"Where am I going to sleep?" Humphrey stumbled after his cousin. "I'm not sleeping on the floor again."

With a great lurch, Pickering threw himself into his bedroom and collapsed onto his bed, instantly unconscious.

"What about me?" Humphrey blundered in and sat down on the end of Pickering's bed with a crash, lifting the other end several feet off the floor. Pickering didn't move and Humphrey fell asleep with his head against the wall, oblivious to the fact that he was sitting on Pickering's legs.

As soon as they heard Humphrey's snores, Darkus and Virginia moved the armchair and crept up to the third floor to check on the cousins. "Look at this," Darkus whispered, standing in the doorway of Pickering's bedroom.

Virginia hung back. "They might wake up!" she mouthed.

Darkus shook his head and beckoned her over. "No, look."

Virginia came up and peered over his shoulder. "Ouch! That's going to be uncomfortable in the morning," she said, seeing Pickering's shins under Humphrey's backside.

"I know." Darkus grinned. "Pity I won't be here to see it." He thought about what he was about to do and felt a surge of energy rush up through his chest.

He was going back into Towering Heights to bring his father home.

He took a deep breath, letting it out slowly. "Right. Phase two. Let's move Beetle Mountain."

Bertolt poked his head out of Humphrey's bedroom as Darkus sped back down. "Did it work?" he asked.

"They're out cold. Sparko," Darkus whispered over his shoulder, racing on down through the kitchen into the Emporium shop and arriving at the manhole. He lifted the board they'd used to cover it.

Screwed into the floor beside the open hole were tracks that supported the heavy iron cover. Inside the rim of the hole was a series of cogs and levers connected to spools of thick wire looped around the metal disc. Bertolt had made a mechanism that would allow Virginia to close and open the manhole cover, using two handles, while standing on the ladder.

"If you aren't enlisting for the battle tomorrow," Darkus said to the seemingly empty shop, "you need to get underground and prepare for the rebuilding of Beetle Mountain."

A pool of beetles bubbled up out of the floorboards, growing and fizzing as it flowed toward him, like a wave of cola. When it reached the edge of the manhole, the wash of beetles became a cascading waterfall.

With Baxter on his shoulder, woozy from the effects of the sleeping powder, Darkus leapt over the stream of beetles and headed back upstairs, taking two steps at a time.

In Humphrey's bedroom, Virginia was standing at the foot of Beetle Mountain, fiddling with the pigtail above her right ear and wondering whether they should bring the butterfly bush with them. There seemed to be lots of beetles on it, and she knew plenty of beetles ate nectar.

"I'm not sure if you can understand me," she said to the mountain, feeling a bit foolish, "but if you burrow under the roots of that tree and work them free, then I could bring it down to your new home."

"They can understand you," Bertolt reassured her.

He was right. The beetles disappeared into the crockery, and gradually the bush tilted toward Virginia. As she reached up to catch it, a shower of beetles flipped, fell, and flew from its branches. A chunky red beetle with a bobblelike head and giant hind legs dropped onto her forehead and clung on.

"Hey!" She went cross-eyed trying to look at it. "How am I supposed to put this tree down with a frog-legged leaf beetle like you hanging off my face?"

The frog-legged leaf beetle didn't move.

Virginia bent her knees and carefully lowered the butterfly bush to the floor. She held her hand up to the bridge of her nose. "Want a ride down?"

The beetle crawled onto her hand. It was about two inches in length—a bit smaller than Newton—and its cherry-red exoskeleton shimmered as it moved, making it look metallic.

"You're a fine-looking fella, and those are some massive legs. I'll bet you can jump."

The red beetle shook its head and crawled off the edge of Virginia's palm, hanging upside down from the back of her hand, all six of its feet clinging to the surface of her skin as if held on by suction cups.

"Oh, I get it, you think you're Spider-Man." Virginia chuckled. "Or Spider-Beetle, I should say, although you look more like a poisonous tree frog." She flipped her hand over so the beetle was standing the right way up. "Humans can go upside down, too, you know." She carefully put the beetle onto the butterfly bush and leaned backward, throwing her arms over her head and dropping into a crablike pose. She flicked her legs up into a handstand. "See?"

"Very impressive." Bertolt clapped.

Darkus walked in. "The pathway down to the sewer is clear," he said, looking amused as she righted herself.

Virginia felt a tickling sensation. The metallic-red beetle had landed on her and was walking up her arm.

"Who's your friend?" Darkus asked.

Virginia lifted her elbow. "This is a spidey-skilled frog-legged leaf beetle. I think he lives in the butterfly tree."

"He's cool!" Darkus peered at the beetle's strong back legs. "He looks like he's made of metal. What are you going to call him?" he asked as the beetle climbed up Virginia's neck.

"Call him?"

Darkus nodded. "He's decided you're his human."

"Really? Do you think so?" Virginia rolled her eyes, trying to look at the frog-legged leaf beetle on her neck. "Maybe he liked my handstand?" She thought for a moment. "If he sticks around, I'll call him Marvin, after Marvin Gaye, the best musician of all time."

The beetle rose up onto its strong hind legs and did a little dance, waggling his front legs like arms and bopping his antennae.

"I think Marvin approves," Darkus laughed.

CHAPTER NINETEEN

Moving a Mountain

*D*arkus stood at the foot of Beetle Mountain.

"It's time," he said to the thousands of waiting insects. "Every beetle who can push, pull, or carry needs to take a mug and move it out of here and down the stairs. Those of you who are strong flyers, go down into the Emporium and help with the mug-drop into the sewer."

At the base of the mountain, Darkus could see dung beetles were already half rolling, half pushing mugs toward the door, three or four beetles to a mug. "Guide the fall of the mugs down the stairs," he suggested, "rather than carrying them. Once you're in the sewer, you'll need to start making the ammunition for tomorrow's battle."

"I'm taking the tree down," Virginia said, lifting the butterfly bush in her arms.

"How're you doing?" Darkus asked Bertolt.

"I don't know. It's hard to judge how much wood the beetles can eat through in one night," Bertolt admitted. "But good, I think." He looked at Virginia. "The floor of Humphrey and Pickering's kitchen isn't being touched. Nor is the supporting wall between the shop and kitchenette. That should stop anything falling on the manhole. We don't want you to get trapped down there."

"Relax—we've got an army of beetles on our side," Virginia said, heading out of the door. "What could possibly go wrong?"

Bertolt looked anxiously at Darkus.

Darkus gave Bertolt's shoulder a reassuring squeeze and nodded at the trail of beetles carrying, dragging, and pushing mugs out of the room and down the stairs. "This is going to take no time at all."

As the night drew on, the initial excitement of helping the beetles and striking a blow against Lucretia Cutter became concentrated into an industrious silence, punctuated with serious looks and nods. Finally, just before dawn, Darkus, Bertolt, and Virginia watched the last mug disappear out of the door on the backs of four orange-and-black harlequin beetles. Humphrey's bedroom was empty except for the stained pink armchair.

Darkus blinked back exhaustion. "We're done!"

The streetlight outside the window flickered off as they tiptoed down to the kitchen. Darkus stopped to whisper to a circle of tiny rust-red beetles he'd gathered together on a work surface.

"Who are those guys?" Virginia asked.

"They're powderpost beetles, wood eaters. They're working on the stairs," Darkus replied.

Bertolt handed Virginia a stopwatch. "This is for you."

"Oh yeah, thanks." Virginia hung it around her neck. "Time check. It's five thirty-two."

"Should we quickly check on the mountain?" Darkus suggested.

They all went down into the shop and peered down the manhole at the new Beetle Mountain.

"It's like it's always been there," Bertolt said. "Look, they've already replanted the butterfly bush!"

"Do you think it's a slightly different shape?" Virginia cocked her head to one side.

"It's hard to say from this angle, but the beetles seem happy," Darkus replied.

"They do, don't they?" Virginia said, pleased.

They could see beetles scurrying over the surface of the mountain, securing mugs and plugging gaps with moss and fluff.

"Who said it was impossible to move mountains?" Darkus smiled.

"So"—Virginia sat up—"I guess it's time for us to split up."

They looked at one another, registering what they were about to do.

"Uncle Max will be waiting for me," Darkus said. "What excuse did you give your parents in the end?"

"I'm staying at his place." Virginia pointed at Bertolt.

"I'm staying with Virginia." Bertolt blinked.

"Are you going to be okay here on your own?" Darkus asked.

"Of course we will." Virginia thumped his arm. "You go get your dad. We'll be fine. You're not the only hero around here with a super-beetle, you know!"

Darkus smiled. Marvin was hanging upside down from one of Virginia's pigtails like a miniature bat, and Newton was sitting on the top of Bertolt's left ear.

"Go on, get out of here." Virginia gave him a gentle shove.

Darkus called out softly, and a cloud of blister beetles flew up out of the manhole, followed by the beautiful jewel beetle who'd volunteered to be Novak's friend. She shimmered all the colors of the rainbow as she landed on Darkus's other shoulder, opposite Baxter. Darkus gave Virginia and Bertolt one last wave, then jogged off through the shop and opened the Emporium door out into the street.

"I brought you something for the battle," Bertolt said to Virginia as they watched Darkus leave. He rummaged in his bag and pulled out a box. "Something with a sting in its tail." He handed her a lighter.

Virginia opened the box and peeped inside. "Deadly!" she said, pocketing the lighter. "Thanks!"

Bertolt threw his arms around Virginia's neck. "Good luck," he said, letting go and then patting her awkwardly.

"You, too." Virginia got to her feet, waving to Bertolt as he disappeared into Furniture Forest. "Right," she said to Marvin, "we'd better find a comfy place to sit and wait for Lucretia Cutter."

Darkus looked around, but the only sign of life was the light in Mr. Patel's newspaper store. The mint-green Renault 4 was sitting in the middle of the road with its engine running. Uncle Max was in the driver's seat, looking at a map. The interior light was on, and Darkus could see that the cream leather of the backseat was covered in giant Hercules and titan beetles. The bombardier beetles were clinging to the roof of the car, and a handful of the larger species of tiger beetle had chosen a perch on Uncle Max's safari hat.

Uncle Max waved, looking uncomfortable surrounded by his beetle passengers.

Darkus and his cloud of blister beetles scrambled into the car.

A bus full of sleepy commuters staring blindly out the windows purred past.

"Pickering and Humphrey are fast asleep," Darkus said as he fastened his seat belt and the blister beetles settled on the dashboard as he did so. "Phase two is complete. Now it's time for phase three."

"Well, then," said Uncle Max, "let's go bring Barty home."

He slammed his foot on the accelerator, released the hand brake, and the car leapt forward with a roar.

CHAPTER TWENTY

Hepburn

*L*ucretia Cutter's bedroom was a cavernous chamber with a floor of ebony parquet and a high ceiling of black Gothic arches. The arches were embellished with gold and reached up a whole story. Hanging from the ceiling were two chandeliers carved from obsidian lava rock. The walls were painted a matte black, and gold arches, echoing those in the ceiling, framed doorways, mirrors, and bookshelves. In the center of the room was a towering four-poster bed, turned from African Blackwood and hung with hand-spun gold lace drapes that glittered as they looped down, offering a glimpse of black silk sheets.

There was a knock at the door. Lucretia Cutter sat up in bed, put on her sunglasses, and pulled a dressing gown over her shoulders. "Come in," she called.

Gerard entered, carrying a silver tray on the fingertips of his left hand. On the tray was a flat-based glass bowl containing a foul-smelling, glutinous brown liquid.

"Your breakfast, Madame," he said, his nostrils curling at the smell.

"Put it on my dressing table," Lucretia Cutter said. She spun around in the bed to get up. This morning she would finally get her hands on those beetles. Then she'd know for certain whether her experiments with human DNA had worked.

Bartholomew was a fool for meddling in her affairs, but when he saw what she'd done—what she was going to do—he'd realize hers was the only way for the human race to progress and survive.

Gerard set down the tray and stood back.

"Madame." He cleared his throat. "May I speak with you about Mademoiselle Novak?"

"What is it, Gerard?"

"The girl is at an age where I feel she may benefit from school-ing . . ." He paused. "She is becoming curious about the world and asking questions."

Lucretia Cutter studied the butler. She was intrigued that he'd given the matter any thought. He must care about the girl.

"The Dotreskolen Academy for Girls in Copenhagen is thought to be very good," he said.

She gave a curt nod. "See to it. And tell Ling Ling to bring the car round at seven thirty."

"Yes, Madame." Gerard bowed and left the room.

Lucretia Cutter got out of bed and sat down in front of her mirror. It irked her that Gerard called her *Madame* and Novak *Mademoiselle*. "Age is a relative concept," she reminded her reflection as she pulled the breakfast tray in front of her, "and I am but newly made."

She lifted her hands to her jawbone, placing her fingertips below each ear, and, opening her mouth impossibly wide, popped her jawbone loose from her skull with a sickening click, letting it hang in the hammock of skin that covered her chin. She lowered her head to the rim of the glass bowl, and a long pair of pink fleshy palps reached out hungrily, scooping the putrid brown vegetation into her mouth.

"Isn't she the loveliest beetle you've ever seen, Baxter?" Novak said, peering down at the rainbow-colored insect crawling across her pale pink bedspread. Its wing cases seemed to flicker from hot pink to emerald green and back again. She reached out her hand, and the jewel beetle stepped up onto it, dropping a miniature scroll onto her palm.

"Is that a message? It's tiny!"

Novak put the beetle down and carefully unraveled the roll of paper.

> *N. I need your help. I'm outside. Can you let me in*
> *the servants' entrance when your mother leaves the*

house? Baxter will bring me back your answer. The
jewel beetle is a friend for you. D.

"He could have put a kiss at the end," Novak harrumphed, but she couldn't keep the smile from her face. "Baxter, go and tell him I'm coming."

The rhinoceros beetle bowed and flew out of the window, back down to Darkus and Uncle Max, who were parked a little way down the road.

Novak got up and pulled a black silk kimono over her pajamas, checking her hair in the mirror. The jewel beetle had also caught sight of herself in the mirror and was parading up and down the bed, admiring her own reflection.

Novak lifted the beetle and placed her on her dressing table. "Are you like Baxter? Can you understand what I'm saying?"

The jewel beetle flicked her antennae gracefully.

"I'm going to take that to mean yes."

The jewel beetle crawled up the dressing-table mirror and clambered onto the postcard of Audrey Hepburn that Novak kept tucked in the corner.

"That's Audrey Hepburn. Isn't she beautiful? She was a movie star."

The beetle opened her wing casings, stretching out her soft wings.

Novak giggled.

"Of course, *you* are much prettier."

The beetle skipped into the air and gracefully looped in a circle, landing on the dressing table facing the mirror and preening her antennae with her mandibles.

"That's what I shall call you." Novak lightly stroked the beetle's elytra. "Hepburn."

Opening the drawer of her dressing table, she rummaged around until she found a gold cone with a clasp on its underside. "This is a dangerous place for beetles, especially one as lovely as you," she said to her new friend, pulling a budding white rose from the vase beside her mirror and cutting the stem with nail scissors. "We need to make you a hiding place." She prized open the flower and plucked out the tightly coiled petals at its center. The outer petals held their shape, enveloping over one another, hiding the rose's hollow heart. Novak pushed the stem into the gold cone and pinned the rose to her dressing gown. "Voilà! A corsage hideaway. Do you think you can fit inside?"

Hepburn flew up, hanging off the bottom petals to open the rose, and crawled in.

"Peep your head out."

Hepburn poked her shiny pink face through the petals.

"Oh! You do understand me! That's wonderful, but you must stay hidden if we meet anyone."

Hepburn disappeared back inside the flower.

Novak examined herself in the dressing-table mirror. The rose didn't look out of place, and anyway the angry bruise on her face drew attention away from the flower.

The familiar sound of car tires on gravel drew her to the window. Ling Ling was opening a car door, and then Mater was there, in a black floor-length dress, wearing her trademark lab coat and sunglasses. She got into the back.

Novak watched, keeping away from the window so that she couldn't be seen. "Let's go and find out what Darkus wants," she whispered to Hepburn.

Lucretia Cutter's car rolled out through the gates of Towering Heights and drove past the empty Renault 4. A white transit van, driven by the two men dressed in black who'd been with her when she'd visited Humphrey and Pickering, followed behind.

Darkus and Uncle Max were crouching behind the Renault 4, and as soon as the vehicles had passed them, they scurried in through the open gates of Towering Heights and pressed themselves into the beech hedge, where their crack commando unit of beetles was waiting for them. The gates swung closed behind them.

"Look, there's Baxter." Darkus pointed.

The rhinoceros beetle flew down from Novak's window, looking like a miniature helicopter, and landed on Darkus's outstretched hand.

"Did you find Novak?" Darkus asked. "Did she get the message? Is she coming?"

The beetle bowed.

Darkus looked up at Uncle Max and took a deep breath. "Well, I'm ready if you are."

"Grit and determination, lad, that's all we need."

Uncle Max winked at him, and Darkus immediately felt calmer.

He put Baxter on his shoulder and then stood with his feet wide and his arms outstretched. First, the big black Hercules beetles clambered up, not stopping until they were perching on top of his head, shoulders, and back, then the green tiger beetles and dung beetles scrambled on. The bombardiers and fire beetles followed, swarming up his legs, and then the blister beetles clung on to the arms of his green sweater.

"Your father is not going to believe his eyes." Uncle Max shook his head and chuckled.

Darkus smiled. "Let's go."

Uncle Max strolled casually up to the front door of Towering Heights. Darkus shadowed him, his head, shoulders, and torso covered with beetles.

Leaning forward, Uncle Max rapped the big silver knocker, and Darkus darted away around the side of the house, running toward the servants' entrance.

Gerard opened the door.

"Good morning, young man," Uncle Max said jovially, wedging his foot in the door.

Darkus could hear Uncle Max shouting. The butler must have answered the front door.

He knocked softly at the servants' entrance. It opened, and Novak was there, smiling shyly, until her mouth dropped open at the sight of Darkus's coat of shimmering beetles.

"Hello," Darkus said. "Can we come in?"

"What are you doing here? And what are you doing with all those beetles?"

"I need you to take me down to the wine cellar," he said, looking about furtively. "To where the cells are."

"What! Why?" Novak took a step back. "I can't . . . I . . ."

Darkus could see she was frightened.

"I wouldn't ask unless it was important." He looked her straight in the eye. "Novak, my dad's down there and I have to rescue him. If I could do it without involving you, I would."

Novak's eyes grew wide.

"Your dad? Are you sure?"

Darkus nodded. "I've come to rescue him."

"But how . . . ?" Novak brushed her hair back from her face. "I mean . . ."

"I need you to help me," Darkus said softly.

"Darkus, I . . ."

"Please, Novak."

She touched her fingers to the purple bruise below her eye, and after a moment's thought, she nodded.

"I brought a few beetle friends along to help us."

Novak giggled. "I can see. You look ridiculous."

"They're surprisingly heavy." He smiled. "You got my message from the jewel beetle?"

"Oh yes, Hepburn." Novak tapped the rose pinned to her dressing gown. "She's simply beautiful."

Hepburn poked her head out and waved her antennae at Darkus.

"Hello," he said to the beetle. "Glad to see you've made yourself at home."

"Come on," Novak said. "We'd better do it quickly. I don't know how long Mater will be gone."

Novak took Darkus through the empty kitchen and toward a spiral staircase that led downward. At the bottom was a door, and behind it a dark, fusty-smelling room.

"This is the wine cellar. On the other side is another door, which leads out to the cells," she whispered.

"Are they guarded?" Darkus asked as they crept through the dark room, stacked high with dusty bottles.

"Dankish, Craven, and Mawling have a schedule. There's an office at the end of the corridor with CCTV, but they never look at it. No one would dare break in here."

"There were two men driving a white van behind your mother's car."

"That would be Dankish and Craven. Mawling's not very clever. Mater never trusts him with anything important. But we don't want to run into him anyway. He's enormous, square like a house, and has a flat nose from when he was a heavyweight boxer."

They reached the door and slipped through it. Darkus found himself standing in exactly the same spot he'd been in when the butler had grabbed him, except that this time the corridor was silent. He looked over his shoulder to the white door with the angry beetles behind it and hoped none were free or roaming the house. He could see the door that his dad's voice had come from. It had the number nine on it.

"Right," Darkus whispered to the beetles clinging to his sweater, "time to do your stuff."

The beetles dropped, fluttered, and crawled to the floor, scurrying forward to the door marked with the number nine. Only Baxter remained on Darkus's shoulder, his antennae held rigid and alert.

"How are you going to open the door without the key?" Novak whispered.

"Leave that to the beetles." Darkus slid back the window in the cell door, but it was pitch-black inside. "Dad?" he called in a loud whisper.

There was no reply.

A line of bombardier beetles climbed up the door and filed through the keyhole. There was a gentle hissing sound as they sprayed their defensive acid into the lock and the metal dissolved. With a heavy clunk, the lock fell out of the door and tumbled to the floor, where it was caught silently by a platoon of dung beetles.

Darkus pushed the door open. He heard some strange sounds—tiny hisses, clicks, and squeals.

Taking a step inside, he waited for his eyes to adjust to the darkness. There were no windows and no electric light.

The fire beetles scurried in, their luminous spots glowing intensely like hundreds of pinpricks of light. They surrounded a dark figure stretched out on the floor.

"Dad?" Darkus whispered, approaching cautiously. "Is that you?"

The figure appeared to be asleep on his stomach.

"Dad?" Darkus dropped down and rolled his father onto his back, pulling his shoulders up onto his knees and cradling his head. "Daddy, it's me. It's Darkus."

"No," his father sobbed quietly, his voice like ash, "she got my boy." His beard was bushy, and his hair wild and matted.

"No, Dad, she didn't. I'm right here."

"I prayed for it to be a dream." His father's voice was a whisper. "Just another of her tortures. All is lost."

As his eyes adjusted, Darkus saw tiny black creatures on and around his father's body. He brushed some away with the back of his hand. He couldn't quite see what they were, but they looked like large ants. Before he could say anything the tiger beetles raced in as quick as lightning, grabbing the creatures with their sharp mandibles, slicing them in two, and throwing them into the shadows. When confronted by the beetles, the insects, whatever they were, retreated into the dark corners of the room. Darkus could feel them watching him and waiting.

"Dad, listen. We're here to rescue you."

His dad clutched his wrist. "Son, you must get out of here. Save yourself."

"We're not going anywhere without you, Dad."

"Darkus, I'm chained to the wall." He moved his feet and Darkus heard the clatter of shackles.

"Bombardiers, I need you," Darkus called softly.

Bartholomew Cuttle looked around, confused.

"Who are you talking to?"

"You mustn't worry, Dad, we're going to get you out of here."

"I don't know where I am."

"You're in Towering Heights, Lucretia Cutter's house," Darkus said. "Do you remember how you got here?"

"I was in the vaults. He was gone. I should have known it wasn't safe . . ." Bartholomew Cuttle shook his head. "I received a letter, a dead specimen; the beetle had been exhibiting strange behavior. I went to check, and . . . and . . ."

"What happened?"

"In the safe, instead of my Goliath, there was a mob of darkling beetles, all waiting . . . hind legs in the air. They blew gas at me, not benzoquinones . . . but I must have that wrong. Then the room was spinning, and specimen drawers were opening on their own, hundreds of Darwin's beetles came teeming out . . . but that can't be right, they're an endangered species . . ."

Darkus thought back to the tanks just down the corridor and knew his father hadn't been imagining the Darwin's beetles.

"I must've been hallucinating, and then the ceiling, and then nothing. When I came to I was in this cell, and she was there." He shuddered. "She was laughing at me. She's a maniac, Darkus." He looked up. "She wasn't like that when I knew her fifteen years ago. She's dangerous. She was saying terrible things about . . ." He shook his head. "You *must* get out of here. NOW!"

"Dad, listen to me. You were kidnapped by Lucretia Cutter's beetles. She's doing some kind of genetic engineering experiments on beetles. I don't know what for, but the beetles that gassed you—they work for her."

"Darkus, beetles can't *work* for anyone. We tried that many years ago—all we managed to make were beetles with personality."

"No, Dad, listen. I've seen her beetles, and they're angry, like hungry wolves, and they did it. They kidnapped you. It's been in all the newspapers. You never left the vault through the door—Eddie was outside the whole time. You just disappeared."

"Disappeared? But . . ."

"Those Darwin's beetles carried you away, down the air-conditioning shaft."

"But that's impossible . . . I would have . . ."

"That's where Baxter found your glasses."

"Baxter?"

"He's a rhinoceros beetle. One of the good beetles that are helping me rescue you, right now. You must listen to me and do what I say. We don't have much time."

CHAPTER TWENTY-ONE

Ambush

Pickering opened his eyes and sat up. His head collided with Humphrey's shoulder.

"Wake up." He pinched Humphrey's arm. "WAKE UP! You're sitting on my legs!"

Humphrey opened his eyes as Pickering's hand slapped his face. He turned and punched Pickering in the head.

Pickering's head bounced back off the mattress and butted Humphrey's shoulder. *"Get off me!"*

"Where am I?" Humphrey groaned. "My head hurts."

"You're on *my* bed, in *my* bedroom, sitting on *my* legs!"

"Keep your hair on," Humphrey said. Leaning forward and grabbing the door frame, he heaved himself to his feet, and the end of the bed that was hanging in the air clattered to the floor.

Pickering wailed. He could see his feet, but he couldn't feel them. *"You've broken my feet!"*

"They do look a bit wrong," Humphrey conceded, scratching his head. Pickering's feet were pointing in the opposite direction to normal.

Pickering tried to stand up and fell over, flipping around the floor like a fish out of water. "I hate you. I hate you. I hate you!"

Humphrey snorted in amusement. "It's not the end of the world, Pickers. They're only feet. They can be fixed."

"Is it eight o'clock yet?" Pickering gabbled. "Lucretia Cutter's coming . . ."

"Oh yeah." Humphrey smiled.

". . . and the beetles are going."

"Oh yeah."

The sound of engines approaching made them lift their heads. Humphrey looked out of the window.

"That's her, and there's a van, too. They're parking opposite."

"Oh no! Are you sure it's her?"

"Uh-huh." Humphrey nodded.

"But I can't walk!" Pickering howled.

"Sorry about that," said Humphrey, unapologetically.

There was a knock at the front door. Humphrey headed out of the room.

"No!" Pickering flapped his arms. "Where are you going?"

"To answer the door."

"Not without me, you're not!"

Humphrey grinned meanly.

"*You* broke my ankles, so *you* are going to have to carry me down the stairs."

Humphrey pretended to be thinking about it for a moment and then shook his head. "Nope."

Pickering started screaming. "Humphrey Winston Gamble, if you don't pick me up and carry me down those stairs, I'm going to tell Lucretia Cutter that you broke my ankles on purpose, and that you can't be trusted, and that you plan to run off with all her money and . . . *WE HAD A DEAL! YOU ODIOUS FATHEAD!*"

Humphrey grunted, picking up Pickering roughly in his arms. "Anything to shut you up," he snarled, and then bellowed down the stairs, "Coming!"

It was the second step that gave way beneath Humphrey's feet. He stumbled forward, dropping Pickering down the stairs. He pulled his left foot free, only to put his right foot through another floorboard, which was dotted with tiny holes.

"What's wrong with this place? It's falling apart!"

"What's wrong with *you*, more like." Pickering rubbed the lump that was already forming on his forehead. "You need to go on a diet!"

"Shut up, or I'll throw you all the way to the bottom." Humphrey grabbed up Pickering again angrily, slinging him over his shoulder. Pickering suddenly found his head resting against Humphrey's enormous buttocks.

Wary of the stairs now, Humphrey descended slowly, testing each one before stepping down.

"Be there in a minute," he bellowed, carefully stepping over each hole-speckled stair. As he made his way down to the front door, he noticed with some satisfaction that his bedroom door was ajar. He must have been confused last night when he thought he couldn't get it open. That boy, the one who had mysteriously escaped them, was haunting him. He'd started to see him everywhere, in the street, in Pickering's junk out in back, he even thought he'd seen him outside Towering Heights yesterday. He shook his head and made a mental note not to kidnap any more children.

"Just a second," he called, almost able to taste the piles of cash that were waiting for him on the other side of the front door.

He opened the door to find two men in black suits.

"Who are you?" Humphrey asked.

"Dankish," said a man who looked like he kicked puppies for fun.

"And I'm Craven," the taller, leaner man said with a nasty smile. "We've come for the beetles."

"Is she here?" Pickering asked Humphrey. "I can't see anything but your huge backside."

Ignoring the two men, Humphrey strode across the road to Lucretia Cutter's car, Pickering slung over his shoulder, oblivious to people's stares. The darkened window dropped to reveal gold lips and dark glasses.

"Hello," Humphrey giggled. "Thanks for the champagne."

"I have no idea what you're talking about." Lucretia Cutter's eyebrows shot up above her glasses. "Have you been drinking?"

"Turn around. Turn around!" Pickering slapped Humphrey's backside.

Humphrey swung him around.

"Hello, my dear Lucretia, fancy seeing you here," Pickering said, trying not to look upside down.

"Stay out of the way," she said, and the black window rose, ending the conversation.

Humphrey dumped Pickering on the pavement outside the Laundromat. "You frightened her away," he complained. "I hadn't finished talking to her."

"They're our beetles." Pickering scowled at Craven and Dankish, who were getting dressed in protective suits beside the back of their open van. "Why do those two get to have all the fun? We should get to do some beetle killing, too. I want a go on one of those poisonous gas guns." He enviously eyed the row of yellow canisters marked with a black skull and crossbones.

"Wouldn't the poisonous gas kill us?" Humphrey asked.

Pickering grabbed Humphrey's ankle and pointed. On the floor of the van was a stack of spare gas masks.

"Not if we're both wearing one of those."

"This is it," Virginia said to Marvin as she peeped through a gap in the boards covering the Emporium window. "There's Lucretia Cutter's car, and there are her henchmen." She looked at the frog-legged leaf beetle in the palm of her hand. "We'd better go and brief the troops."

Virginia tiptoed back through the shop to the stairwell behind the cupboard door and crept up to Pickering and Humphrey's kitchen. She pushed open the door and gasped.

Legions of armored beetles were lined up before her in orderly rows, prepared for war. Every beetle with jaws or claws, antlers or horns, weaponry or skill was there, gathered into regiments, hissing and spitting and flicking their antennae defiantly.

On the floor, a multitude of black-armored rhinoceros beetles—Baxter's brothers—were lined up beside stag beetles, who shook their monstrous antlerlike mandibles, eager for a fight. On the sink draining board, ranks of emerald-green tiger beetles, who move faster than the eye can see and whose scythelike jaws tear their prey apart, were shoulder to shoulder with titan beetles, equal in voracity but huge and mighty, with mandibles that can cut human flesh. Beside them were the courageous and carefree blister beetles lined up alongside the diabolical ironclad horde and the bombardier beetles. On the front line of the beetle army, in shining bronze, were the dung beetles, bringing powerful ball rollers to the battlefield.

Awestruck, Virginia knelt down before them. "They're outside now," she whispered clearly, hoping the beetles understood her. "There are two men wearing helmets and protective suits. They each have a tank of poison on their backs. We need to get those helmets off their heads. They can't use the gas if they're not wearing a helmet.

"Once the front door is closed, I'll signal the attack. Dung beetles and bombardier beetles, you take the offensive positions at the top of the stairs. Remember, we have the advantage of surprise. They aren't expecting a fight."

The beetle horde vibrated to show they understood.

"Blister beetles, tigers, and those of you with a strong bite"—Virginia looked around—"you need to get into position on the ceiling of the front hall. You are the downpour squadron. Darkus has told you what you need to do?"

The harlequin beetles reared up and the tiger beetles chittered to one another.

"Blister beetles, you're in charge of opening up those escape routes for your fellow soldiers. We don't want to leave casualties behind if we can help it. Diabolical ironclad, you and I have a special mission to complete from the banisters. Stags, rhinos, Atlas, Hercules, the final offensive is down to you."

A familiar vibrating noise came up the stairwell behind her. Virginia got to her feet as Goliath flew into the room.

"Sir," she saluted.

The regal beetle landed and took his position in the heart of the front line.

This is how an adventure feels, Virginia thought as her heart roared like a lion in her chest. Taking a deep breath, she opened the door onto the landing and took up her position at the top of the stairs as the beetles marched out behind her, sounding like a storm of hailstones on a tin roof.

Bertolt checked the clock. It was eight a.m. The Laundromat should have just opened. Trying his best to look normal, he left Uncle Max's flat, carrying a laundry basket.

He crossed the street, walking nervously past Lucretia Cutter's car, and was relieved to see the OPEN sign on the Laundromat door.

Once inside, he called out, "Hello?" checking to see that the Laundromat was empty, and then dropped down behind the washing machines in the window, lifting the towel that covered his backpack in the laundry basket.

Newton flitted and flickered nervously above his head.

"You need to stay hidden, Newton," Bertolt whispered as he pulled out a detonator board the size of a coloring book. "Someone could come in at any minute."

Screwed to the detonator were four switches, a bunch of wires, and an antenna. He reached into the backpack and pulled out his stopwatch, getting into a position where he could see the action in the street.

Lucretia Cutter's henchmen were wearing what looked like space suits and checking bright yellow canisters strapped to each other's backs.

Bertolt felt his heart tap-dancing on his rib cage. He wondered if they sent children to prison for colluding with insects to blow up buildings.

CHAPTER TWENTY-TWO
The Battle of Nelson Parade

*C*lipping down their goldfish-bowl helmets, Dankish and Craven strolled through the door of number five. On their backs they each carried a yellow-and-black cylinder of poisonous gas, which led to a gunlike nozzle holstered in their belts.

Virginia's lip curled with disgust and her fists clenched as she watched the two men silently from the landing above. She was going to teach those beetle murderers a lesson they'd never forget.

"Here we go," she whispered to Marvin, who was hanging by his back legs from one of her pigtails. As the front door swung shut, she swiped her hand down, signaling the attack, and pressed the start button on her stopwatch.

Like an enormous black dagger, the first beetle squadron dived down, flying straight at the invaders' heads, blocking out all the light.

Startled by the sudden attack, Craven and Dankish cried out as they twisted and turned, trying to swat the beetles away.

A chain of dung beetles speedily rolled balls of poo forward, pushing them into position between the banisters, where stag beetles waited to lift them. Once the first squadron had retreated to the hall ceiling and they had a clear shot, the dung bombs rained down.

The hall quickly became a slurry pit.

Virginia flapped her hands with delight at the yells of alarm and disgust that came from the muck-splattered helmets of Craven and Dankish.

Unable to see out of their visors, Craven and Dankish collided and grabbed on to each other as they slid, slipped, and fell. Each time they wiped their helmets, a new poo ball obliterated their view.

Virginia hugged her arms tightly around her chest, barely able to contain her glee. This was the funniest thing she'd ever seen in her life, and it was painful trying not to laugh.

"What the hell's going on?" Dankish yelled, lifting his helmet a fraction.

That was the moment the bombardier and blister beetles had been waiting for: They zoomed down in a phalanx toward his exposed Adam's apple, dividing before impact and skimming either side of his neck, releasing a generous spray of boiling acid onto his bare skin.

Dankish shrieked like Virginia's mother when she saw a mouse, and jerked his hands up, knocking his helmet off his head and to the floor. The beetles waiting on the ceiling plummeted down into his suit like a malicious shower of hungry piranha.

Dankish screamed again and again as the acid squirters and the vicious biters went to work. He fell to the floor writhing, punching himself, trying to crush the beetles through the suit, and as he howled in agony the stag beetles scored a direct hit, dropping a brown dung ball into his open mouth.

Virginia punched the air.

Craven couldn't see what was happening, because his helmet was covered in poo, but he could hear Dankish's screams. As if in slow motion, Virginia watched his hands move to the neck clips of the protective suit and snap them open. Craven's helmet only popped up a fraction of an inch before the bombardier beetles shot down for a second attack. His nasal howls soon echoed Dankish's, and his helmet fell to the floor as a furious downpour of angry insects tumbled into his suit.

Virginia leapt up in delight as Craven, too, fell to the floor, screaming. She looked at the stopwatch. Three minutes to go. Peering over the banisters, she could see Dankish and Craven squirming around in a quagmire of poo, retching and howling as they were bitten and stung. The beetles were already streaming out of the holes in the heels of their suits, making good their escape.

They had done it! They had stopped Lucretia's men!

Suddenly, the front door flew open and Humphrey thundered through it, with Pickering strapped to his back inside a cylinder harness, his broken ankles dangling at awkward angles. They were wearing gas masks they'd taken from the van.

"Ha-HA!" Pickering cried. "Thought you'd keep all the fun to yourselves, did you? Well, think again, because we're here to show you how beetle killing should be done!"

Pickering's crowing petered out when he saw Dankish and Craven. Humphrey stared.

"*Dear God*, it stinks in here!" Pickering's nose wrinkled.

Virginia's heart sank as the cousins charged into the hallway, and before she could stop herself from leaning too far forward, she lost her balance and clattered noisily against the banisters.

Humphrey raised his head, looking up. "There's someone up there!" he cried. "IT'S THE BOY!"

"Get him!" Pickering screeched. "KILL HIM!"

Virginia spun around in a panic. This wasn't in the plan. There was no one to rescue her.

Humphrey tore a tank of poisonous gas from Craven's back and swung it over his shoulder to Pickering, who hugged it. There was a cracking sound and a terrible scream as Humphrey charged forward over the fallen men, ignoring the storm of beetles biting and stinging his flesh. Impervious to the deluge of dung balls fired at him, he reached the bottom of the stairs.

"Oh no," Virginia whispered to Marvin. "What do I do now?"

A screech sounded behind her: It was Goliath calling out an order. Three rhinoceros beetles climbed onto his wing cases, linking their horns and serrated legs around him. Four stags ran up and grabbed on to his underbelly. Together as one they began to roll toward the stairs, picking up Atlas, Hercules, and titan beetles, gathering momentum and beetles as they went. Virginia's jaw dropped as she watched. By the time the beetle ball reached the top of the stairs, it was the size of a giant Space Hopper.

On the command of Goliath, another screech from the center of the ball, the beetles on the outside rose up onto their back legs, linking their arms together, their vicious horns sticking out.

Virginia grabbed Bertolt's rockets, laying them on the floor so that they poked out over the stairwell, and looked at the stopwatch—thirty seconds.

She pulled the lighter from her pocket, quickly lighting the fuses before sprinting into the kitchen, throwing herself down the stairs into the shop, running to the manhole, and scrambling down the ladder. She rotated the handles at a furious speed, pulling the metal cover over the hole until it clunked into place, and strapped the climbing harness she was wearing over her tracksuit to the ladder.

Clinging to the rings of the iron ladder, above Beetle Mountain, Virginia closed her eyes.

"Do it, Bertolt!" she whispered. "Get the scumbags!"

"Someone's coming," Novak hissed from the doorway.

Bartholomew Cuttle grabbed his son's hand. "Who's that?"

"Don't worry." Darkus frantically pulled at the shackles around his father's feet, and one of them broke open. "She's my friend."

"Mawling has started the morning round of the cells." Novak tugged at her kimono belt anxiously.

"Are there are other prisoners?"

Novak bit her lip and didn't answer. "Darkus, when Mawling gets here, he'll see the lock is gone. What shall I do?"

"We need more time." Darkus tugged at the other shackle, but it held firm.

Hepburn flew up to Novak and looped the loop.

"Good idea, Hepburn." Novak held out her hand for the beetle to land. "We'll give you as much time as we can."

"What are you going to do?"

"Hepburn and I are going to put on a show," Novak replied.

Darkus heard the patter of her feet as she ran up the hall. He struggled in vain with the iron cuff, finally hitting it in frustration. It broke open.

"Yes!" Darkus scrambled to his father's head. "Dad, your feet are free. Can you get up?"

Bartholomew Cuttle rolled over onto all fours and slid onto his knees. Darkus noticed he was still wearing the blue shirt and corduroy trousers that he'd been dressed in the day he had disappeared, except that now the shirt was dirty and ripped.

His father crossed his arms and shivered. Darkus pulled off the green sweater.

"Here."

Bartholomew looked at his son as if he had never seen him before and took the sweater, pulling it over his head.

"How did you find me?" he asked.

"I found the beetles first, or rather they found me," Darkus replied, smiling down at his dad. "It's going to be okay now, Dad. Uncle Max is waiting outside with the car." He took one of his father's arms and rested it over his shoulder. "Let's get you on your feet. Hup!"

Bartholomew Cuttle tried to stand, but his knees gave way and he fell forward, landing back on his hands.

"This isn't going to work," he said. "I'm too weak."

Darkus looked at the door anxiously.

His father gently pushed Darkus away. "You'll never be able to carry me. You must leave before she sees you."

"I will not," Darkus said, gritting his teeth and pushing his father back.

Surprised by the shove, and terribly weak, Bartholomew Cuttle fell back. There was a dull thud as his head hit the floor.

"Dad! I'm sorry." Darkus dropped down by his father's face. "Dad?"

His father's eyes were closed.

"No!" Darkus's breath was sucked out of his lungs by the shock of realizing he'd knocked his dad unconscious. "No, no, no!"

He shook his shoulders, then tried to lift him, growing more frantic, until he realized he couldn't lift his father on his own.

A sob of desperation burst from his chest as he sank to his knees. It was hopeless. Covering his face with his hands, he felt his body shaking and hot tears rolling down his cheeks, making his palms wet.

A familiar weight on his shoulder and the gentle scratching of Baxter's horn under his chin made him wipe his eyes, and then he heard a familiar sound, like sugar pouring into a bowl. He looked down.

The beetles were surging together and crawling underneath Bartholomew Cuttle's exhausted body. Dung, Hercules, and titan beetles formed a raft of elytra with their backs. Together they lifted Darkus's father off the floor and carried him forward on thousands of tiny serrated legs.

Darkus let out a laugh of surprise and relief as he watched the beetles carry his father out of the cell door. He sprang to his feet and ran to join them.

"You are the best beetles in the world," he whispered as they made their way down the corridor and into the wine cellar. "Baxter, go and tell Novak we're out of the cell."

Baxter leapt off his shoulder into the air and was gone. Darkus opened the door at the other end of the cellar, and they marched to the spiral staircase. Novak ran up, with Hepburn and Baxter flying above her.

"I did the best I could, but he's going to see the cell door any second now," she gasped. "We must hurry."

Darkus heard a distant bellowing roar, then a strange high-pitched noise that seemed to really bother the beetles, who flicked their antennae and forelegs angrily at it.

"Mawling's found the cell!" Novak grabbed Darkus's arm. "He's coming. He'll release the assassin bugs! We've got to get out of here!"

"Assassin bugs?" Darkus's mind flicked back to the room with the yellow ladybugs and angry stags.

"They drink blood." Novak looked terrified.

Darkus spun around. "Beetles, can you get Dad up the stairs?"

Every single beetle—Baxter, dung, Hercules, titan, bombardier, blister, fire, and tiger—climbed on top of his dad now. Clutching the unconscious Bartholomew Cuttle with each of their six legs, they all flipped up their elytra on Darkus's command and spread their vibrating wings. Slowly, the body of the unconscious man rose, ghostlike, up the stairwell to the kitchen.

Hearing a terrified scream, Novak and Darkus rushed up the stairs to find the cook staring wide-eyed at the floating specter.

"Close your eyes, Millie," Novak cried. "It's not real. Don't look. I can explain everything. Please stop screaming."

Darkus rushed across the room, into the hall full of crates, and threw back the bolts of the servants' door, pushing it open. The levitating body of his unconscious father, held aloft by thousands of tiny wings, glided out into the morning sunlight.

He paused in the doorway.

"Get out of here," Novak gasped.

Darkus grabbed her hand. "Come with us."

Novak looked longingly at Darkus but shook her head. "I can't," she whispered, and took a step back.

"But if she finds out . . ." Darkus's stomach churned at the thought of what Lucretia Cutter would do to her rebellious daughter. "Novak, she's a monster."

"But she's my mother," Novak said, and closed the door.

Humphrey stood at the foot of the stairs, looking up at the giant black spiky beetle boulder teetering at the top of the stairs.

"Pickers, what is that!?"

Pickering mounted the nozzle of the gas hose onto his shoulder.

"Who cares? Let's kill it."

Humphrey stepped up. The stair was slippery and he lost his balance, causing him to take a hurried second step. The next stair dissolved into powder beneath him. He lurched forward, and his back foot slid away.

As he fell, Humphrey saw the beetle boulder tip forward, shedding beetles—armed with horns, claws, and pincers—onto each stair.

His face hit the floor with a crash just as the beetle boulder hit him in the face. Angry beetles were catapulted forward, and he and Pickering were covered in a blanket of attacking arthropods.

"Shoot the gun!" howled Humphrey. "Gas them!"

"NO!" screamed Craven from the floor. "We don't have our helmets on! You'll kill us!"

"Put them on, then!" Pickering screamed. "*I'm going to fire this thing!*"

Humphrey watched Craven speedily drag his body to the front door and pull it open. He looked at Dankish, who grabbed his helmet and pulled it over his head, wailing as a batallion of black beetles inside advanced toward his nose.

"*DO IT!*" Humphrey roared, every bit of his body in pain.

Pickering raised the barrel of the gas gun and took aim at the beetles on Humphrey's bald head.

"*DIE! DIE! DIE! DIE!*" Pickering screamed. He fiddled with the tap, trying to release the gas, but his fingers were slippery.

"*What are you waiting for?*" Humphrey howled, then froze as he heard a terrifying shriek rushing toward his ears.

Something was being fired at his head! He heard a terrifying series of loud bangs.

"I've been shot!" Pickering wailed. "I'm dying!"

Humphrey's arms and legs flailed. The boy had a gun!

"Retreat! Retreat! RETREAT!" Pickering screamed, repeatedly punching the back of Humphrey's head.

Bertolt's eyes were locked on his stopwatch.

"Seven, six, five . . ." he counted down in a whisper.

Underground, Virginia was staring at her stopwatch. *Three, two* . . . She closed her eyes and held on tight.

"One!" Bertolt flicked the first switch.

There was a moment of silence.

A muffled boom.

And the Emporium windows exploded out of their frames.

Bertolt leapt to his feet, ran to the pay phone on the Laundromat wall, and dialed 999.

"Hello, can I have the police, please?" He thought about what Virginia had told him to say. She'd be safely underground by now, if she'd followed the plan . . . "Hello? Yes. I live on Nelson Parade. I thought you should know there's a girl tied to a chair in a room above the Emporium. I can see her through the window. It's very strange, because the two men who live there don't have any children."

He let the operator reassure him, then hung up before dialing again.

"Hello, can I have the fire brigade, please? I'd like to report an explosion at the Emporium on Nelson Parade."

He held out the receiver and flicked down the second switch, blowing the ceiling off Humphrey's bedroom and sending a wave of brick dust rippling out into the street.

"Oh my! Did you hear that? There was another one. Please come quickly. I think it might be terrorists!"

CHAPTER TWENTY-THREE

Goliath's Fall

Uncle Max was doing his best to make a horrendous racket. "I'm not leaving until that monstrous woman has explained herself," he shouted loudly, banging his fist against the open door. "She took a potshot at my nephew, and I intend to tell the police! Do you hear me? She's not above the law, you know!"

He leaned toward the butler and shouted over his shoulder, up the stairs. "I said, YOU'RE NOT ABOVE THE LAW, YOU KNOW!"

"Sir, as I said before"—Gerard put his hand to Uncle Max's chest and tried to push him back onto the doorstep—"Madame Cutter is not at home at present."

"Don't you touch me!" Uncle Max held up his fists and started boxing the air to show that he meant business. "I might be an old man, but I can still throw a punch."

"Please, sir, calm yourself." Gerard held up his hands.

A scream sounded from the kitchen.

"CALM MYSELF?" Uncle Max shouted.

Gerard looked over his shoulder at the door to the kitchen and then back at Uncle Max.

Millie screamed again, and Gerard took a step backward.

There was no choice: Uncle Max drew his fist back and threw a punch that connected with the butler's jaw and sent him flying backward.

"OUCH!" Uncle Max hopped about, waving his fist. He hadn't hit a man for at least twenty years. He'd forgotten how much it hurt.

The butler was out cold on the hall floor. "That's for clobbering my nephew," Uncle Max said, stepping into the house to check that the butler wasn't seriously hurt. "Sorry, old bean. You did save him, too, I know that," he whispered to the unconscious man. "You're going to have a sore jaw and a lump on your head when you wake up, but I suspect it's better she finds you this way."

Leaving the front door wide open, Uncle Max went back out onto the doorstep as Darkus appeared around the side of the house. Max ran to his nephew and relieved the beetles of their heavy human cargo, pulling his brother onto his broad shoulders.

"Run, lad. Get the car open."

Darkus ran ahead, and the beetles followed him like a storm cloud.

They reached the car and gently laid Bartholomew down on the backseat. Darkus covered him with a blanket. In the morning light, his dad looked deathly pale.

The beetles piled into the trunk.

Bartholomew Cuttle's eyes flickered open.

"Max?"

"Listen to me, Barty." Uncle Max leaned in over Darkus's shoulder. "We need to get you to a hospital, but first there are two children who need protecting from Lucretia Cutter. Can you hold on?"

"Yes." Bartholomew smiled at Darkus. "I'm okay now."

"Good. We need to get back to Nelson Parade," Uncle Max said, getting in behind the wheel. "Hurry!"

He revved the engine as Darkus slid into the passenger seat and slammed the door.

As they drove away from Towering Heights, Darkus looked back and saw a flood of dark shapes like giant ants sweep across the white gravel of the driveway, stopping at the gates.

Lucretia Cutter stepped out of her car, her chitin feet clicking as they struck the pavement, the sound deadened by the dense black fabric of her skirt. Her head swung from left to right and back again. Something wasn't right.

Ling Ling, her chauffeur, hurried around with her canes. She took them, adopting a pose of fragility, but barely leaned on them as she lurched across the road.

"Craven," she barked at the man in the gutter, "explain."

"They attacked us," he bleated.

"Who did?"

"The beetles."

"Where's Dankish?"

"Inside."

"What's that stench?" Lucretia Cutter recoiled.

"Poo," Craven whispered.

Humphrey lumbered out into the street, with Pickering still strapped to his back and a broken Dankish clinging to his ankle. The men were covered from head to toe in biting, scratching beetles. As Humphrey reached the curb, the Goliath beetle dropped to the ground and gave a commanding screech. All the beetles scurried and flew down the drain by the side of the road, swift and fluid as water.

"Stop them!" Lucretia Cutter swung round. "They're escaping!"

As the beetles disappeared down the drain, Lucretia Cutter bounded forward and swiped at the Goliath beetle with one of her canes, knocking it over onto its back. Its legs pawed at the air. Lifting her arm high, she hammered her cane down onto its abdomen, piercing its armor and killing it dead.

"Get up, you fools!" she barked at the men on the ground, lifting her cane and shaking it for them to see. "They're just beetles!"

From his position inside the Laundromat, Bertolt choked back tears at the sight of Goliath impaled on Lucretia Cutter's stick, and a surge of anger exploded in his chest. "They are *not* just beetles!" he murmured, grabbing his detonator board and flicking down another switch. "For Goliath."

Lucretia Cutter stumbled, dropping the cane with the skewered beetle as a third explosion rocked the street.

"What is happening?" she shouted angrily. Spinning around, she realized there were clusters of people on the pavement watching her. The wail of sirens rose in the distance, and the number of concerned people gathering around Lucretia Cutter was growing.

A news van drove up the street and screeched to a stop. A blond girl in a smart suit scrambled out, clutching a microphone. Hot on her heels was a bald man carrying a camera.

"Emma Lamb from News Desk BBTV," the girl called out as she ran toward Lucretia Cutter.

Ling Ling moved into a defensive stance between her boss and the cameraman, ready for a fight. The crowd surged forward to look at the enigmatic woman standing in the middle of the road.

Three police cars drove up one end of the street and two fire engines approached from the other. Emma Lamb ushered her cameraman forward to capture the scene.

Lucretia Cutter inhaled deeply through her nose to calm the rage that was building up inside her. She leaned her head to the right until her neck made a crunching noise. "Humans," she hissed as an ambulance arrived behind the fire engines.

Bertolt slipped out of the Laundromat and into the street, merging with the crowd.

"And *this* is for kidnapping Darkus's dad," Bertolt whispered, flicking his last switch.

The final explosion dropped the shop ceiling on the ground, carrying the weight of all the floors above. It made a deafening *boom* that sent the boards flying off the front of the Emporium and caused a mushroom cloud of dust to rise up into the sky above the building. Everyone in the street screamed and scurried backward as a red-and-black metal sign with MR. GAMBLE'S EXOTIC PIE SHOP scrawled on it came flying out of the building and embedded itself into the roof of a police car. The screams became wails and gasps as the crowd stared at the place where the Emporium had stood. A series of hanging walls and toothless stairs was all that was left inside the empty brick shell.

There was a minute of stunned silence. Then a ripple of murmurs and anxious shouts were accompanied by more gasps as a girl in a red tracksuit stumbled out of the rubble. It was Virginia, smeared with dirt and covered in dust.

She locked eyes with Bertolt and winked. Then:

"Help me!" she cried, and fainted.

Three firemen came running forward, followed by the cameraman. A blanket was wrapped around Virginia's shoulders and she was carried out of the ruins of the building. As she passed Humphrey and Pickering, she pointed and started screaming hysterically.

"It was them! They kidnapped me!" she cried, and then pretended to faint again.

"Wait! What? No!" Pickering cried, confused. "We kidnapped a boy, but he disappeared."

Two police officers marched over and slammed handcuffs onto his wrists.

"This is a mistake—it was a boy, it was a boy!" Humphrey protested. The policemen shoved him into the back of their van and closed the door. "I've never seen that girl before in my life!"

Lucretia Cutter stood frozen in the midst of the chaos, holding on to her canes and staring at the girl who had clambered out of the rubble. She carefully studied the people around her, but none of the faces were familiar.

She could feel unseen forces working against her.

An old mint-green car pulled up behind the fire engine, and a boy got out of the passenger seat. Lucretia Cutter's mind whirled, synapses firing messages back and forth as she tried to make sense of what she saw. She recognized the boy; he was Novak's companion, the one who had inexplicably escaped from her house yesterday.

A man she faintly remembered from her past—a man who'd stood taller when she'd last seen him—scrambled out of the driver's seat of the car and opened the back door.

"No!" she screeched with rage as she saw Maximilian Cuttle lift his brother up and help him to stand.

All three of the Cuttles turned to face her, defiant.

"How . . . ?" Lucretia Cutter choked.

"It's over, Lucy," Bartholomew Cuttle said in a voice as strong as stone. "I should have put an end to this before you became toxic with power and greed."

She snarled, her face contorting with hate.

But Bartholomew Cuttle only smiled. "I'm going to bend heaven and earth to stop you," he said. "I will tell the world who you are, and when they see the truth, all of humanity will rise up and sweep your abominable empire off the face of this planet."

Darkus looked at his father with shock. He'd never heard him sound so angry and serious.

Lucretia Cutter looked scornfully at the man she'd kept imprisoned in her cell for six weeks. Barking out a humorless laugh, she raised one of her canes, flicked down a trigger from its stem, and pointed it at Bartholomew Cuttle's heart.

"NO!" Virginia screamed, struggling to get away from the fireman holding her.

"*NO!*" Bertolt cried, hurling himself forward, crashing into Lucretia Cutter's legs just as Darkus flew across the hood of the car, pushing his father to the ground.

A shot rang out as Lucretia Cutter fell.

"Dad?"

"Hellfire!" Uncle Max scrambled to his feet.

"Darkus! Darkus, are you okay?" Bartholomew grabbed his son. "Oh no! NO! My boy!"

Darkus sank into his father's arms, gripping his shoulder, blood oozing between his fingers.

Uncle Max turned and shouted, "MEDICS, HERE! NOW!"

Lucretia Cutter's head hit the road, her trademark sunglasses bouncing away across the tarmac. Covering her face with her hands, she kicked viciously at Bertolt, who was clinging desperately to her legs.

Virginia saw an enraged, hissing Baxter fly at Lucretia Cutter, stabbing between her fingers at her naked eyes with his sharp horn.

Lucretia Cutter made a hideous sound, part scream, part hiss, as if she were burning.

And then there was a lithe body in black, springing in, grabbing Bertolt around the waist and tossing him aside. Ling Ling whirled around gracefully, kicking Baxter away from Lucretia Cutter's face, dropping down and windmilling her arms under her boss's armpits and lifting her effortlessly onto her back.

Before anyone could figure out what had happened, the ambulance crew had surrounded Darkus, and Ling Ling was running to the car with Lucretia Cutter.

"Stop her!" Virginia cried out. "She's a murderer!"

But no one was listening. She watched, helpless, as Ling Ling deposited Lucretia Cutter into the passenger seat of the car, slammed the door, slid around the hood, and disappeared into the driving seat.

With a thunderous roar, the engine inside the mechanical scarab revved, and the car climbed the pavement, circumnavigating the emergency service vehicles and disappearing up Nelson Road.

CHAPTER TWENTY-FOUR

Back to Base Camp

*D*arkus dragged the ladder from the shed and leaned it against the wall. His right arm and shoulder were tightly bandaged and hung in a sling. His shoulder hurt so badly if he jogged or jarred it that it made him suck air through his teeth, but he was determined to get over that wall.

"Right, I'm going up," he said to Baxter, stepping onto the ladder.

Since the shooting, the rhinoceros beetle had taken to perching on Darkus's head or his other shoulder, but couldn't settle in either position, so he kept clambering between the two.

Once up on the wall, Darkus gingerly slid down the other side, landing on a stack of drawers, and carefully picked his way down into

Furniture Forest. As he passed the Rat Trap, Darkus shook his head. He couldn't believe it had only been a week since they'd found Uncle Max in there. It seemed much longer than that.

Crawling slowly through the tunnels, with Baxter flying before him, Darkus noticed that some of the beetles had taken up residence in the bedsteads and tables that made up the forest. He could see the punched holes of woodworm in the furniture. When they saw him the tok-tokkies and deathwatch beetles hammered their abdomens and heads against the nearest hard surfaces as he passed by, like miniature woodpeckers, to show their appreciation for what he and Virginia and Bertolt had done for them.

Darkus smiled. Despite the awkward and sometimes painful effort of crawling, it was good to be heading back to Base Camp victorious.

He only had a blurred memory of what had happened after he was shot. He remembered being lifted onto a stretcher and the ambulance team fitting a drip into his arm, then the sound of sirens blaring. Uncle Max had been by his side, holding his hand the whole time.

There were faces and cameras flashing, voices shouting.

"Darkus! Darkus! How does it feel to be reunited with your father?"

"Who shot you, Darkus?"

The bullet had gone straight through his shoulder and, remarkably, done little damage, but he'd lost a lot of blood. He'd been in the hospital for five days before the doctors agreed to discharge him into the care of Uncle Max.

Dad hadn't fared as well.

Darkus remembered the medical team lifting off Dad's sweater in the back of the ambulance and cutting away the stained shirt from his body. He remembered seeing hundreds of bleeding lesions and sores all over his father's chest.

Dad was still in the hospital now, being treated for an infection. Darkus wondered for the hundredth time what the antlike creatures in the cell were. They definitely weren't beetles. Novak had called them assassin bugs.

He stopped. There it was—the black front door with the silver 73.

He climbed to his feet. With his good right hand he turned the handle and walked into Base Camp.

"DARKUS!" Virginia shouted, then whooped with joy.

"Hello!" Bertolt's voice was breathless, his eyes shining. "We've been here every day after school. We didn't know if you'd come back," he gabbled. Newton was flicking and fizzing above his head.

Darkus laughed, delighted to see them both, and came to sit with them on the couch. "Are you okay?" he asked, seeing Bertolt's bandaged arms. "What happened to you?"

"Lucretia Cutter's legs. Didn't you see?" Bertolt replied. "You were right. She's got claws and spikes, like a beetle, and they're as sharp as knives! When I grabbed her legs, the spikes cut my arms."

"The battle plan." Darkus looked at Virginia. "Did it work?"

"Like a dream." Virginia nodded, her eyes sparkling. "The beetles were amazing, and so brave. Marvin was with me the whole time." She reached up to where he sat on her hair and tickled his red thorax.

"I wish you could have seen Lucretia Cutter's men sliding around and screaming, covered in poo," she chuckled. "It was the funniest thing. And Bertolt's rockets were brilliant. When the firecrackers went off, Pickering thought he was being shot . . ." Her voice trailed off as she looked at Darkus's shoulder. "Does it hurt?" she asked.

"A bit." Darkus nodded. "I get really tired in the evenings. But being shot's not as bad as you think it's going to be."

Virginia looked so impressed that Darkus blushed.

"Baxter was brave, too," Bertolt said, looking affectionately at the rhinoceros beetle as he settled on Darkus's good shoulder. "When Lucretia Cutter shot you, he went for her face."

"Yeah." Virginia nodded. "I think he got her in the eye with his horn."

"Everything happened so fast," Darkus marveled. "I didn't see anything at all."

"When she pointed her cane, I knocked her over. Her glasses fell off . . . and her eyes . . . they were bulging out of her head like shiny black marbles." Bertolt looked suddenly scared. "Darkus, they were like beetle eyes."

"Compound eyes." Virginia nodded.

"She's got compound eyes?" Darkus shook his head. "What is she?"

"She's not human, that's for sure," Virginia said grimly.

"Then her bodyguard jumped in and pulled her out of there, and they drove off," Bertolt added.

"She escaped?" Darkus couldn't believe what he was hearing. "After shooting me?"

"The police went after her," Virginia said.

"Is your uncle angry about what we did to the Emporium?" Bertolt asked nervously. "Is his flat okay?"

Darkus laughed. "Is that why you didn't come to see me in the hospital—in case he shouted at you?"

"No." Bertolt looked flustered. "I wasn't allowed. Our parents were very angry with us for lying about where we were."

Virginia nodded. "I'm grounded forever."

"So how come you're here now?"

Virginia snorted. "I'm *not* here now," she said. "I'm in the library, studying."

Darkus laughed. "Well, you don't need to worry. The flat is fine. Uncle Max has had some men come around to check. It's not going to fall down."

"Phew!" said Bertolt.

"He told me that because it was only the middles of the floors that fell down, and all the walls were left alone, the Emporium is condemned, but there was no damage to the buildings on either side."

"Really?" Bertolt looked surprised.

"He said you should get a degree in engineering for not pulling down the whole street."

"That's nice." Bertolt pushed his glasses up on his nose. "Does this mean you're going to go back to your old school now that your dad's back?"

"Not yet." Darkus shook his head. "Dad's still in the hospital, and when he does come out, he'll need looking after, so Uncle Max has said we can both stay here until he's back on his feet."

"Oh, that's wonderful news." Bertolt's face lit up, and Newton looped the loop and flashed his tail.

"There is some bad news, though," Virginia said.

"What?" Darkus asked.

Bertolt bit his lip. "They didn't catch Lucretia Cutter."

"What?" Darkus stood up.

"She escaped," Virginia said, "and Humphrey and Pickering have been charged by the police with attempted murder, for shooting you."

"But that's crazy! They didn't shoot me; Lucretia Cutter did."

"I know," Bertolt agreed.

"She's still out there somewhere?" Darkus asked.

Virginia nodded. "But the beetles are safe," she reminded him. "Beetle Mountain is hidden in the sewer, and Pickering and Humphrey are in prison, so Furniture Forest is ours."

"Do you think she'll come back?" Bertolt asked.

Darkus sat down and sighed.

"I don't know. She's up to something, and whatever it is, it's dark. I can see it in my dad's face." He looked up at the light-speckled tarpaulin ceiling of Base Camp. "But it doesn't matter what she comes at us with," he said, turning from Virginia to Bertolt. "We've got the beetles." His hand went up to Baxter on his shoulder.

"Don't forget your good friends . . ." Virginia added with a grin.

"Yes." Bertolt nodded.

"And with a bit of grit and determination," Darkus smiled, "we're unbeatable."

HERE ENDS

BEETLE BOY

An Entomologist's Dictionary

ABDOMEN: The part of the body behind the thorax (human abdomens are usually referred to as tummy or belly). It is the largest of the three body segments of an insect..

ANTENNAE (SINGULAR: ANTENNA): A pair of sensory appendages on the head sometimes called *feelers.* They are used to sense many things, including odor, taste, heat, wind speed, and direction.

ARTHROPOD: Means *jointed leg* and refers to a group of animals that includes insects (known as hexapods), crustaceans, myriapods (millipedes and centipedes), and chelicerates (spiders, scorpions, horseshoe crabs, and their relatives). Arthropod bodies are usually in segments, and all arthropods have an exoskeleton and are invertebrates.

BEETLE: One type (or *order*) of insect with the front pair of wing cases modified into hardened elytra. There are more species of beetle than any other animal on the planet.

CHITIN: The material that makes up the exoskeletons of most arthropods, including insects.

COLEOPTERA: The scientific name for beetles.

COLEOPTERIST: A scientist who studies beetles.

COMPOUND EYE: Can be made up of thousands of individual visual receptors, and is common in arthropods. It enables many arthropods to see very well, but they see the world as a pixelated image—like the pixels on a computer screen.

DNA (DEOXYRIBONUCLEIC ACID): The blueprint for almost every living creature. It is the molecule that carries genetic information. A length of DNA is called a gene.

DOUBLE HELIX: The shape that DNA forms when the individual components of DNA join together. It looks like a twisted ladder.

ELYTRA (SINGULAR: ELYTRON): The hardened forewings of beetles that serve as protective wing-cases for the delicate, membranous hind wings underneath, which are used for flying. Some beetles can't fly; their elytra are fused together, and they don't have hind wings.

ENTOMOLOGIST: A scientist who studies insects.

EXOSKELETON: An external skeleton—a skeleton on the outside of the body, rather than on the inside like mammals. Insects have exoskeletons made largely from chitin. The exoskeleton is very strong and can be jam-packed with muscles, meaning that insects (especially beetles that have extremely tough exoskeletons) can be very strong for their size.

HABITAT: The area in which an organism lives. This is not the specific location. For example, a stag beetle's habitat is a broad-leaved woodland and not London.

INSECT: An organism in the class Insecta, with over 1.8 million different species known and more to discover. Insects have three main body parts—the head, thorax, and abdomen. The head has antennae and a pair of compound eyes. Insects have six legs and many have wings. They have a complex life cycle called metamorphosis.

INVERTEBRATE: An animal that does not have a spine (backbone).

LARVAE (SINGULAR: LARVA): Immature insects. Beetle larvae are often called grubs. Larvae look completely different to adult insects and often feed on different things than their parents, meaning that they don't compete with their parents for food.

MANDIBLES: Mouthparts. Mandibles can grasp, crush, or cut food, or defend against predators and rivals.

METAMORPHOSIS: Means *change*; it involves a total transformation of the insect between the different life stages (egg, larva, pupa, and adult; or egg, nymph, and adult). For example, imagine a big, fat, cream-colored grub: It looks nothing like an adult beetle. Many insects (including beetles) metamorphosize inside a pupa or cocoon: they enter the pupa as a grub, are blended into beetle soup, re-form as an adult beetle, and break their way out of the pupa. Adult beetles never molt and, as they are encased in a hard exoskeleton that doesn't stretch or grow, they can never grow bigger. Therefore, if you see an adult beetle, it can never grow any bigger than it is.

PALPS: A pair of sensory appendages near the mouth of an insect. They are used to touch/feel and sense chemicals in the surroundings.

SETAE (SINGULAR: SETA): Tiny hairlike projections covering parts of an insect's body. They may be protective, can be used for defense, camouflage, and adhesion (sticking to things), and can be sensitive to moisture and vibration.

SPECIES: The scientific, Latin name for an organism; helps define what type of organism something is, regardless of what language you speak. For example, across the world, Baxter is known as *Chalcosoma caucasus*. However, depending on what language you speak, you call him a different common name. The species name is always written with its genus name in front of it and is always typed in italics, with the genus starting with a capital letter and the species all in lowercase type. If you are writing by hand, it should all be underlined instead of italicized. See "Taxonomy."

STRIDULATION: A loud squeaking or scratching noise made by an insect rubbing its body parts together to attract a mate, as a territorial sound, or as a warning sign.

TAXONOMY: The practice of identifying, describing, and naming organisms. It uses a system called *biological classification*, with similar organisms grouped together. It starts off with a broad grouping (the kingdom) and gets more specific, with the species as the most specific group. No two species names (when combined with their genus) are the same: kingdom → phylum → class → order → family → genus → species. This system avoids the confusion caused by common names, which vary in different languages or even different households. For example, Baxter is a species of rhinoceros beetle: some people may call him an Atlas beetle, Hercules beetle, or unicorn beetle, and there are lots of different species of rhinoceros beetle. So how do we know what Baxter really is? If you use biological classification, you can classify Baxter as: kingdom = Animalia (animal) → phylum = Arthropoda (arthropod) → class = Insecta (insect) → order = Coleoptera (beetle) → family = Scarabaeidae → genus = *Chalcosoma* → species = *caucasus*. But all you really need to say is the genus and species, so Baxter is a *Chalcosoma caucasus*.

THORAX: The part of an insect's body between the head and the abdomen.

TRANSGENIC: An animal can be described as transgenic if scientists have added DNA from another species.

Acknowledgments

*W*riting your first book is like playing blindman's bluff. You know what you have to do, but you can't see where you're going. I am indebted to many people for pushing me in the right direction. Above all others, I need to thank Sam Harmsworth Sparling for the love, enthusiasm, and unwavering support. He always knew I could do it, especially when I did not, and without him there would be no *Beetle Boy*.

This book is factually accurate, thanks to the expertise of Dr. Sarah Beynon, entomologist extraordinaire. A massive thanks goes to her for generously giving her time and knowledge to *Beetle Boy*. If you are interested in learning more about beetles, then you should take a trip to her Bug Farm in Pembrokeshire. You can find out about it here: www.thebugfarm.co.uk.

Heartfelt love and thanks go to Claire Rakich, a true friend. Honest to a fault, she read every draft and told me when I was going awry. And it's impossible to write a book with children clambering on your head, and so thank you, Nana Jane, for giving me the gift of time and looking after my boys. A generous sprinkle of gratitude goes to the beta readers who gave me the confidence to keep on going. That's you: Hannah Gabrielle, Jude Bloor, Jacob Bloor, Adam Rakich, Sarah Dustagheer, Gwilym Jones, Dominic Fennell, Emma Beaty, Sophie Lilley, Will Richmond, Dom Brouard, Lorna Hosler, Ivor Talbot, and Emma Keith. And I must thank David Sabel and the gang at the National Theatre for the good advice (that's you, Bash), support, and encouragement.

I owe a debt of gratitude to Jenny Saville for pointing me in the direction of the Golden Egg Academy. It was Imogen Cooper, and her Golden Egg Academy, that threw me into the head of Barry Cunningham, and there the magic happened. Thank you, thank you, thank you, Imogen.

Thank you, Kirsty McLachlan and DGA, for helping me negotiate my foothold in the publishing industry.

Thanks to Chicken House editor Rachel Leyshon for ironing out the wrinkles and making me think about the story I wanted to tell. Thanks to Rachel Hickman, Elinor Bagenal, and everyone at Chicken House for the support and enthusiasm for *Beetle Boy*. I'm very lucky to have landed in your coop. In particular, thank you to Barry for the beetle-browed passion right from the word *go*. To be championed by you is a writer's dream.

About the Author

M. G. Leonard is senior digital media producer at the National Theatre of Great Britain, where she creates podcasts and documentaries about making theater. *Beetle Boy* is her debut novel and book one of The Beetle Trilogy. She lives in Brighton, England, with her family. You can visit her online at www.mgleonard.com and follow her on Twitter at @MGLnrd.